THE NICK ADAMS STORIES

BOOKS BY ERNEST HEMINGWAY

THE
Nick Adams
STORIES

BY

ERNEST HEMINGWAY

PREFACE BY PHILIP YOUNG

A CHARLES SCRIBNER'S SONS BOOK

Macmillan Publishing Company

NEW YORK

First Scribner/Macmillan Hudson River Edition 1986

ISBN 0-02-550780-X

10 9 8 7 6 5

PRINTED IN THE UNITED STATES OF AMERICA

HALF-TITLE PAGE DECORATION BY WALTER FERRO

PREFACE

"Of the place where he had been a boy he had written well enough. As well as he could then." So thought a dying writer in an early version of "The Snows of Kilimanjaro." The writer of course was Hemingway. The place was the Michigan of his boyhood summers, where he remembered himself as Nick Adams. As well as he could write then was very well indeed.

Until now, however, the stories involving Nick have always appeared so many to a book, in jumbled sequence. As a result the coherence of his adventures has been obscured, and their impact fragmented. In *Men Without Women*, Hemingway's second collection of stories, Nick appears first as a soldier in Italy, next as an adolescent in Summit, Illinois, then in turn as a younger boy in Michigan, a married man in Austria, and a soldier back in Italy. Or consider the trouble with "Big Two-Hearted River," one of the best-known Hemingway stories. Placed where it was—at the end of *In Our Time*, the first collection—it puzzled a good many readers. Put where it goes chronologically, following the stories of World War I, its submerged tensions—the impression that Nick is exorcising some nameless anxiety—become perfectly understandable. But "A Way You'll Never Be," which precedes "Big Two-Hearted River" in time and explains it, was published eight years and several books after it.

Arranged in chronological sequence, the events of Nick's life make up a meaningful narrative in which a memorable character grows from child to adolescent to soldier, veteran, writer, and parent—a sequence closely paralleling the events of Hemingway's own life. In this arrangement Nick Adams, who for a long time was not widely recognized as a consistent character at all, emerges clearly as the first in a long line of Hemingway's fictional selves. Later versions, from Jake Barnes and Frederic Henry to Richard Cantwell and Thomas Hudson, were all to have behind them part of Nick's history and, correspondingly, part of Hemingway's.

As is true for many writers of fiction, the relationship between Hemingway's work and the events of his own life is an immediate and intricate one. In some stories he appears to report details of actual experience as faithfully as he might have entered them in a diary. In others the play of his imagination has transformed experience into a new and different reality. Exploring the connections between actuality and fiction in Hemingway can be an absorbing activity, and readers who wish to pursue it are referred to the biographical studies listed at the end of this preface. But Hemingway naturally intended his stories to be understood and enjoyed without regard for such considerations—as they have been for a long time.

The first Nick Adams fiction appeared almost a half-century ago, the last in 1933, and over the years a great deal has been written about it. Among the unpublished manuscripts Hemingway left behind him, however, eight new contributions to the over-all narrative were discovered. Presented here for the first time, inserted in the places in time where the events fall, they are varied in length and apparent purpose. Three accounts—of how the Indians left the country of Nick's boyhood, of his first sight of the Mississippi, and of what happened just before and after his wedding—are quite brief. If the author had larger plans for any of them, such are unknown; they might be read simply as sketches in an artist's notebook. In two other cases his plans are self-evident, for here we have the beginnings of works that were never completed. Nick on board the *Chicago*, bound for France during World War I, was the start of a novel called *Along with Youth* that was abandoned long ago. Similarly, though much later, the plot of "The Last Good Country" was left in mid-air, and many pages would have been required to resolve it. Two other pieces are known to have originated in Nick stories already published. "Three Shots" tells how the young boy became frightened while on a camping trip. It once preceded the story called "Indian Camp." And Nick's "stream of consciousness" reflections on his writing career once (anachronistically) concluded "Big Two-Hearted River." Of these new works only "Summer People," very likely the first fiction Hemingway wrote about Nick Adams, can be regarded as a full-length, completed story.

To distinguish them from previously published works, all the new materials in this book have been printed in a special "oblique" type. If the decision to publish them at all is questioned, justification is available. For one thing, the plan for rearranging the Nick Adams stories coherently benefits from material that fills substantial gaps in the narrative. Further, all this new fiction relates in one way or another to events in the author's life, in which his readers continue to be interested. Last and most important is the fact that these pieces throw new light on the work and personality of one of our foremost writers and genuinely increase our understanding of him. The typography suggests an oblique introduction, but a warm reception is expected.

—PHILIP YOUNG

BIOGRAPHICAL STUDIES

BAKER, CARLOS. *Ernest Hemingway: A Life Story*. New York: Charles Scribner's Sons, 1969.

HEMINGWAY, LEICESTER. *My Brother, Ernest Hemingway*. New York: World Publishing Company, 1962.

MONTGOMERY, CONSTANCE CAPPEL. *Hemingway in Michigan*. New York: Fleet Press Corporation, 1966.

SANFORD, MARCELLINE HEMINGWAY. *At the Hemingways: A Family Portrait*. Boston: Little, Brown and Company, 1962.

CONTENTS

CONTENTS

THE NORTHERN WOODS

Three Shots

Nick was undressing in the tent. He saw the shadows of his father and Uncle George cast by the fire on the canvas wall. He felt very uncomfortable and ashamed and undressed as fast as he could, piling his clothes neatly. He was ashamed because undressing reminded him of the night before. He had kept it out of his mind all day.

His father and uncle had gone off across the lake after supper to fish with a jack light. Before they shoved the boat out his father told him that if any emergency came up while they were gone he was to fire three shots with the rifle and they would come right back. Nick went back from the edge of the lake through the woods to the camp. He could hear the oars of the boat in the dark. His father was rowing and his uncle was sitting in the stern trolling. He had taken his seat with his rod ready when his father shoved the boat out. Nick listened to them on the lake until he could no longer hear the oars.

Walking back through the woods Nick began to be frightened. He was always a little frightened of the woods at night. He opened the flap of the tent and undressed and lay very quietly between the blankets in the dark. The fire was burned down to a bed of coals outside. Nick lay still and tried to go to sleep. There was no noise anywhere. Nick felt if he could only hear a fox bark or an owl or anything he would be all right. He was not afraid of anything definite as yet. But he was getting very afraid. Then suddenly he was afraid of dying. Just a few weeks before at home, in church, they had sung a hymn, "Some day the silver cord will break." While they were singing the hymn Nick had realized that some day he must die. It made him feel quite sick. It was the first time he had ever realized that he himself would have to die sometime.

That night he sat out in the hall under the night light trying to read Robinson Crusoe to keep his mind off the fact that some day the silver cord must break. The nurse found him there and threatened to tell his father on him if he did not go to bed. He went in to bed and as soon as the nurse was in her room came out again and read under the hall light until morning.

Last night in the tent he had had the same fear. He never had it except at night. It was more a realization than a fear at first. But it was always on the edge of fear and became fear very quickly when it started. As soon as he began to be really frightened he took the rifle and poked the muzzle out the front of the tent and shot three times. The rifle kicked badly. He heard the shots rip off through the trees. As soon as he had fired the shots it was all right.

He lay down to wait for his father's return and was asleep before his father and uncle had put out their jack light on the other side of the lake.

"Damn that kid," Uncle George said as they rowed back. "What did you tell him to call us in for? He's probably got the heebie-jeebies about something."

Uncle George was an enthusiastic fisherman and his father's younger brother.

"Oh, well. He's pretty small," his father said.

"That's no reason to bring him into the woods with us."

"I know he's an awful coward," his father said, "but we're all yellow at that age."

"I can't stand him," George said. "He's such an awful liar."

"Oh, well, forget it. You'll get plenty of fishing anyway."

They came into the tent and Uncle George shone his flashlight into Nick's eyes.

"What was it, Nickie?" said his father. Nick sat up in bed.

"It sounded like a cross between a fox and a wolf and it was fooling around the tent," Nick said. "It was a little like a fox but more like a wolf." He had learned the phrase "cross between" that same day from his uncle.

"He probably heard a screech owl," Uncle George said.

In the morning his father found two big basswood trees that leaned across each other so that they rubbed together in the wind.

"Do you think that was what it was, Nick?" his father asked.

"Maybe," Nick said. He didn't want to think about it.

"You don't want to ever be frightened in the woods, Nick. There is nothing that can hurt you."

"Not even lightning?" Nick asked.

"No, not even lightning. If there is a thunder storm get out into the open. Or get under a beech tree. They're never struck."

"Never?" Nick asked.

"I never heard of one," said his father.

"Gee, I'm glad to know that about beech trees," Nick said.

Now he was undressing again in the tent. He was conscious of the two shadows on the wall although he was not watching them. Then he heard a boat being pulled up on the beach and the two shadows were gone. He heard his father talking with someone.

Then his father shouted, "Get your clothes on, Nick."

He dressed as fast as he could. His father came in and rummaged through the duffel bags.

"Put your coat on, Nick," his father said.

Indian Camp

At the lake shore there was another rowboat drawn up. The two Indians stood waiting.

Nick and his father got in the stern of the boat and the Indians shoved it off and one of them got in to row. Uncle George sat in the stern of the camp rowboat. The young Indian shoved the camp boat off and got in to row Uncle George.

The two boats started off in the dark. Nick heard the oarlocks of the other boat quite a way ahead of them in the mist. The Indians rowed with quick choppy strokes. Nick lay back with his father's arm around him. It was cold on the water. The Indian who was rowing them was working very hard, but the other boat moved farther ahead in the mist all the time.

"Where are we going, Dad?" Nick asked.

"Over to the Indian camp. There is an Indian lady very sick."

"Oh," said Nick.

Across the bay they found the other boat beached. Uncle George was smoking a cigar in the dark. The young Indian pulled the boat way up the beach. Uncle George gave both the Indians cigars.

They walked up from the beach through a meadow that

was soaking wet with dew, following the young Indian who carried a lantern. Then they went into the woods and followed a trail that led to the logging road that ran back into the hills. It was much lighter on the logging road as the timber was cut away on both sides. The young Indian stopped and blew out his lantern and they all walked on along the road.

They came around a bend and a dog came out barking. Ahead were the lights of the shanties where the Indian bark-peelers lived. More dogs rushed out at them. The two Indians sent them back to the shanties. In the shanty nearest the road there was a light in the window. An old woman stood in the doorway holding a lamp.

Inside on a wooden bunk lay a young Indian woman. She had been trying to have her baby for two days. All the old women in the camp had been helping her. The men had moved off up the road to sit in the dark and smoke out of range of the noise she made. She screamed just as Nick and the two Indians followed his father and Uncle George into the shanty. She lay in the lower bunk, very big under a quilt. Her head was turned to one side. In the upper bunk was her husband. He had cut his foot very badly with an ax three days before. He was smoking a pipe. The room smelled very bad.

Nick's father ordered some water to be put on the stove, and while it was heating he spoke to Nick.

"This lady is going to have a baby, Nick," he said.

"I know," said Nick.

"You don't know," said his father. "Listen to me. What she is going through is called being in labor. The baby wants to be born and she wants it to be born. All her muscles are trying to get the baby born. That is what is happening when she screams."

"I see," Nick said.

Just then the woman cried out.

"Oh, Daddy, can't you give her something to make her stop screaming?" asked Nick.

"No. I haven't any anesthetic," his father said. "But her screams are not important. I don't hear them because they are not important."

The husand in the upper bunk rolled over against the wall.

The woman in the kitchen motioned to the doctor that the water was hot. Nick's father went into the kitchen and poured about half of the water out of the big kettle into a basin. Into the water left in the kettle he put several things he unwrapped from a handkerchief.

"Those must boil," he said, and began to scrub his hands in the basin of hot water with a cake of soap he had brought from the camp. Nick watched his father's hands scrubbing each other with the soap. While his father washed his hands very carefully and thoroughly, he talked.

"You see, Nick, babies are supposed to be born head first but sometimes they're not. When they're not they make a lot of trouble for everybody. Maybe I'll have to operate on this lady. We'll know in a little while."

When he was satisfied with his hands he went in and went to work.

"Pull back that quilt, will you, George?" he said. "I'd rather not touch it."

Later when he started to operate Uncle George and three Indian men held the woman still. She bit Uncle George on the arm and Uncle George said, "Damn squaw bitch!" and the young Indian who had rowed Uncle George over laughed at him. Nick held the basin for his father. It all took a long time.

His father picked the baby up and slapped it to make it breathe and handed it to the old woman.

"See, it's a boy, Nick," he said. "How do you like being an intern?"

Nick said, "All right." He was looking away so as not to see what his father was doing.

"There. That gets it," said his father and put something into the basin.

Nick didn't look at it.

"Now," his father said, "there's some stitches to put in. You can watch this or not, Nick, just as you like. I'm going to sew up the incision I made."

Nick did not watch. His curiosity had been gone for a long time.

His father finished and stood up. Uncle George and the three Indian men stood up. Nick put the basin out in the kitchen.

Uncle George looked at his arm. The young Indian smiled reminiscently.

"I'll put some peroxide on that, George," the doctor said.

He bent over the Indian woman. She was quiet now and her eyes were closed. She looked very pale. She did not know what had become of the baby or anything.

"I'll be back in the morning," the doctor said, standing up. "The nurse should be here from St. Ignace by noon and she'll bring everything we need."

He was feeling exalted and talkative as football players are in the dressing room after a game.

"That's one for the medical journal, George," he said. "Doing a Caesarian with a jackknife and sewing it up with nine-foot, tapered gut leaders."

Uncle George was standing against the wall, looking at his arm.

"Oh, you're a great man, all right," he said.

"Ought to have a look at the proud father. They're usually the worst sufferers in these little affairs," the doctor said. "I must say he took it all pretty quietly."

He pulled back the blanket from the Indian's head. His hand came away wet. He mounted on the edge of the lower bunk with the lamp in one hand and looked in. The Indian lay with his face toward the wall. His throat had been cut from ear to ear. The blood had flowed down into a pool where his body sagged the bunk. His head rested on his left arm. The open razor lay, edge up, in the blankets.

"Take Nick out of the shanty, George," the doctor said.

There was no need of that. Nick, standing in the door of the kitchen, had a good view of the upper bunk when his father, the lamp in one hand, tipped the Indian's head back.

It was just beginning to be daylight when they walked along the logging road back toward the lake.

"I'm terribly sorry I brought you along, Nickie," said his father, all his postoperative exhilaration gone. "It was an awful mess to put you through."

"Do ladies always have such a hard time having babies?" Nick asked.

"No, that was very, very exceptional."

"Why did he kill himself, Daddy?"

"I don't know, Nick. He couldn't stand things, I guess."

"Do many men kill themselves, Daddy?"

"Not very many, Nick."

"Do many women?"

"Hardly ever."

"Don't they ever?"

"Oh, yes. They do sometimes."

"Daddy?"

"Yes."

[20]

"Where did Uncle George go?"

"He'll turn up all right."

"Is dying hard, Daddy?"

"No, I think it's pretty easy, Nick. It all depends."

They were seated in the boat, Nick in the stern, his father rowing. The sun was coming up over the hills. A bass jumped, making a circle in the water. Nick trailed his hand in the water. It felt warm in the sharp chill of the morning.

In the early morning on the lake sitting in the stern of the boat with his father rowing, he felt quite sure that he would never die.

The Doctor
and the Doctor's Wife

Dick Boulton came from the Indian camp to cut up logs for Nick's father. He brought his son Eddy and another Indian named Billy Tabeshaw with him. They came in through the back gate out of the woods, Eddy carrying the long crosscut saw. It flopped over his shoulder and made a musical sound as he walked. Billy Tabeshaw carried two big cant hooks. Dick had three axes under his arm.

He turned and shut the gate. The others went on ahead of him down to the lake shore where the logs were buried in the sand.

The logs had been lost from the big log booms that were towed down the lake to the mill by the steamer *Magic*. They had drifted up onto the beach and if nothing were done about them sooner or later the crew of the *Magic* would come along the shore in a rowboat, spot the logs, drive an iron spike with a ring on it into the end of each one and then tow them out into the lake to make a new boom. But the lumbermen might never come for them because a few logs were not worth the price of a crew to gather them. If no one came for them they would be left to waterlog and rot on the beach.

Nick's father always assumed that this was what would happen and hired the Indians to come down from the camp and cut the logs up with the crosscut saw and split them with a wedge to make cord wood and chunks for the open fire-place. Dick Boulton walked around past the cottage down to the lake. There were four big beech logs lying almost buried in the sand. Eddy hung the saw up by one of its handles in the crotch of a tree. Dick put the three axes down on the little dock. Dick was a half-breed and many of the farmers around the lake believed he was really a white man. He was very lazy but a great worker once he was started. He took a plug of tobacco out of his pocket, bit off a chew and spoke in Ojibway to Eddy and Billy Tabeshaw.

They sunk the ends of their cant hooks into one of the logs and swung against it to loosen it in the sand. They swung their weight against the shafts of the cant hooks. The log moved in the sand. Dick Boulton turned to Nick's father.

"Well, Doc," he said, "that's a nice lot of timber you've stolen."

"Don't talk that way, Dick," the doctor said. "It's drift-wood."

Eddy and Billy Tabeshaw had rocked the log out of the wet sand and rolled it toward the water.

"Put it right in," Dick Boulton shouted.

"What are you doing that for?" asked the doctor.

"Wash it off. Clean off the sand on account of the saw. I want to see who it belongs to," Dick said.

The log was just awash in the lake. Eddy and Billy Tabeshaw leaned on their cant hooks, sweating in the sun. Dick kneeled down in the sand and looked at the mark of the scaler's hammer in the wood at the end of the log.

"It belongs to White and McNally," he said, standing up and brushing off his trousers knees.

The doctor was very uncomfortable.

"You'd better not saw it up then, Dick," he said, shortly.

"Don't get huffy, Doc," said Dick. "Don't get huffy. I

don't care who you steal from. It's none of my business."

"If you think the logs are stolen, leave them alone and take your tools back to the camp," the doctor said. His face was red.

"Don't go off at half cock, Doc," Dick said. He spat tobacco juice on the log. It slid off, thinning in the water. "You know they're stolen as well as I do. It don't make any difference to me."

"All right. If you think the logs are stolen, take your stuff and get out."

"Now, Doc—"

"Take your stuff and get out."

"Listen, Doc."

"If you call me Doc once again, I'll knock your eye teeth down your throat."

"Oh, no, you won't, Doc."

Dick Boulton looked at the doctor. Dick was a big man. He knew how big a man he was. He liked to get into fights. He was happy. Eddy and Billy Tabeshaw leaned on their cant hooks and looked at the doctor. The doctor chewed the beard on his lower lip and looked at Dick Boulton. Then he turned away and walked up the hill to the cottage. They could see from his back how angry he was. They all watched him walk up the hill and go inside the cottage.

Dick said something in Ojibway. Eddy laughed but Billy Tabeshaw looked very serious. He did not understand English but he had sweat all the time the row was going on. He was fat, with only a few hairs of mustache like a Chinaman. He picked up the two cant hooks. Dick picked up the axes and Eddy took the saw down from the tree. They started off and walked up past the cottage and out the back gate into the woods. Dick left the gate open. Billy Tabeshaw went back and fastened it. They were gone through the woods.

In the cottage the doctor, sitting on the bed in his room, saw a pile of medical journals on the floor by the bureau. They were still in their wrappers, unopened. It irritated him.

"Aren't you going back to work, dear?" asked the doctor's wife from the room where she was lying with the blinds drawn.

"No!"

"Was anything the matter?"

"I had a row with Dick Boulton."

"Oh," said his wife. "I hope you didn't lose your temper, Henry."

"No," said the doctor.

"Remember, that he who ruleth his spirit is greater than he that taketh a city," said his wife. She was a Christian Scientist. Her Bible, her copy of *Science and Health* and her *Quarterly* were on a table beside her bed in the darkened room.

Her husband did not answer. He was sitting on his bed now, cleaning a shotgun. He pushed the magazine full of the heavy yellow shells and pumped them out again. They were scattered on the bed.

"Henry," his wife called. Then paused a moment. "Henry!"

"Yes," the doctor said.

"You didn't say anything to Boulton to anger him, did you?"

"No," said the doctor.

"What was the trouble about, dear?"

"Nothing much."

"Tell me, Henry. Please don't try and keep anything from me. What was the trouble about?"

"Well, Dick owes me a lot of money for pulling his squaw through pneumonia and I guess he wanted a row so he wouldn't have to take it out in work."

His wife was silent. The doctor wiped his gun carefully with a rag. He pushed the shells back in against the spring of the magazine. He sat with the gun on his knees. He was very fond of it. Then he heard his wife's voice from the darkened room.

"Dear, I don't think, I really don't think that anyone would really do a thing like that."

"No?" the doctor said.

"No. I can't really believe that anyone would do a thing of that sort intentionally."

The doctor stood up and put the shotgun in the corner behind the dresser.

"Are you going out, dear?" his wife said.

"I think I'll go for a walk," the doctor said.

"If you see Nick, dear, will you tell him his mother wants to see him?" his wife said.

The doctor went out on the porch. The screen door slammed behind him. He heard his wife catch her breath when the door slammed.

"Sorry," he said, outside her window with the blinds drawn.

"It's all right, dear," she said.

He walked in the heat out the gate and along the path into the hemlock woods. It was cool in the woods even on such a hot day. He found Nick sitting with his back against a tree, reading.

"Your mother wants you to come and see her," the doctor said.

"I want to go with you," Nick said.

His father looked down at him.

"All right. Come on, then," his father said. "Give me the book; I'll put it in my pocket."

"I know where there's black squirrels, Daddy," Nick said.

"All right," said his father. "Let's go there."

Ten Indians

After one Fourth of July, Nick, driving home late from town in the big wagon with Joe Garner and his family, passed nine drunken Indians along the road. He remembered there were nine because Joe Garner, driving along in the dusk, pulled up the horses, jumped down into the road and dragged an Indian out of the wheel rut. The Indian had been asleep, face down in the sand. Joe dragged him into the bushes and got back up on the wagon box.

"That makes nine of them," Joe said, "just between here and the edge of town."

"Them Indians," said Mrs. Garner.

Nick was on the back seat with the two Garner boys. He was looking out from the back seat to see the Indian where Joe had dragged him alongside of the road.

"Was it Billy Tabeshaw?" Carl asked.

"No."

"His pants looked mighty like Billy."

"All Indians wear the same kind of pants."

"I didn't see him at all," Frank said. "Pa was down into the road and back up again before I seen a thing. I thought he was killing a snake."

"Plenty of Indians'll kill snakes tonight, I guess," Joe Garner said.

"Them Indians," said Mrs. Garner.

They drove along. The road turned off from the main high-way and went up into the hills. It was hard pulling for the horses and the boys got down and walked. The road was sandy. Nick looked back from the top of the hill by the schoolhouse. He saw the lights of Petoskey and, off across Little Traverse Bay, the lights of Harbor Springs. They climbed back in the wagon again.

"They ought to put some gravel on that stretch," Joe Garner said. The wagon went along the road through the woods. Joe and Mrs. Garner sat close together on the front seat. Nick sat between the two boys. The road came out into a clearing.

"Right here was where Pa ran over the skunk."

"It was further on."

"It don't make no difference where it was," Joe said with-out turning his head. "One place is just as good as another to run over a skunk."

"I saw two skunks last night," Nick said.

"Where?"

"Down by the lake. They were looking for dead fish along the beach."

"They were coons probably," Carl said.

"They were skunks. I guess I know skunks."

"You ought to," Carl said. "You got an Indian girl."

"Stop talking that way, Carl," said Mrs. Garner.

"Well, they smell about the same."

Joe Garner laughed.

"You stop laughing, Joe," Mrs. Garner said. "I won't have Carl talk that way."

"Have you got an Indian girl, Nickie?" Joe asked.

"No."

"He has too, Pa," Frank said. "Prudence Mitchell's his girl."

"She's not."

"He goes to see her every day."

"I don't." Nick, sitting between the two boys in the dark, felt hollow and happy inside himself to be teased about Prudence Mitchell. "She ain't my girl," he said.

"Listen to him," said Carl. "I see them together every day."

"Carl can't get a girl," his mother said, "not even a squaw." Carl was quiet.

"Carl ain't no good with girls," Frank said.

"You shut up."

"You're all right, Carl," Joe Garner said. "Girls never got a man anywhere. Look at your pa."

"Yes, that's what you would say," Mrs. Garner moved close to Joe as the wagon jolted. "Well, you had plenty of girls in your time."

"I'll bet Pa wouldn't ever have had a squaw for a girl."

"Don't you think it," Joe said. "You better watch out to keep Prudie, Nick."

His wife whispered to him and Joe laughed.

"What you laughing at?" asked Frank.

"Don't you say it, Garner," his wife warned. Joe laughed again.

"Nickie can have Prudence," Joe Garner said. "I got a good girl."

"That's the way to talk," Mrs. Garner said.

The horses were pulling heavily in the sand. Joe reached out in the dark with the whip.

"Come on, pull into it. You'll have to pull harder than this tomorrow."

They trotted down the long hill, the wagon jolting. At the farmhouse everybody got down. Mrs. Garner unlocked the door, went inside, and came out with a lamp in her hand. Carl and Nick unloaded the things from the back of the wagon.

Frank sat on the front seat to drive to the barn and put up the horses. Nick went up the steps and opened the kitchen door. Mrs. Garner was building a fire in the stove. She turned from pouring kerosene on the wood.

"Good-by, Mrs. Garner," Nick said. "Thanks for taking me."

"Oh, shucks, Nickie."

"I had a wonderful time."

"We like to have you. Won't you stay and eat some supper?"

"I better go. I think Dad probably waited for me."

"Well, get along then. Send Carl up to the house, will you?"

"All right."

"Good night, Nickie."

"Good night, Mrs. Garner."

Nick went out the farmyard and down to the barn. Joe and Frank were milking.

"Good night," Nick said. "I had a swell time."

"Good night, Nick," Joe Garner called. "Aren't you going to stay and eat?"

"No, I can't. Will you tell Carl his mother wants him?"

"All right. Good night, Nickie."

Nick walked barefoot along the path through the meadow below the barn. The path was smooth and the dew was cool on his bare feet. He climbed a fence at the end of the meadow, went down through a ravine, his feet wet in the swamp mud, and then climbed up through the dry beech woods until he saw the lights of the cottage. He climbed over the fence and walked around to the front porch. Through the window he saw his father sitting by the table, reading in the light from the big lamp. Nick opened the door and went in.

"Well, Nickie," his father said, "was it a good day?"

"I had a swell time, Dad. It was a swell Fourth of July."

"Are you hungry?"

"You bet."

"What did you do with your shoes?"

"I left them in the wagon at Garner's."

"Come on out to the kitchen."

Nick's father went ahead with the lamp. He stopped and lifted the lid of the icebox. Nick went on into the kitchen. His father brought in a piece of cold chicken on a plate and a pitcher of milk and put them on the table before Nick. He put down the lamp.

"There's some pie, too," he said. "Will that hold you?"

"It's grand."

His father sat down in a chair beside the oilcloth-covered table. He made a big shadow on the kitchen wall.

"Who won the ball game?"

"Petoskey. Five to three."

His father sat watching him eat and filled his glass from the milk pitcher. Nick drank and wiped his mouth on his napkin. His father reached over to the shelf for the pie. He cut Nick a big piece. It was huckleberry pie.

"What did you do, Dad?"

"I went out fishing in the morning."

"What did you get?"

"Only perch."

His father sat watching Nick eat the pie.

"What did you do this afternoon?" Nick asked.

"I went for a walk up by the Indian camp."

"Did you see anybody?"

"The Indians were all in town getting drunk."

"Didn't you see anybody at all?"

"I saw your friend, Prudie."

"Where was she?"

"She was in the woods with Frank Washburn. I ran onto them. They were having quite a time."

His father was not looking at him.

"What were they doing?"

"I didn't stay to find out."

"Tell me what they were doing."

"I don't know," his father said. "I just heard them threshing around."

"How did you know it was them?"

"I saw them."

"I thought you said you didn't see them."

"Oh, yes, I saw them."

"Who was it with her?" Nick asked.

"Frank Washburn."

"Were they—were they——"

"Were they what?"

"Were they happy?"

"I guess so."

His father got up from the table and went out the kitchen screen door. When he came back Nick was looking at his plate. He had been crying.

"Have some more?" His father picked up the knife to cut the pie.

"No," said Nick.

"You better have another piece."

"No, I don't want any."

His father cleared off the table.

"Where were they in the woods?" Nick asked.

"Up back of the camp." Nick looked at his plate. His father said, "You better go to bed, Nick."

"All right."

Nick went into his room, undressed, and got into bed. He heard his father moving around in the living room. Nick lay in the bed with his face in the pillow.

"My heart's broken," he thought. "If I feel this way my heart must be broken."

After a while he heard his father blow out the lamp and go into his own room. He heard a wind come up in the trees outside and felt it come in cool through the screen. He lay for a long time with his face in the pillow, and after a while he forgot to think about Prudence and finally he went to sleep. When he awoke in the night he heard the wind in the hemlock trees outside the cottage and the waves of the lake coming in on the shore, and he went back to sleep. In the morning there was a big wind blowing and the waves were running high up on the beach and he was awake a long time before he remembered that his heart was broken.

The Indians Moved Away

The Petoskey road ran straight uphill from Grandpa Bacon's farm. His farm was at the end of the road. It always seemed, though, that the road started at his farm and ran to Petoskey, going along the edge of the trees up the long hill, steep and sandy, to disappear into the woods where the long slope of fields stopped short against the hardwood timber.

After the road went into the woods it was cool and the sand firm underfoot from the moisture. It went up and down hills through the woods with berry bushes and beech saplings on either side that had to be periodically cut back to keep them from effacing the road altogether. In the summer the Indians picked the berries along the road and brought them down to the cottage to sell them, packed in the buckets, wild red raspberries crushing with their own weight, covered with basswood leaves to keep them cool; later blackberries, firm and fresh shining, pails of them. The Indians brought them, coming through the woods to the cottage by the lake. You never heard them come but there they were, standing by the kitchen door with the tin buckets full of berries. Sometimes Nick, lying reading in the hammock, smelt the Indians coming through the gate past the woodpile and around the house. Indians all smelled alike. It was a sweetish smell that all Indians had. He had smelled it first when Grandpa Bacon rented the shack by the point to Indians and after they had left he went inside the shack and it all smelled that way. Grandpa Bacon could never rent the shack to white people after that and no more Indians rented it because the Indian who had lived there had gone into Petoskey to get drunk on the Fourth of July and, coming back, had lain down to go to sleep on the Pere Marquette railway tracks and been run over by the midnight train. He was a very tall Indian and had made Nick an ash canoe paddle. He had lived alone in the shack and drank pain killer and walked through the woods alone at night. Many Indians were that way.

There were no successful Indians. Formerly there had been —old Indians who owned farms and worked them and grew old and fat with many children and grandchildren. Indians like Simon Green who lived on Hortons Creek and had a big farm. Simon Green was dead, though, and his children had sold the farm to divide the money and gone off somewhere.

Nick remembered Simon Green sitting in a chair in front of the blacksmith shop at Hortons Bay, perspiring in the sun while his horses were being shod inside. Nick spading up the cool moist dirt under the eaves of the shed for worms dug with his fingers in the dirt and heard the quick clang of the iron being hammered. He sifted dirt into his can of worms and filled back the earth he had spaded, patting it smooth with the spade. Outside in the sun Simon Green sat in the chair.

"Hello, Nick," he said as Nick came out.

"Hello, Mr. Green."

"Going fishing?"

"Yes."

"Pretty hot day," Simon smiled. "Tell your dad we're going to have lots of birds this fall."

Nick went on across the field back of the shop to the house to get his cane pole and creel. On his way down to the creek Simon Green passed along the road in his buggy. Nick was just going into the brush and Simon did not see him. That was the last he had seen of Simon Green. He died that winter and the next summer his farm was sold. He left nothing besides his farm. Everything had been put back into the farm. One of the boys wanted to go on farming but the others overruled him and the farm was sold. It did not bring one half as much as everyone expected.

The Green boy, Eddy, who had wanted to go on farming, bought a piece of land over back of Spring Brook. The other two boys bought a poolroom in Pellston. They lost money and were sold out. That was the way the Indians went.

ON HIS OWN

The Light of the World

When he saw us come in the door the bartender looked up and then reached over and put the glass covers on the two free-lunch bowls.

"Give me a beer," I said. He drew it, cut the top off with the spatula and then held the glass in his hand. I put the nickel on the wood and he slid the beer toward me.

"What's yours?" he said to Tom.

"Beer."

He drew that beer and cut it off and when he saw the money he pushed the beer across to Tom.

"What's the matter?" Tom asked.

The bartender didn't answer him. He just looked over our heads and said, "What's yours?" to a man who'd come in.

"Rye," the man said. The bartender put out the bottle and glass and a glass of water.

Tom reached over and took the glass off the free-lunch bowl. It was a bowl of pickled pig's feet and there was a wooden thing that worked like a scissors, with two wooden forks at the end to pick them up with.

"No," said the bartender and put the glass cover back on the bowl. Tom held the wooden scissors fork in his hand. "Put it back," said the bartender.

"You know where," said Tom.

The bartender reached a hand forward under the bar, watching us both. I put fifty cents on the wood and he straightened up.

"What was yours?" he said.

"Beer," I said, and before he drew the beer he uncovered both the bowls.

"Your goddam pig's feet stink," Tom said, and spit what he had in his mouth on the floor. The bartender didn't say anything. The man who had drunk the rye paid and went out without looking back.

"You stink yourself," the bartender said. "All you punks stink."

"He says we're punks," Tommy said to me.

"Listen," I said. "Let's get out."

"You punks clear the hell out of here," the bartender said.

"I said we were going out," I said. "It wasn't your idea."

"We'll be back," Tommy said.

"No you won't," the bartender told him.

"Tell him how wrong he is," Tom turned to me.

"Come on," I said.

Outside it was good and dark.

"What the hell kind of place is this?" Tommy said.

"I don't know," I said. "Let's go down to the station."

We'd come in that town at one end and we were going out the other. It smelled of hides and tan bark and the big piles of sawdust. It was getting dark as we came in and now that it was dark it was cold and the puddles of water in the road were freezing at the edges.

Down at the station there were five whores waiting for the train to come in, and six white men and four Indians. It was crowded and hot from the stove and full of stale smoke. As we came in nobody was talking and the ticket window was down.

[40]

"Shut the door, can't you?" somebody said.

I looked to see who said it. It was one of the white men. He wore stagged trousers and lumbermen's rubbers and a Mackinaw shirt like the others, but he had no cap and his face was white and his hands were white and thin.

"Aren't you going to shut it?"

"Sure," I said, and shut it.

"Thank you," he said. One of the other men snickered.

"Ever interfere with a cook?" he said to me.

"No."

"You interfere with this one," he looked at the cook. "He likes it."

The cook looked away from him, holding his lips tight together.

"He puts lemon juice on his hands," the man said. "He wouldn't get them in dishwater for anything. Look how white they are."

One of the whores laughed out loud. She was the biggest whore I ever saw in my life and the biggest woman. And she had on one of those silk dresses that change colors. There were two other whores that were nearly as big but the big one must have weighed three hundred and fifty pounds. You couldn't believe she was real when you looked at her. All three had those changeable silk dresses. They sat side by side on the bench. They were huge. The other two were just ordinary-looking whores, peroxide blondes.

"Look at his hands," the man said and nodded his head at the cook. The whore laughed again and shook all over.

The cook turned and said to her quickly, "You big disgusting mountain of flesh."

She just kept on laughing and shaking.

"Oh, my Christ," she said. She had a nice voice. "Oh, my sweet Christ."

The two other whores, the big ones, acted very quiet and placid as though they didn't have much sense, but they were big, nearly as big as the biggest one. They'd have both gone well over two hundred and fifty pounds. The other two were dignified.

Of the men, besides the cook and the one who talked, there were two other lumberjacks, one that listened, interested but bashful, and the other that seemed getting ready to say something, and two Swedes. Two Indians were sitting down at the end of the bench and one standing up against the wall.

The man who was getting ready to say something spoke to me very low, "Must be like getting on top of a hay mow."

I laughed and said it to Tommy.

"I swear to Christ I've never been anywhere like this," he said. "Look at the three of them." Then the cook spoke up.

"How old are you boys?"

"I'm ninety-six and he's sixty-nine," Tommy said.

"Ho! Ho! Ho!" the big whore shook with laughing. She had a really pretty voice. The other whores didn't smile.

"Oh, can't you be decent?" the cook said. "I asked just to be friendly."

"We're seventeen and nineteen," I said.

"What's the matter with you?" Tommy turned to me.

"That's all right."

"You can call me Alice," the big whore said and then she began to shake again.

"Is that your name?" Tommy asked.

"Sure," she said. "Alice. Isn't it?" she turned to the man who sat by the cook.

"Alice. That's right."

"That's the sort of name you'd have," the cook said.

"It's my real name," Alice said.

"What's the other girls' names?" Tom asked.

"Hazel and Ethel," Alice said. Hazel and Ethel smiled. They weren't very bright.

"What's your name?" I said to one of the blondes.

"Frances," she said.

"Frances what?"

"Frances Wilson. What's it to you?"

"What's yours?" I asked the other one.

"Oh, don't be fresh," she said.

"He just wants us all to be friends," the man who talked said. "Don't you want to be friends?"

"No," the peroxide one said. "Not with you."

"She's just a spitfire," the man said. "A regular little spitfire."

The one blonde looked at the other and shook her head.

"Goddamned mossbacks," she said.

Alice commenced to laugh again and to shake all over.

"There's nothing funny," the cook said. "You all laugh but there's nothing funny. You two young lads, where are you bound for?"

"Where are you going yourself?" Tom asked him.

"I want to go to Cadillac," the cook said. "Have you ever been there? My sister lives there."

"He's a sister himself," the man in the stagged trousers said.

"Can't you stop that sort of thing?" the cook asked. "Can't we speak decently?"

"Cadillac is where Steve Ketchel came from and where Ad Wolgast is from," the shy man said.

"Steve Ketchel," one of the blondes said in a high voice as though the name had pulled a trigger in her. "His own father shot and killed him. Yes, by Christ, his own father. There aren't any more men like Steve Ketchel."

"Wasn't his name Stanley Ketchel?" asked the cook.

"Oh, shut up," said the blonde. "What do you know about

Steve? Stanley. He was no Stanley. Steve Ketchel was the finest and most beautiful man that ever lived. I never saw a man as clean and as white and as beautiful as Steve Ketchel. There never was a man like that. He moved just like a tiger and he was the finest, free-est spender that ever lived."

"Did you know him?" one of the men asked.

"Did I know him? Did I know him? Did I love him? You ask me that? I knew him like you know nobody in the world and I loved him like you love God. He was the greatest, finest, whitest, most beautiful man that ever lived, Steve Ketchel, and his own father shot him down like a dog."

"Were you out on the coast with him?"

"No. I knew him before that. He was the only man I ever loved."

Every one was very respectful to the peroxide blonde, who said all this in a high stagey way, but Alice was beginning to shake again. I felt it, sitting by her.

"You should have married him," the cook said.

"I wouldn't hurt his career," the peroxide blonde said. "I wouldn't be a drawback to him. A wife wasn't what he needed. Oh, my God, what a man he was."

"That was a fine way to look at it," the cook said. "Didn't Jack Johnson knock him out though?"

"It was a trick," Peroxide said. "That big dinge took him by surprise. He'd just knocked Jack Johnson down, the big black bastard. That nigger beat him by a fluke."

The ticket window went up and the three Indians went over to it.

"Steve knocked him down," Peroxide said. "He turned to smile at me."

"I thought you said you weren't on the coast," someone said.

"I went out just for that fight. Steve turned to smile at me and that black son of a bitch from hell jumped up and hit him by surprise. Steve could lick a hundred like that black bastard."

"He was a great fighter," the lumberjack said.

"I hope to God he was," Peroxide said. "I hope to God they don't have fighters like that now. He was like a god, he was. So white and clean and beautiful and smooth and fast and like a tiger or like lightning."

"I saw him in the moving pictures of the fight," Tom said. We were all very moved. Alice was shaking all over and I looked and saw she was crying. The Indians had gone outside on the platform.

"He was more than any husband could ever be," Peroxide said. "We were married in the eyes of God and I belong to him right now and always will and all of me is his. I don't care about my body. They can take my body. My soul belongs to Steve Ketchel. By God, he was a man."

Everybody felt terribly. It was sad and embarrassing. Then Alice, who was still shaking, spoke. "You're a dirty liar," she said in that low voice. "You never layed Steve Ketchel in your life and you know it."

"How can you say that?" Peroxide said proudly.

"I say it because it's true," Alice said. "I'm the only one here that ever knew Steve Ketchel and I come from Mancelona and I knew him there and it's true and you know it's true and God can strike me dead if it isn't true."

"He can strike me, too," Peroxide said.

"This is true, true, true, and you know it. Not just made up and I know exactly what he said to me."

"What did he say?" Peroxide asked, complacently.

Alice was crying so she could hardly speak from shaking so.

"He said, 'You're a lovely piece, Alice.' That's exactly what he said."

"It's a lie," Peroxide said.

"It's true," Alice said. "That's truly what he said."

[45]

"It's a lie," Peroxide said proudly.

"No, it's true, true, true, to Jesus and Mary true."

"Steve couldn't have said that. It wasn't the way he talked," Peroxide said happily.

"It's true," Alice said in her nice voice. "And it doesn't make any difference to me whether you believe it or not." She wasn't crying any more and she was calm.

"It would be impossible for Steve to have said that," Peroxide declared.

"He said it," Alice said and smiled. "And I remember when he said it and I was a lovely piece then exactly as he said, and right now I'm a better piece than you, you dried-up old hot-water bottle."

"You can't insult me," said Peroxide. "You big mountain of pus. I have my memories."

"No," Alice said in that sweet lovely voice, "you haven't got any real memories except having your tubes out and when you started C. and M. Everything else you just read in the papers. I'm clean and you know it and men like me, even though I'm big, and you know it, and I never lie and you know it."

"Leave me with my memories," Peroxide said. "With my true, wonderful memories."

Alice looked at her and then at us and her face lost that hurt look and she smiled and she had about the prettiest face I ever saw. She had a pretty face and a nice smooth skin and a lovely voice and she was nice all right and really friendly. But, my God, she was big. She was as big as three women. Tom saw me looking at her and he said, "Come on. Let's go."

"Good-by," said Alice. She certainly had a nice voice.

"Good-by," I said.

"Which way are you boys going?" asked the cook.

"The other way from you," Tom told him.

The Battler

Nick stood up. He was all right. He looked up the track at the lights of the caboose going out of sight around a curve. There was water on both sides of the track, then tamarack swamp.

He felt of his knee. The pants were torn and the skin was barked. His hands were scraped and there were sand and cinders driven up under his nails. He went over to the edge of the track, down the little slope to the water and washed his hands. He washed them carefully in the cold water, getting the dirt out from the nails. He squatted down and bathed his knee.

That lousy crut of a brakeman. He would get him some day. He would know him again. That was a fine way to act.

"Come here, kid," he said. "I got something for you."

He had fallen for it. What a lousy kid thing to have done. They would never suck him in that way again.

"Come here, kid, I got something for you." Then wham and he lit on his hands and knees beside the track.

Nick rubbed his eye. There was a big bump coming up. He would have a black eye, all right. It ached already. That son of a crutting brakeman.

He touched the bump over his eye with his fingers. Oh, well, it was only a black eye. That was all he had gotten out of it. Cheap at the price. He wished he could see it. Could not see it looking into the water, though. It was dark and he was a long way off from anywhere. He wiped his hands on his trousers and stood up, then climbed the embankment to the rails.

He started up the track. It was well ballasted and made easy walking, sand and gravel packed between the ties, solid walking. The smooth roadbed like a causeway went on ahead through the swamp. Nick walked along. He must get to somewhere.

Nick had swung on to the freight train when it slowed down for the yards outside of Walton Junction. The train, with Nick on it, had passed through Kalkaska as it started to get dark. Now he must be nearly to Mancelona. Three or four miles of swamp. He stepped along the track, walking so he kept on the ballast between the ties, the swamp ghostly in the rising mist. His eye ached and he was hungry. He kept on hiking, putting the miles of track back of him. The swamp was all the same on both sides of the track.

Ahead there was a bridge. Nick crossed it, his boots ringing hollow on the iron. Down below the water showed black between the slits of ties. Nick kicked a loose spike and it dropped into the water. Beyond the bridge were hills. It was high and dark on both sides of the track. Up the track Nick saw a fire.

He came up the track toward the fire carefully. It was off to one side of the track, below the railway embankment. He had only seen the light from it. The track came out through a cut and where the fire was burning the country opened out and fell away into woods. Nick dropped carefully down the embankment and cut into the woods to come up to the fire through the trees. It was a beechwood forest and the fallen beechnut burrs were under his shoes as he walked between the trees. The fire was bright now, just at the edge of the trees.

There was a man sitting by it. Nick waited behind the tree and watched. The man looked to be alone. He was sitting there with his head in his hands, looking at the fire. Nick stepped out and walked into the firelight.

The man sat there looking into the fire. When Nick stopped quite close to him he did not move.

"Hello!" Nick said.

The man looked up.

"Where did you get the shiner?" he said.

"A brakeman busted me."

"Off the through freight?"

"Yes."

"I saw the bastard," the man said. "He went through here 'bout an hour and a half ago. He was walking along the top of the cars, slapping his arms and singing."

"The bastard!"

"It must have made him feel good to bust you," the man said seriously.

"I'll bust him."

"Get him with a rock sometime when he's going through," the man advised.

"I'll get him."

"You're a tough one, aren't you?"

"No," Nick answered.

"All you kids are tough."

"You got to be tough," Nick said.

"That's what I said."

The man looked at Nick and smiled. In the firelight Nick saw that his face was misshapen. His nose was sunken, his eyes were slits, he had queer-shaped lips. Nick did not perceive all this at once; he only saw the man's face was queerly formed and mutilated. It was like putty in color. Dead-looking in the firelight.

"Don't you like my pan?" the man asked.

Nick was embarrassed.

"Sure," he said.

"Look here!" the man took off his cap.

He had only one ear. It was thickened and tight against the side of his head. Where the other ear should have been there was a stump.

"Ever see one like that?"

"No," said Nick. It made him a little sick.

"I could take it," the man said. "Don't you think I could take it, kid?"

"You bet!"

"They all bust their hands on me," the little man said. "They couldn't hurt me."

He looked at Nick. "Sit down," he said. "Want to eat?"

"Don't bother," Nick said. "I'm going on to the town."

"Listen!" the man said. "Call me Ad."

"Sure!"

"Listen," the little man said. "I'm not quite right."

"What's the matter?"

"I'm crazy."

He put on his cap. Nick felt like laughing.

"You're all right," he said.

"No, I'm not. I'm crazy. Listen, you ever been crazy?"

"No," Nick said. "How does it get you?"

"I don't know," Ad said. "When you got it you don't know about it. You know me, don't you?"

"No."

"I'm Ad Francis."

"Honest to God?"

"Don't you believe it?"

"Yes."

Nick knew it must be true.

"You know how I beat them?"

"No," Nick said.

"My heart's slow. It only beats forty a minute. Feel it."

Nick hesitated.

"Come on," the man took hold of his hand. "Take hold of my wrist. Put your fingers there."

The little man's wrist was thick and the muscles bulged above the bone. Nick felt the slow pumping under his fingers.

"Got a watch?"

"No."

"Neither have I," Ad said. "It ain't any good if you haven't got a watch."

Nick dropped his wrist.

"Listen," Ad Francis said. "Take ahold again. You count and I'll count up to sixty."

Feeling the slow hard throb under his fingers Nick started to count. He heard the little man counting slowly, one, two, three, four, five, and on—aloud.

"Sixty," Ad finished. "That's a minute. What did you make it?"

"Forty," Nick said.

"That's right," Ad said happily. "She never speeds up."

A man dropped down the railroad embankment and came across the clearing to the fire.

"Hello, Bugs!" Ad said.

"Hello!" Bugs answered. It was a Negro's voice. Nick knew from the way he walked that he was a Negro. He stood with his back to them, bending over the fire. He straightened up.

"This is my pal Bugs," Ad said. "He's crazy, too."

"Glad to meet you," Bugs said. "Where you say you're from?"

"Chicago," Nick said.

"That's a fine town," the Negro said. "I didn't catch your name."

"Adams. Nick Adams."

[51]

"He says he's never been crazy, Bugs," Ad said.

"He's got a lot coming to him," the Negro said. He was unwrapping a package by the fire.

"When are we going to eat, Bugs?" the prizefighter asked.

"Right away."

"Are you hungry, Nick?"

"Hungry as hell."

"Hear that, Bugs?"

"I hear most of what goes on."

"That ain't what I asked you."

"Yes. I heard what the gentleman said."

Into a skillet he was laying slices of ham. As the skillet grew hot the grease sputtered and Bugs, crouching on long nigger legs over the fire, turned the ham and broke eggs into the skillet, tipping it from side to side to baste the eggs with the hot fat.

"Will you cut some bread out of that bag, Mister Adams?" Bugs turned from the fire.

"Sure."

Nick reached in the bag and brought out a loaf of bread. He cut six slices. Ad watched him and leaned forward.

"Let me take your knife, Nick," he said.

"No, you don't," the Negro said. "Hang onto your knife, Mister Adams."

The prizefighter sat back.

"Will you bring me the bread, Mister Adams?" Bugs asked. Nick brought it over.

"Do you like to dip your bread in the ham fat?" the Negro asked.

"You bet!"

"Perhaps we'd better wait until later. It's better at the finish of the meal. Here."

The Negro picked up a slice of ham and laid it on one of the pieces of bread, then slid an egg on top of it.

"Just close that sandwich, will you, please, and give it to Mister Francis."

Ad took the sandwich and started eating.

"Watch out how that egg runs," the Negro warned. "This is for you, Mister Adams. The remainder for myself."

Nick bit into the sandwich. The Negro was sitting opposite him beside Ad. The hot fried ham and eggs tasted wonderful.

"Mister Adams is right hungry," the Negro said. The little man whom Nick knew by name as a former champion fighter was silent. He had said nothing since the Negro had spoken about the knife.

"May I offer you a slice of bread dipped right in the hot ham fat?" Bugs said.

"Thanks a lot."

The little white man looked at Nick.

"Will you have some, Mister Adolph Francis?" Bugs offered from the skillet.

Ad did not answer. He was looking at Nick.

"Mister Francis?" came the nigger's soft voice.

Ad did not answer. He was looking at Nick.

"I spoke to you, Mister Francis," the nigger said softly.

Ad kept on looking at Nick. He had his cap down over his eyes. Nick felt nervous.

"How the hell do you get that way?" came out from under the cap sharply at Nick.

"Who the hell do you think you are? You're a snotty bastard. You come in here where nobody asks you and eat a man's food and when he asks to borrow a knife you get snotty."

He glared at Nick, his face was white and his eyes almost out of sight under the cap.

"You're a hot sketch. Who the hell asked you to butt in here?"

"Nobody."

"You're damn right nobody did. Nobody asked you to

stay either. You come in here and act snotty about my face and smoke my cigars and drink my liquor and then talk snotty. Where the hell do you think you get off?"

Nick said nothing. Ad stood up.

"I'll tell you, you yellow-livered Chicago bastard. You're going to get your can knocked off. Do you get that?"

Nick stepped back. The little man came toward him slowly, stepping flat-footed forward, his left foot stepping forward, his right dragging up to it.

"Hit me," he moved his head. "Try and hit me."

"I don't want to hit you."

"You won't get out of it that way. You're going to take a beating, see? Come on and lead at me."

"Cut it out," Nick said.

"All right, then, you bastard."

The little man looked down at Nick's feet. As he looked down the Negro, who had followed behind him as he moved away from the fire, set himself and tapped him across the base of the skull. He fell forward and Bugs dropped the cloth-wrapped blackjack on the grass. The little man lay there, his face in the grass. The Negro picked him up, his head hanging, and carried him to the fire. His face looked bad, the eyes open. Bugs laid him down gently.

"Will you bring me the water in the bucket, Mister Adams," he said. "I'm afraid I hit him just a little hard."

The Negro splashed water with his hand on the man's face and pulled his ears gently. The eyes closed.

Bugs stood up.

"He's all right," he said. "There's nothing to worry about. I'm sorry, Mister Adams."

"It's all right." Nick was looking down at the little man. He saw the blackjack on the grass and picked it up. It had a flexible handle and was limber in his hand. Worn black leather with a handkerchief wrapped around the heavy end.

"That's a whalebone handle," the Negro smiled. "They don't make them any more. I didn't know how well you could take care yourself and, anyway, I didn't want you to hurt him or mark him up no more than he is."

The Negro smiled again.

"You hurt him yourself."

"I know how to do it. He won't remember nothing of it. I have to do it to change him when he gets that way."

Nick was still looking down at the little man, lying, his eyes closed, in the firelight. Bugs put some wood on the fire.

"Don't you worry about him none, Mister Adams. I seen him like this plenty of times before."

"What made him crazy?" Nick asked.

"Oh, a lot of things," the Negro answered from the fire. "Would you like a cup of this coffee, Mister Adams?"

He handed Nick the cup and smoothed the coat he had placed under the unconscious man's head.

"He took too many beatings, for one thing," the Negro sipped the coffee. "But that just made him sort of simple. Then his sister was his manager and they was always being written up in the papers all about brothers and sisters and how she loved her brother and how he loved his sister, and then they got married in New York and that made a lot of unpleasantness."

"I remember about it."

"Sure. Of course they wasn't brother and sister no more than a rabbit, but there was a lot of people didn't like it either way and they commenced to have disagreements, and one day she just went off and never come back."

He drank the coffee and wiped his lips with the pink palm of his hand.

"He just went crazy. Will you have some more coffee, Mister Adams?"

"Thanks."

"I seen her a couple of times," the Negro went on. "She was an awful good-looking woman. Looked enough like him to be twins. He wouldn't be bad-looking without his face all busted."

He stopped. The story seemed to be over.

"Where did you meet him?" asked Nick.

"I met him in jail," the Negro said. "He was busting people all the time after she went away and they put him in jail. I was in for cuttin' a man."

He smiled, and went on soft-voiced: "Right away I liked him and when I got out I looked him up. He likes to think I'm crazy and I don't mind. I like to be with him and I like seeing the country and I don't have to commit no larceny to do it. I like living like a gentleman."

"What do you all do?" Nick asked.

"Oh, nothing. Just move around. He's got money."

"He must have made a lot of money."

"Sure. He spent all his money, though. Or they took it away from him. She sends him money."

He poked up the fire.

"She's a mighty fine woman," he said. "She looks enough like him to be his own twin."

The Negro looked over at the little man, lying breathing heavily. His blond hair was down over his forehead. His mutilated face looked childish in repose.

"I can wake him up any time now, Mister Adams. If you don't mind I wish you'd sort of pull out. I don't like to not be hospitable, but it might disturb him back again to see you. I hate to have to thump him and it's the only thing to do when he gets started. I have to sort of keep him away from people. You don't mind, do you, Mister Adams? No, don't thank me, Mister Adams. I'd have warned you about him but he seemed to have taken such a liking to you and I thought things were going to be all right. You'll hit a town about two miles up the track. Mancelona they call it. Good-by. I wish we could ask you to stay the night but it's just out of the question. Would you like to take some of that ham and some bread with you? No? You better take a sandwich," all this in a low, smooth, polite nigger voice.

"Good. Well, good-by, Mister Adams. Good-by and good luck!"

Nick walked away from the fire across the clearing to the railway tracks. Out of the range of the fire he listened. The low soft voice of the Negro was talking. Nick could not hear the words. Then he heard the little man say, "I got an awful headache, Bugs."

"You'll feel better, Mister Francis," the Negro's voice soothed. "Just you drink a cup of this hot coffee."

Nick climbed the embankment and started up the track. He found he had a ham sandwich in his hand and put it in his pocket. Looking back from the mounting grade before the track curved into the hills he could see the firelight in the clearing.

The Killers

The door of Henry's lunchroom opened and two men came in. They sat down at the counter.

"What's yours?" George asked them.

"I don't know," one of the men said. "What do you want to eat, Al?"

"I don't know," said Al. "I don't know what I want to eat."

Outside it was getting dark. The streetlight came on outside the window. The two men at the counter read the menu. From the other end of the counter Nick Adams watched them. He had been talking to George when they came in.

"I'll have a roast pork tenderloin with applesauce and mashed potatoes," the first man said.

"It isn't ready yet."

"What the hell do you put it on the card for?"

"That's the dinner," George explained. "You can get that at six o'clock."

George looked at the clock on the wall behind the counter.

"It's five o'clock."

"The clock says twenty minutes past five," the second man said.

"It's twenty minutes fast."

"Oh, to hell with the clock," the first man said. "What have you got to eat?"

"I can give you any kind of sandwiches," George said. "You can have ham and eggs, bacon and eggs, liver and bacon, or a steak."

"Give me chicken croquettes with green peas and cream sauce and mashed potatoes."

"That's the dinner."

"Everything we want's the dinner, eh? That's the way you work it."

"I can give you ham and eggs, bacon and eggs, liver——"

"I'll take ham and eggs," the man called Al said. He wore a derby hat and a black overcoat buttoned across the chest. His face was small and white and he had tight lips. He wore a silk muffler and gloves.

"Give me bacon and eggs," said the other man. He was about the same size as Al. Their faces were different, but they were dressed like twins. Both wore overcoats too tight for them. They sat leaning forward, their elbows on the counter.

"Got anything to drink?" Al asked.

"Silver beer, bevo, ginger ale," George said.

"I mean you got anything to *drink?*"

"Just those I said."

"This is a hot town," said the other. "What do they call it?"

"Summit."

"Ever hear of it?" Al asked his friend.

"No," said the friend.

"What do you do here nights?" Al asked.

"They eat the dinner," his friend said. "They all come here and eat the big dinner."

"That's right," George said.

"So you think that's right?" Al asked George.

"Sure."

"You're a pretty bright boy, aren't you?"

"Sure," said George.

"Well, you're not," said the other little man. "Is he, Al?"

"He's dumb," said Al. He turned to Nick. "What's your name?"

"Adams."

"Another bright boy," Al said. "Ain't he a bright boy, Max?"

"The town's full of bright boys," Max said.

George put the two platters, one of ham and eggs, the other of bacon and eggs, on the counter. He set down two side dishes of fried potatoes and closed the wicket into the kitchen.

"Which is yours?" he asked Al.

"Don't you remember?"

"Ham and eggs."

"Just a bright boy," Max said. He leaned forward and took the ham and eggs. Both men ate with their gloves on. George watched them eat.

"What are you looking at?" Max looked at George.

"Nothing."

"The hell you were. You were looking at me."

"Maybe the boy meant it for a joke, Max," Al said.

George laughed.

"You don't have to laugh," Max said to him. "You don't have to laugh at all, see?"

"All right," said George.

"So he thinks it's all right." Max turned to Al. "He thinks it's all right. That's a good one."

"Oh, he's a thinker," Al said. They went on eating.

"What's the bright boy's name down the counter?" Al asked Max.

"Hey, bright boy," Max said to Nick. "You go around on the other side of the counter with your boy friend."

"What's the idea?" Nick asked.

"There isn't any idea."

"You better go around, bright boy," Al said. Nick went around behind the counter.

"What's the idea?" George asked.

"None of your damn business," Al said. "Who's out in the kitchen?"

"The nigger."

"What do you mean, the nigger?"

"The nigger that cooks."

"Tell him to come in."

"What's the idea?"

"Tell him to come in."

"Where do you think you are?"

"We know damn well where we are," the man called Max said. "Do we look silly?"

"You talk silly," Al said to him. "What the hell do you argue with this kid for? Listen," he said to George, "tell the nigger to come out here."

"What are you going to do to him?"

"Nothing. Use your head, bright boy. What would we do to a nigger?"

George opened the slit that opened back into the kitchen. "Sam," he called. "Come in here a minute."

The door to the kitchen opened and the nigger came in. "What was it?" he asked. The two men at the counter took a look at him.

"All right, nigger. You stand right there," Al said.

Sam, the nigger, standing in his apron, looked at the two men sitting at the counter. "Yes, sir," he said. Al got down from his stool.

"I'm going back to the kitchen with the nigger and bright boy," he said. "Go on back to the kitchen, nigger. You go with him, bright boy." The little man walked after Nick and Sam, the cook, back into the kitchen. The door shut after them. The man called Max sat at the counter opposite George. He didn't look at George but looked in the mirror that ran along back of the counter. Henry's had been made over from a saloon into a lunch counter.

"Well, bright boy," Max said, looking into the mirror, "why don't you say something?"

"What's it all about?"

"Hey, Al," Max called, "bright boy wants to know what it's all about."

"Why don't you tell him?" Al's voice came from the kitchen.

"What do you think it's all about?"

"I don't know."

"What do you think?"

Max looked into the mirror all the time he was talking.

"I wouldn't say."

"Hey, Al, bright boy says he wouldn't say what he thinks it's all about."

"I can hear you, all right," Al said from the kitchen. He had propped open the slit that dishes passed through into the kitchen with a catsup bottle. "Listen, bright boy," he said from the kitchen to George. "Stand a little further along the bar. You move a little to the left, Max." He was like a photographer arranging for a group picture.

"Talk to me, bright boy," Max said. "What do you think's going to happen?"

George did not say anything.

"I'll tell you," Max said. "We're going to kill a Swede. Do you know a big Swede named Ole Andreson?"

"Yes."

"He comes here to eat every night, don't he?"

"Sometimes he comes here."

"He comes here at six o'clock, don't he?"

"If he comes."

"We know all that, bright boy," Max said. "Talk about something else. Ever go to the movies?"

"Once in a while."

"You ought to go to the movies more. The movies are fine for a bright boy like you."

"What are you going to kill Ole Andreson for? What did he ever do to you?"

"He never had a chance to do anything to us. He never even seen us."

"And he's only going to see us once," Al said from the kitchen.

"What are you going to kill him for, then?" George asked.

"We're killing him for a friend. Just to oblige a friend, bright boy."

"Shut up," said Al from the kitchen. "You talk too goddam much."

"Well, I got to keep bright boy amused. Don't I, bright boy?"

"You talk too damn much," Al said. "The nigger and my bright boy are amused by themselves. I got them tied up like a couple of girl friends in the convent."

"I suppose you were in a convent."

"You never know."

"You were in a kosher convent. That's where you were."

George looked up at the clock.

"If anybody comes in you tell them the cook is off, and if they keep after it, you tell them you'll go back and cook yourself. Do you get that, bright boy?"

"All right," George said. "What you going to do with us afterward?"

"That'll depend," Max said. "That's one of those things you never know at the time."

George looked up at the clock. It was a quarter past six. The door from the street opened. A streetcar motorman came in.

[63]

"Hello, George," he said. "Can I get supper?"

"Sam's gone out," George said. "He'll be back in about half an hour."

"I'd better go up the street," the motorman said. George looked at the clock. It was twenty minutes past six.

"That was nice, bright boy," Max said. "You're a regular little gentleman."

"He knew I'd blow his head off," Al said from the kitchen.

"No," said Max. "It ain't that. Bright boy is nice. He's a nice boy. I like him."

At six fifty-five George said: "He's not coming."

Two other people had been in the lunchroom. Once George had gone out to the kitchen and made a ham-and-egg sandwich "to go" that a man wanted to take with him. Inside the kitchen he saw Al, his derby hat tipped back, sitting on a stool beside the wicket with the muzzle of a sawed-off shotgun resting on the ledge. Nick and the cook were back to back in the corner, a towel tied in each of their mouths. George had cooked the sandwich, wrapped it up in oiled paper, put it in a bag, brought it in, and the man had paid for it and gone out.

"Bright boy can do everything," Max said. "He can cook and everything. You'd make some girl a nice wife, bright boy."

"Yes?" George said. "Your friend, Ole Andreson, isn't going to come."

"We'll give him ten minutes," Max said.

Max watched the mirror and the clock. The hands of the clock marked seven o'clock, and then five minutes past seven.

"Come on, Al," said Max. "We better go. He's not coming."

"Better give him five minutes," Al said from the kitchen.

In the five minutes a man came in, and George explained that the cook was sick.

"Why the hell don't you get another cook?" the man asked. "Aren't you running a lunch counter?" He went out.

"Come on, Al," Max said.

"What about the two bright boys and the nigger?"

"They're all right."

"You think so?"

"Sure. We're through with it."

"I don't like it," said Al. "It's sloppy. You talk too much."

"Oh, what the hell," said Max. "We got to keep amused, haven't we?"

"You talk too much, all the same," Al said. He came out from the kitchen. The cut-off barrels of the shotgun made a slight bulge under the waist of his too tight-fitting overcoat. He straightened his coat with his gloved hands.

"So long, bright boy," he said to George. "You got a lot of luck."

"That's the truth," Max said. "You ought to play the races, bright boy."

The two of them went out the door. George watched them, through the window, pass under the arc light and cross the street. In their tight overcoats and derby hats they looked like a vaudeville team. George went back through the swinging door into the kitchen and untied Nick and the cook.

"I don't want any more of that," said Sam, the cook. "I don't want any more of that."

Nick stood up. He had never had a towel in his mouth before.

"Say," he said. "What the hell?" He was trying to swagger it off.

"They were going to kill Ole Andreson," George said. "They were going to shoot him when he came in to eat."

"Ole Andreson?"

"Sure."

The cook felt the corners of his mouth with his thumbs.

"They all gone?" he asked.

[65]

"Yeah," said George. "They're gone now."

"I don't like it," said the cook. "I don't like any of it at all."

"Listen," George said to Nick. "You better go see Ole Andreson."

"All right."

"You better not have anything to do with it at all," Sam, the cook, said. "You better stay way out of it."

"Don't go if you don't want to," George said.

"Mixing up in this ain't going to get you anywhere," the cook said. "You stay out of it."

"I'll go see him," Nick said to George. "Where does he live?"

The cook turned away.

"Little boys always know what they want to do," he said.

"He lives up at Hirsch's rooming house," George said to Nick.

"I'll go up there."

Outside the arc light shone through the bare branches of a tree. Nick walked up the street beside the car tracks and turned at the next arc light down a side street. Three houses up the street was Hirsch's rooming house. Nick walked up the two steps and pushed the bell. A woman came to the door.

"Is Ole Andreson here?"

"Do you want to see him?"

"Yes, if he's in."

Nick followed the woman up a flight of stairs and back to the end of a corridor. She knocked on the door.

"Who is it?"

"It's somebody to see you, Mr. Andreson," the woman said.

"It's Nick Adams."

"Come in."

Nick opened the door and went into the room. Ole Andreson was lying on the bed with all his clothes on. He had been a heavyweight prizefighter and he was too long for the bed. He lay with his head on two pillows. He did not look at Nick.

"What was it?" he asked.

"I was up at Henry's," Nick said, "and two fellows came in and tied up me and the cook, and they said they were going to kill you."

It sounded silly when he said it. Ole Andreson said nothing.

"They put us out in the kitchen," Nick went on. "They were going to shoot you when you came in to supper."

Ole Andreson looked at the wall and did not say anything.

"George thought I better come and tell you about it."

"There isn't anything I can do about it," Ole Andreson said.

"I'll tell you what they were like."

"I don't want to know what they were like," Ole Andreson said. He looked at the wall. "Thanks for coming to tell me about it."

"That's all right."

Nick looked at the big man lying on the bed.

"Don't you want me to go and see the police?"

"No," Ole Andreson said. "That wouldn't do any good."

"Isn't there something I could do?"

"No. There ain't anything to do."

"Maybe it was just a bluff."

"No. It ain't just a bluff."

Ole Andreson rolled over toward the wall.

"The only thing is," he said, talking toward the wall, "I just can't make up my mind to go out. I been in here all day."

"Couldn't you get out of town?"

"No," Ole Andreson said. "I'm through with all that running around."

He looked at the wall.

"There ain't anything to do now."

"Couldn't you fix it up some way?"

"No. I got in wrong." He talked in the same flat voice. "There ain't anything to do. After a while I'll make up my mind to go out."

"I better go back and see George," Nick said.

"So long," said Ole Andreson. He did not look toward Nick. "Thanks for coming around."

Nick went out. As he shut the door he saw Ole Andreson with all his clothes on, lying on the bed looking at the wall.

"He's been in his room all day," the landlady said downstairs. "I guess he don't feel well. I said to him: 'Mr. Andreson, you ought to go out and take a walk on a nice fall day like this,' but he didn't feel like it."

"He doesn't want to go out."

"I'm sorry he don't feel well," the woman said. "He's an awfully nice man. He was in the ring, you know."

"I know it."

"You'd never know it except from the way his face is," the woman said. They stood talking just inside the street door. "He's just as gentle."

"Well, good night, Mrs. Hirsch," Nick said.

"I'm not Mrs. Hirsch," the woman said. "She owns the place. I just look after it for her. I'm Mrs. Bell."

"Well, good night, Mrs. Bell," Nick said.

"Good night," the woman said.

Nick walked up the dark street to the corner under the arc light, and then along the car tracks to Henry's eating house. George was inside, back of the counter.

"Did you see Ole?"

"Yes," said Nick. "He's in his room and he won't go out."

The cook opened the door from the kitchen when he heard Nick's voice.

"I don't even listen to it," he said and shut the door.

"Did you tell him about it?" George asked.

"Sure. I told him but he knows what it's all about."

"What's he going to do?"

"Nothing."

"They'll kill him."

"I guess they will."

"He must have got mixed up in something in Chicago."

"I guess so," said Nick.

"It's a hell of a thing."

"It's an awful thing," Nick said.

They did not say anything. George reached down for a towel and wiped the counter.

"I wonder what he did?" Nick said.

"Double-crossed somebody. That's what they kill them for."

"I'm going to get out of this town," Nick said.

"Yes," said George. "That's a good thing to do."

"I can't stand to think about him waiting in the room and knowing he's going to get it. It's too damned awful."

"Well," said George, "you better not think about it."

The Last Good Country

"Nickie," his sister said to him. "Listen to me, Nickie."

"I don't want to hear it."

He was watching the bottom of the spring where the sand rose in small spurts with the bubbling water. There was a tin cup on a forked stick that was stuck in the gravel by the spring and Nick Adams looked at it and at the water rising and then flowing clear in its gravel bed beside the road.

He could see both ways on the road and he looked up the hill and then down to the dock and the lake, the wooded point across the bay and the open lake beyond where there were white caps running. His back was against a big cedar tree and behind him there was a thick cedar swamp. His sister was sitting on the moss beside him and she had her arm around his shoulders.

"They're waiting for you to come home to supper," his sister said. "There's two of them. They came in a buggy and they asked where you were."

"Did anybody tell them?"

"Nobody knew where you were but me. Did you get many, Nickie?"

"I got twenty-six."

"Are they good ones?"

"Just the size they want for the dinners."

"Oh, Nickie, I wish you wouldn't sell them."

"She gives me a dollar a pound," Nick Adams said.

His sister was tanned brown and she had dark brown eyes and dark brown hair with yellow streaks in it from the sun. She and Nick loved each other and they did not love the others. They always thought of everyone else in the family as the others.

"They know about everything, Nickie," his sister said hopelessly. "They said they were going to make an example of you and send you to the reform school."

"They've only got proof on one thing," Nick told her. "But I guess I have to go away for a while."

"Can I go?"

"No. I'm sorry, Littless. How much money have we got?"

"Fourteen dollars and sixty-five cents. I brought it."

"Did they say anything else?"

"No. Only that they were going to stay till you came home."

"Our mother will get tired of feeding them."

"She gave them lunch already."

"What were they doing?"

"Just sitting around on the screen porch. They asked our mother for your rifle but I'd hid it in the woodshed when I saw them by the fence."

"Were you expecting them?"

"Yes. Weren't you?"

"I guess so. Goddam them."

"Goddam them for me, too," his sister said. "Aren't I old enough to go now? I hid the rifle. I brought the money."

"I'd worry about you," Nick Adams told her. "I don't even know where I'm going."

"Sure you do."

"If there's two of us they'd look harder. A boy and a girl show up."

"I'd go like a boy," she said. "I always wanted to be a boy anyway. They couldn't tell anything about me if my hair was cut."

"No," Nick Adams said. "That's true."

"Let's think something out good," she said. "Please, Nick, please. I could be lots of use and you'd be lonely without me. Wouldn't you be?"

"I'm lonely now thinking about going away from you."

"See? And we may have to be away for years. Who can tell? Take me, Nickie. Please take me." She kissed him and held onto him with both her arms. Nick Adams looked at her and tried to think straight. It was difficult. But there was no choice.

"I shouldn't take you. But then I shouldn't have done any of it," he said. "I'll take you. Maybe only for a couple of days, though."

"That's all right," she told him. "When you don't want me I'll go straight home. I'll go home anyway if I'm a bother or a nuisance or an expense."

"Let's think it out," Nick Adams told her. He looked up and down the road and up at the sky where the big high afternoon clouds were riding and at the white caps on the lake out beyond the point.

"I'll go through the woods down to the inn beyond the point and sell her the trout," he told his sister. "She ordered them for dinners tonight. Right now they want more trout dinners than chicken dinners. I don't know why. The trout are in good shape. I gutted them and they're wrapped in cheese-cloth and they'll be cool and fresh. I'll tell her I'm in some trouble with the game wardens and that they're looking for me and I have to get out of the country for a while. I'll get her to give me a small skillet and some salt and pepper and some bacon and some shortening and some corn meal. I'll get her to give me a sack to put everything in and I'll get some dried apricots and some prunes and some tea and plenty of matches and a hatchet. But I can only get one blanket. She'll help me because buying trout is just as bad as selling them."

"I can get a blanket," his sister said. "I'll wrap it around the rifle and I'll bring your moccasins and my moccasins and I'll change to different overalls and a shirt and hide these so they'll think I'm wearing them and I'll bring soap and a comb and a pair of scissors and something to sew with and Lorna Doone and Swiss Family Robinson."

"Bring all the .22's you can find," Nick Adams said. Then quickly, "Come on back. Get out of sight." He had seen a buggy coming down the road.

Behind the cedars they lay flat against the springy moss with their faces down and heard the soft noise of the horses' hooves in the sand and the small noise of the wheels. Neither of the men in the buggy was talking but Nick Adams smelled them as they went past and he smelled the sweated horses. He sweated himself until they were well past on their way to the dock because he thought they might stop to water at the spring or to get a drink.

"Is that them, Littless?" he asked.

"Yeah," she said.

"Crawl way back in," Nick Adams said. He crawled back into the swamp, pulling his sack of fish. The swamp was mossy and not muddy there. Then he stood up and hid the sack behind the trunk of a cedar and motioned the girl to come further in. They went into the cedar swamp, moving as softly as deer.

"I know the one," Nick Adams said. "He's a no good son of a bitch."

"He said he'd been after you for four years."

"I know."

"The other one, the big one with the spit tobacco face and the blue suit, is the one from down state."

[73]

"Good," Nick said. "Now we've had a look at them I better get going. Can you get home all right?"

"Sure. I'll cut up to the top of the hill and keep off the road. Where will I meet you tonight, Nickie?"

"I don't think you ought to come, Littless."

"I've got to come. You don't know how it is. I can leave a note for our mother and say I went with you and you'll take good care of me."

"All right," Nick Adams said. "I'll be where the big hemlock is that was struck by lightning. The one that's down. Straight up from the cove. Do you know the one? On the short cut to the road."

"That's awfully close to the house."

"I don't want you to have to carry the stuff too far."

"I'll do what you say. But don't take chances, Nickie."

"I'd like to have the rifle and go down now to the edge of the timber and kill both of those bastards while they're on the dock and wire a piece of iron on them from the old mill and sink them in the channel."

"And then what would you do?" his sister asked. "Somebody sent them."

"Nobody sent that first son of a bitch."

"But you killed the moose and you sold the trout and you killed what they took from your boat."

"That was all right to kill that."

He did not like to mention what that was, because that was the proof they had.

"I know. But you're not going to kill people and that's why I'm going with you."

"Let's stop talking about it. But I'd like to kill those two sons of bitches."

"I know," she said. "So would I. But we're not going to kill people, Nickie. Will you promise me?"

"No. Now I don't know whether it's safe to take her the trout."

"I'll take them to her."

"No. They're too heavy. I'll take them through the swamp and to the woods in back of the hotel. You go straight to the hotel and see if she's there and if everything's all right. And if it is you'll find me there by the big basswood tree."

"It's a long way there through the swamp, Nicky."

"It's a long way back from reform school, too."

"Can't I come with you through the swamp? I'll go in then and see her while you stay out and come back out with you and take them in."

"All right," Nick said. "But I wish you'd do it the other way."

"Why, Nickie?"

"Because you'll see them maybe on the road and you can tell me where they've gone. I'll see you in the second-growth wood lot in back of the hotel where the big basswood is."

Nick waited more than an hour in the second-growth timber and his sister had not come. When she came she was excited and he knew she was tired.

"They're at our house," she said. "They're sitting out on the screen porch and drinking whiskey and ginger ale and they've unhitched and put their horses up. They say they're going to wait till you come back. It was our mother told them you'd gone fishing at the creek. I don't think she meant to. Anyway I hope not."

"What about Mrs. Packard?"

"I saw her in the kitchen of the hotel and she asked me if I'd seen you and I said no. She said she was waiting for you to bring her some fish for tonight. She was worried. You might as well take them in."

"Good," he said. "They're nice and fresh. I repacked them in ferns."

"Can I come in with you?"

"Sure," Nick said.

The hotel was a long wooden building with a porch that fronted on the lake. There were wide wooden steps that led down to the pier that ran far out into the water and there were natural cedar railings alongside the steps and natural cedar railings around the porch. There were chairs made of natural cedar on the porch and in them sat middle-aged people wearing white clothes. There were three pipes set on the lawn with spring water bubbling out of them, and little paths led to them. The water tasted like rotten eggs because these were mineral springs and Nick and his sister used to drink from them as a matter of discipline. Now coming toward the rear of the hotel, where the kitchen was, they crossed a plank bridge over a small brook running into the lake beside the hotel, and slipped into the back door of the kitchen.

"Wash them and put them in the ice box, Nickie," Mrs. Packard said. "I'll weigh them later."

"Mrs. Packard," Nick said. "Could I speak to you a minute?"

"Speak up," she said. "Can't you see I'm busy?"

"If I could have the money now."

Mrs. Packard was a handsome woman in a gingham apron. She had a beautiful complexion and she was very busy and her kitchen help were there as well.

"You don't mean you want to sell trout. Don't you know that's against the law?"

"I know," Nick said. "I brought you the fish for a present. I mean my time for the wood I split and corded."

"I'll get it," she said. "I have to go to the annex."

Nick and his sister followed her outside. On the board sidewalk that led to the icehouse from the kitchen she stopped

[76]

and put her hands in her apron pocket and took out a pocket-book.

"You get out of here," she said quickly and kindly. "And get out of here fast. How much do you need?"

"I've got sixteen dollars," Nick said.

"Take twenty," she told him. "And keep that tyke out of trouble. Let her go home and keep an eye on them until you're clear."

"When did you hear about them?"

She shook her head at him.

"Buying is as bad or worse than selling," she said. "You stay away until things quiet down. Nickie, you're a good boy no matter what anybody says. You see Packard if things get bad. Come here nights if you need anything. I sleep light. Just knock on the window."

"You aren't going to serve them tonight are you, Mrs. Packard? You're not going to serve them for the dinners?"

"No," she said. "But I'm not going to waste them. Packard can eat half a dozen and I know other people that can. Be careful, Nickie, and let it blow over. Keep out of sight."

"Littless wants to go with me."

"Don't you dare take her," Mrs. Packard said. "You come by tonight and I'll have some stuff made up for you."

"Could you let me take a skillet?"

"I'll have what you need. Packard knows what you need. I don't give you any more money so you'll keep out of trouble."

"I'd like to see Mr. Packard about getting a few things."

"He'll get you anything you need. But don't you go near the store, Nick."

"I'll get Littless to take him a note."

"Anytime you need anything," Mrs. Packard said. "Don't you worry. Packard will be studying things out."

"Goodby, Aunt Halley."

"Goodby," she said and kissed him. She smelt wonderful when she kissed him. It was the way the kitchen smelled when they were baking. Mrs. Packard smelled like her kitchen and her kitchen always smelled good.

"Don't worry and don't do anything bad."

"I'll be all right."

"Of course," she said. "And Packard will figure out something."

They were in the big hemlocks on the hill behind the house now. It was evening and the sun was down beyond the hills on the other side of the lake.

"I've found everything," his sister said. "It's going to make a pretty big pack, Nickie."

"I know it. What are they doing?"

"They ate a big supper and now they're sitting out on the porch and drinking. They're telling each other stories about how smart they are."

"They aren't very smart so far."

"They're going to starve you out," his sister said. "A couple of nights in the woods and you'll be back. You hear a loon holler a couple of times when you got an empty stomach and you'll be back."

"What did our mother give them for supper?"

"Awful," his sister said.

"Good."

"I've located everything on the list. Our mother's gone to bed with a sick headache. She wrote our father."

"Did you see the letter?"

"No. It's in her room with the list of stuff to get from the store tomorrow. She's going to have to make a new list when she finds everything is gone in the morning."

"How much are they drinking?"

"They've drunk about a bottle, I guess."

"I wish we could put knockout drops in it."

"I could put them in if you'll tell me how. Do you put them in the bottle?"

"No. In the glass. But we haven't got any."

"Would there be any in the medicine cabinet?"

"No."

"I could put paragoric in the bottle. They have another bottle. Or calomel. I know we've got those."

"No," said Nick. "You try to get me about half the other bottle when they're asleep. Put it in any old medicine bottle."

"I better go and watch them," his sister said. "My, I wish we had knockout drops. I never even heard of them."

"They aren't really drops," Nick told her. "It's chloral hydrate. Whores give it to lumberjacks in their drinks when they're going to jack roll them."

"It sounds pretty bad," his sister said. "But we probably ought to have some for in emergencies."

"Let me kiss you," her brother said. "Just for in an emergency. Let's go down and watch them drinking. I'd like to hear them talk sitting in our own house."

"Will you promise not to get angry and do anything bad?"

"Sure."

"Nor to the horses. It's not the horses' fault."

"Not the horses either."

"I wish we had knockout drops," his sister said loyally.

"Well, we haven't," Nick told her. "I guess there aren't any this side of Boyne City."

They sat in the woodshed and they watched the two men sitting at the table on the screen porch. The moon had not risen and it was dark, but the outlines of the men showed against the lightness that the lake made behind them. They were not talking now but were both leaning forward on the table. Then Nick heard the clink of ice against a bucket.

"The ginger ale's gone," one of the men said.

[79]

"I said it wouldn't last," the other said. "But you were the one said we had plenty."

"Get some water. There's a pail and a dipper in the kitchen."

"I've drunk enough. I'm going to turn in."

"Aren't you going to stay up for that kid?"

"No. I'm going to get some sleep. You stay up."

"Do you think he'll come in tonight?"

"I don't know. I'm going to get some sleep. You wake me when you get sleepy."

"I can stay up all night," the local warden said. "Many's the night I've stayed up all night for jack lighters and never shut an eye."

"Me, too," the down-state man said. "But now I'm going to get a little sleep."

Nick and his sister watched him go in the door. Their mother had told the two men they could sleep in the bedroom next to the living room. They saw when he struck a match. Then the window was dark again. They watched the other warden sitting at the table until he put his head on his arms. Then they heard him snoring.

"We'll give him a little while to make sure he's solid asleep. Then we'll get the stuff," Nick said.

"You get over outside the fence," his sister said. "It doesn't matter if I'm moving around. But he might wake up and see you."

"All right," Nick agreed. "I'll get everything out of here. Most of it's here."

"Can you find everything without a light?"

"Sure. Where's the rifle?"

"Flat on the back upper rafter. Don't slip or make the wood fall down, Nick."

"Don't you worry."

She came out to the fence at the far corner where Nick was making up his pack beyond the big hemlock that had been struck by lightning the summer before and had fallen in a storm that autumn. The moon was just rising now behind the far hills and enough moonlight came through the trees for Nick to see clearly what he was packing. His sister put down the sack she was carrying and said, "They're sleeping like pigs, Nickie."

"Good."

"The down-state one was snoring just like the one outside. I think I got everything."

"You good old Littless."

"I wrote a note to our mother and told her I was going with you to keep you out of trouble and not to tell anybody and that you'd take good care of me. I put it under her door. It's locked."

"Oh, shit," Nick said. Then he said, "I'm sorry, Littless."

"Now it's not your fault and I can't make it worse for you."

"You're awful."

"Can't we be happy now?"

"Sure."

"I brought the whiskey," she said hopefully. "I left some in the bottle. One of them can't be sure the other didn't drink it. Anyway they have another bottle."

"Did you bring a blanket for you?"

"Of course."

"We better get going."

"We're all right if we're going where I think. The only thing makes the pack bigger is my blanket. I'll carry the rifle."

"All right. What kind of shoes have you?"

"I've got my work-moccasins."

"What did you bring to read?"

"Lorna Doone and Kidnapped and Wuthering Heights."

"They're all too old for you but Kidnapped."

"Lorna Doone isn't."

"We'll read it out loud," Nick said. "That way it lasts longer. But, Littless, you've made things sort of hard now and we better go. Those bastards can't be as stupid as they act. Maybe it was just because they were drinking."

Nick had rolled the pack now and tightened the straps and he sat back and put his moccasins on. He put his arm around his sister. "You sure you want to go?"

"I have to go, Nickie. Don't be weak and undecisive now. I left the note."

"All right," Nick said. "Let's go. You can take the rifle until you get tired of it."

"I'm all ready to go," his sister said. "Let me help you strap the pack."

"You know you haven't had any sleep at all and that we have to travel?"

"I know. I'm really like the snoring one at the table says he was."

"Maybe he was that way once, too," Nick said. "But what you have to do is keep your feet in good shape. Do the moccasins chafe?"

"No. And my feet are tough from going barefoot all summer."

"Mine are good, too," said Nick. "Come on. Let's go."

They started off walking on the soft hemlock needles and the trees were high and there was no brush between the tree trunks. They walked uphill and the moon came through the trees and showed Nick with the very big pack and his sister carrying the .22 rifle. When they were at the top of the hill they looked back and saw the lake in the moonlight. It was clear enough so they could see the dark point, and beyond were the high hills of the far shore.

"We might as well say goodby to it," Nick Adams said.

"Goodby, lake," Littless said. "I love you, too."

They went down the hill and across the long field and through the orchard and then through a rail fence and into a field of stubble. Going through the stubble field they looked to the right and saw the slaughterhouse and the big barn in the hollow and the old log farmhouse on the other high land that overlooked the lake. The long road of Lombardy poplars that ran to the lake was in the moonlight.

"Does it hurt your feet, Littless?" Nick asked.

"No," his sister said.

"I came this way on account of the dogs," Nick said. "They'd shut up as soon as they knew it was us. But somebody might hear them bark."

"I know," she said. "And as soon as they shut up afterwards they'd know it was us."

Ahead they could see the dark of the rising line of hills beyond the road. They came to the end of one cut field of grain and crossed the little sunken creek that ran down to the springhouse. Then they climbed across the rise of another stubble field and there was another rail fence and the sandy road with the second-growth timber solid beyond it.

"Wait till I climb over and I'll help you," Nick said. "I want to look at the road."

From the top of the fence he saw the roll of the country and the dark timber by their own house and the brightness of the lake in the moonlight. Then he was looking at the road.

"They can't track us the way we've come and I don't think they would notice tracks in this deep sand," he said to his sister. "We can keep to the two sides of the road if it isn't too scratchy."

"Nickie, honestly I don't think they're intelligent enough to track anybody. Look how they just waited for you to come back and then practically got drunk before supper and afterwards."

"They came down to the dock," Nick said. "That was where

I was. If you hadn't told me they would have picked me up."

"They didn't have to be so intelligent to figure you would be on the big creek when our mother let them know you might have gone fishing. After I left they must have found all the boats were there and that would make them think you were fishing the creek. Everybody knows you usually fish below the grist mill and the cider mill. They were just slow thinking it out."

"All right," Nick said. "But they were awfully close then."

His sister handed him the rifle through the fence, butt toward him, and then crawled between the rails. She stood beside him on the road and he put his hand on her head and stroked it.

"Are you awfully tired, Littless?"

"No. I'm fine. I'm too happy to be tired."

"Until you're too tired you walk in the sandy part of the road where their horses made holes in the sand. It's so soft and dry tracks won't show and I'll walk on the side where it's hard."

"I can walk on the side, too."

"No. I don't want you to get scratched."

They climbed, but with constant small descents, toward the height of land that separated the two lakes. There was close, heavy, second-growth timber on both sides of the road and blackberry and raspberry bushes grew from the edge of the road to the timber. Ahead they could see the top of each hill as a notch in the timber. The moon was well on its way down now.

"How do you feel, Littless?" Nick asked his sister.

"I feel wonderful. Nickie, is it always this nice when you run away from home?"

"No. Usually it's lonesome."

"How lonesome have you ever been?"

"Bad black lonesome. Awful."

"Do you think you'll get lonesome with me?"

"No."

"You don't mind you're with me instead of going to Trudy?"

"What do you talk about her for all the time?"

"I haven't been. Maybe you were thinking about her and you thought I was talking."

"You're too smart," Nick said. "I thought about her because you told me where she was and when I knew where she was I wondered what she would be doing and all that."

"I guess I shouldn't have come."

"I told you that you shouldn't come."

"Oh, hell," his sister said. "Are we going to be like the others and have fights? I'll go back now. You don't have to have me."

"Shut up," Nick said.

"Please don't say that, Nickie. I'll go back or I'll stay just as you want. I'll go back whenever you tell me to. But I won't have fights. Haven't we seen enough fights in families?"

"Yes," said Nick.

"I know I forced you to take me. But I fixed it so you wouldn't get in trouble about it. And I did keep them from catching you."

They had reached the height of land and from here they could see the lake again although from here it looked narrow now and almost like a big river.

"We cut across country here," Nick said. "Then we'll hit that old logging road. Here's where you go back from if you want to go back."

He took off his pack and put it back into the timber and his sister leaned the rifle on it.

"Sit down, Littless, and take a rest," he said. "We're both tired."

Nick lay with his head on the pack and his sister lay by him with her head on his shoulder.

"I'm not going back, Nickie, unless you tell me to," she said. "I just don't want fights. Promise me we won't have fights?"

"Promise."

"I won't talk about Trudy."

"The hell with Trudy."

"I want to be useful and a good partner."

"You are. You won't mind if I get restless and mix it up with being lonesome?"

"No. We'll take good care of each other and have fun. We can have a lovely time."

"All right. We'll start to have it now."

"I've been having it all the time."

"We just have one pretty hard stretch and then a really hard stretch and then we'll be there. We might as well wait until it gets light to start. You go to sleep, Littless. Are you warm enough?"

"Oh yes, Nickie. I've got my sweater."

She curled up beside him and was asleep. In a little while Nick was sleeping, too. He slept for two hours until the morning light woke him.

Nick had circled around through the second-growth timber until they had come onto the old logging road.

"We couldn't leave tracks going into it from the main road," he told his sister.

The old road was so overgrown that he had to stoop many times to avoid hitting branches.

"It's like a tunnel," his sister said.

"It opens up after a while."

"Have I ever been here before?"

"No. This goes up way beyond where I ever took you hunting."

"Does it come out on the secret place?"

"No, Littless. We have to go through some long bad slash-ings. Nobody gets in where we're going."

They kept on along the road and then took another road that was even more overgrown. Then they came out into a clearing. There was fireweed and brush in the clearing and the old cabins of the logging camp. They were very old and some of the roofs had fallen in. But there was a spring by the road and they both drank at it. The sun wasn't up yet and they both felt hollow and empty in the early morning after the night of walking.

"All this beyond was hemlock forest," Nick said. "They only cut it for the bark and they never used the logs."

"But what happens to the road?"

"They must have cut up at the far end first and hauled and piled the bark by the road to snake it out. Then finally they cut everything right to the road and piled the bark here and then pulled out."

"Is the secret place beyond all this slashing?"

"Yes. We go through the slashing and then some more road and then another slashing and then we come to virgin timber."

"How did they leave it when they cut all this?"

"I don't know. It belonged to somebody that wouldn't sell, I guess. They stole a lot from the edges and paid stump-age on it. But the good part's still there and there isn't any passable road into it."

"But why can't people go down the creek? The creek has to come from somewhere?"

They were resting before they started the bad traveling through the slashing and Nick wanted to explain.

"Look, Littless. The creek crosses the main road we were on and it goes through a farmer's land. The farmer has it fenced for a pasture and he runs people off that want to fish. So they stop at the bridge on his land. On the section of the creek where they would hit if they cut across his pasture on the other side from his house he runs a bull. The bull is mean and he really runs everybody off. He's the meanest bull I ever saw and he just stays there, mean all the time, and hunts for people. Then after him the farmer's land ends and there's a section of cedar swamp with sink holes and you'd have to know it to get through. And then, even if you know it, it's bad. Below that is the secret place. We're going in over the hills and sort of in the back way. Then below the secret place there's real swamp. Bad swamp that you can't get through. Now we better start the bad part."

The bad part and the part that was worse were behind them now. Nick had climbed over many logs that were higher than his head and others that were up to his waist. He would take the rifle and lay it down on the top of the log and pull his sister up and then she would slide down on the far side or he would lower himself down and take the rifle and help the girl down. They went over and around piles of brush and it was hot in the slashing, and the pollen from the ragweed and the fireweed dusted the girl's hair and made her sneeze.

"Damn slashings," she said to Nick. They were resting on top of a big log ringed where they sat by the cutting of the barkpeelers. The ring was gray in the rotting gray log and all around were other long gray trunks and gray brush and branches with the brilliant and worthless weeds growing.

"This is the last one," Nick said.

"I hate them," his sister said. "And the damn weeds are like flowers in a tree cemetery if nobody took care of it."

"You see why I didn't want to try to make it in the dark."

"We couldn't."

"No. And nobody's going to chase us through here. Now we come into the good part."

They came from the hot sun of the slashings into the shade

of the great trees. The slashings had run up to the top of a ridge and over and then the forest began. They were walking on the brown forest floor now and it was springy and cool under their feet. There was no underbrush and the trunks of the trees rose sixty feet high before there were any branches. It was cool in the shade of the trees and high up in them Nick could hear the breeze that was rising. No sun came through as they walked and Nick knew there would be no sun through the high top branches until nearly noon. His sister put her hand in his and walked close to him.

"I'm not scared, Nickie. But it makes me feel very strange."

"Me, too," Nick said. "Always."

"I never was in woods like these."

"This is all the virgin timber left around here."

"Do we go through it very long?"

"Quite a way."

"I'd be afraid if I were alone."

"It makes me feel strange. But I'm not afraid."

"I said that first."

"I know. Maybe we say it because we are afraid."

"No. I'm not afraid because I'm with you. But I know I'd be afraid alone. Did you ever come here with anyone else?"

"No. Only by myself."

"And you weren't afraid?"

"No. But I always feel strange. Like the way I ought to feel in church."

"Nickie, where we're going to live isn't as solemn as this, is it?"

"No. Don't you worry. There it's cheerful. You just enjoy this, Littless. This is good for you. This is the way forests were in the olden days. This is about the last good country there is left. Nobody gets in here ever."

"I love the olden days. But I wouldn't want it all this solemn."

"It wasn't all solemn. But the hemlock forests were."

"It's wonderful walking. I thought behind our house was wonderful. But this is better. Nickie, do you believe in God? You don't have to answer if you don't want to."

"I don't know."

"All right. You don't have to say it. But you don't mind if I say my prayers at night?"

"No. I'll remind you if you forget."

"Thank you. Because this kind of woods makes me feel awfully religious."

"That's why they build cathedrals to be like this."

"You've never seen a cathedral, have you?"

"No. But I've read about them and I can imagine them. This is the best one we have around here."

"Do you think we can go to Europe some time and see cathedrals?"

"Sure we will. But first I have to get out of this trouble and learn how to make some money."

"Do you think you'll ever make money writing?"

"If I get good enough."

"Couldn't you maybe make it if you wrote cheerfuller things? That isn't my opinion. Our mother said everything you write is morbid."

"It's too morbid for the St. Nicholas," Nick said. "They didn't say it. But they didn't like it."

"But the St. Nicholas is our favorite magazine."

"I know," said Nick. "But I'm too morbid for it already. And I'm not even grown-up."

"When is a man grown-up? When he's married?"

"No. Until you're grown-up they send you to reform school. After you're grown-up they send you to the penitentiary."

"I'm glad you're not grown-up then."

"They're not going to send me anywhere," Nick said. "And let's not talk morbid even if I write morbid."

"I didn't say it was morbid."

"I know. Everybody else does, though."

"Let's be cheerful, Nickie," his sister said. "These woods make us too solemn."

"We'll be out of them pretty soon," Nick told her. "Then you'll see where we're going to live. Are you hungry, Littless?"

"A little."

"I'll bet," Nick said. "We'll eat a couple of apples."

They were coming down a long hill when they saw sunlight ahead through the tree trunks. Now, at the edge of the timber there was wintergreen growing and some partridge-berries and the forest floor began to be alive with growing things. Through the tree trunks they saw an open meadow that sloped to where white birches grew along the stream. Below the meadow and the line of the birches there was the dark green of a cedar swamp and far beyond the swamp there were dark blue hills. There was an arm of the lake between the swamp and the hills. But from here they could not see it. They only felt from the distances that it was there.

"Here's the spring," Nick said to his sister. "And here's the stones where I camped before."

"It's a beautiful, beautiful place, Nickie," his sister said. "Can we see the lake, too?"

"There's a place where we can see it. But it's better to camp here. I'll get some wood and we'll make breakfast."

"The firestones are very old."

"It's a very old place," Nick said. "The firestones are Indian."

"How did you come to it straight through the woods with no trail and no blazes?"

"Didn't you see the direction sticks on the three ridges?"

"No."

"*I'll show them to you sometime.*"

"*Are they yours?*"

"*No. They're from the old days.*"

"*Why didn't you show them to me?*"

"*I don't know,*" Nick said. "*I was showing off I guess.*"

"*Nickie, they'll never find us here.*"

"*I hope not,*" Nick said.

At about the time that Nick and his sister were entering the first of the slashings the warden who was sleeping on the screen porch of the house that stood in the shade of the trees above the lake was wakened by the sun that, rising above the slope of open land behind the house, shone full on his face.

During the night the warden had gotten up for a drink of water and when he had come back from the kitchen he had lain down on the floor with a cushion from one of the chairs for a pillow. Now he waked, realized where he was, and got to his feet. He had slept on his right side because he had a .38 Smith and Wesson revolver in a shoulder holster under his left armpit. Now, awake, he felt for the gun, looked away from the sun, which hurt his eyes, and went into the kitchen where he dipped up a drink of water from the pail beside the kitchen table. The hired girl was building a fire in the stove and the warden said to her, "What about some breakfast?"

"No breakfast," she said. She slept in a cabin out behind the house and had come into the kitchen a half an hour before. The sight of the warden lying on the floor of the screen porch and the nearly empty bottle of whiskey on the table had frightened and disgusted her. Then it had made her angry.

"What do you mean, no breakfast?" the warden said, still holding the dipper.

"Just that."

"Why?"

"Nothing to eat."

"What about coffee?"

"No coffee."

"Tea?"

"No tea. No bacon. No corn meal. No salt. No pepper. No coffee. No Borden's canned cream. No Aunt Jemima buckwheat flour. No nothing."

"What are you talking about? There was plenty to eat last night."

"There isn't now. Chipmunks must have carried it away."

The warden from down state had gotten up when he heard them talking and had come into the kitchen.

"How do you feel this morning?" the hired girl asked him.

The warden ignored the hired girl and said, "What is it, Evans?"

"That son of a bitch came in here last night and got himself a pack load of grub."

"Don't you swear in my kitchen," the hired girl said.

"Come out here," the down-state warden said. They both went out on the screen porch and shut the kitchen door.

"What does that mean, Evans?" the down-state man pointed at the quart of Old Green River which had less than a quarter left in it. "How skunk-drunk were you?"

"I drank the same as you. I sat up by the table—"

"Doing what?"

"Waiting for the goddam Adams boy if he showed."

"And drinking."

"Not drinking. Then I got up and went in the kitchen and got a drink of water about half past four and I lay down here in front of the door to take it easier."

"Why didn't you lie down in front of the kitchen door?"

"I could see him better from here if he came."

"So what happened?"

[93]

"He must have come in the kitchen, through a window maybe, and loaded that stuff."

"Bullshit."

"What were you doing?" the local warden asked.

"I was sleeping the same as you."

"Okay. Let's quit fighting about it. That doesn't do any good."

"Tell that hired girl to come out here."

The hired girl came out and the down-state man said to her, "You tell Mrs. Adams we want to speak to her."

The hired girl did not say anything but went into the main part of the house, shutting the door after her.

"You better pick up the full and the empty bottles," the down-state man said. "There isn't enough of this to do any good. You want a drink of it?"

"No thanks. I've got to work today."

"I'll take one," the down-state man said. "It hasn't been shared right."

"I didn't drink any of it after you left," the local warden said doggedly.

"Why do you keep on with that bullshit?"

"It isn't bullshit."

The down-state man put the bottle down. "All right," he said to the hired girl, who had opened and shut the door behind her. "What did she say?"

"She has a sick headache and she can't see you. She says you have a warrant. She says for you to search the place if you want to and then go."

"What did she say about the boy?"

"She hasn't seen the boy and she doesn't know anything about him."

"Where are the other kids?"

"They're visiting at Charlevoix."

"Who are they visiting?"

"I don't know. She doesn't know. They went to the dance and they were going to stay over Sunday with friends."

"Who was that kid that was around here yesterday?"

"I didn't see any kid around here yesterday."

"There was."

"Maybe some friend of the children asking for them. Maybe some resorter's kid. Was it a boy or a girl?"

"A girl about eleven or twelve. Brown hair and brown eyes. Freckles. Very tanned. Wearing overalls and a boy's shirt. Barefooted."

"Sounds like anybody," the hired girl said. "Did you say eleven or twelve years old?"

"Oh, shit," said the man from down state. "You can't get anything out of these mossbacks."

"If I'm a mossback what's he?" the hired girl looked at the local warden. "What's Mr. Evans? His kids and me went to the same schoolhouse."

"Who was the girl?" Evans asked her. "Come on, Suzy. I can find out anyway."

"I wouldn't know," Suzy, the hired girl, said. "It seems like all kinds of people come by here now. I feel just like I'm in a big city."

"You don't want to get in any trouble, do you, Suzy?" Evans said.

"No, sir."

"I mean it."

"You don't want to get in any trouble either, do you?" Suzy asked him.

Out at the barn after they were hitched up the down-state man said, "We didn't do so good, did we?"

"He's loose now," Evans said. "He's got grub and he must have his rifle. But he's still in the area. I can get him. Can you track?"

"No. Not really. Can you?"

"In snow," the other warden laughed.

"But we don't have to track. We have to think out where he'll be."

"He didn't load up with all that stuff to go south. He'd just take a little something and head for the railway."

"I couldn't tell what was missing from the woodshed. But he had a big pack load from the kitchen. He's heading in somewhere. I got to check on all his habits and his friends and where he used to go. You block him off at Charlevoix and Petoskey and St. Ignace and Sheboygan. Where would you go if you were him?"

"I'd go to the Upper Peninsula."

"Me, too. He's been up there, too. The ferry is the easiest place to pick him up. But there's an awful big country between here and Sheboygan and he knows that country, too."

"We better go down and see Packard. We were going to check that today."

"What's to prevent him going down by East Jordan and Grand Traverse?"

"Nothing. But that isn't his country. He'll go some place that he knows."

Suzy came out when they were opening the gate in the fence.

"Can I ride down to the store with you? I've got to get some groceries."

"What makes you think we're going to the store?"

"Yesterday you were talking about going to see Mr. Packard."

"How are you going to get your groceries back?"

"I guess I can get a lift with somebody on the road or coming up the lake. This is Saturday."

"All right. Climb up," the local warden said.

"Thank you, Mr. Evans," Suzy said.

At the general store and post office Evans hitched the team at the rack and he and the down-state man stood and talked before they went in.

"I couldn't say anything with that damned Suzy."

"Sure."

"Packard's a fine man. There isn't anybody better-liked in this country. You'd never get a conviction on that trout business against him. Nobody's going to scare him and we don't want to antagonize him."

"Do you think he'll cooperate?"

"Not if you act rough."

"We'll go see him."

Inside the store Suzy had gone straight through past the glass showcases, the opened barrels, the boxes, the shelves of canned goods, seeing nothing nor anyone until she came to the post office with its lockboxes and it's general delivery and stamp window. The window was down and she went straight on to the back of the store. Mr. Packard was opening a packing box with a crowbar. He looked at her and smiled.

"Mr. John," the hired girl said, speaking very fast. "There's two wardens coming in that's after Nickie. He cleared out last night and his kid sister's gone with him. Don't let on about that. His mother knows it and it's all right. Anyhow she isn't going to say anything."

"Did he take all your groceries?"

"Most of them."

"You pick out what you need and make a list and I'll check it over with you."

"They're coming in now."

"You go out the back and come in the front again. I'll go and talk to them."

Suzy walked around the long frame building and climbed the front steps again. This time she noticed everything as she came in. She knew the Indians who had brought in the baskets and she knew the two Indian boys who were looking at the fishing tackle in the first showcases on the left. She knew all the patent medicines in the next case and who usually bought them. She had clerked one summer in the store and she knew what the penciled code letters and numbers meant that were on the cardboard boxes that held shoes, winter overshoes, wool socks, mittens, caps and sweaters. She knew what the baskets were worth that the Indians had brought in and that it was too late in the season for them to bring a good price.

"Why did you bring them in so late, Mrs. Tabeshaw?" she asked.

"Too much fun Fourth of July," the Indian woman laughed.

"How's Billy?" Suzy asked.

"I don't know, Suzy. I no see him four weeks now."

"Why don't you take them down to the hotel and try and sell them to the resorters?" Suzy said.

"Maybe," Mrs. Tabeshaw said. "I took once."

"You ought to take them every day."

"Long walk," Mrs. Tabeshaw said.

While Suzy was talking to the people she knew and making a list of what she needed for the house the two wardens were in the back of the store with Mr. John Packard.

Mr. John had gray-blue eyes and dark hair and a dark mustache and he always looked as though he had wandered into a general store by accident. He had been away from northern Michigan once for eighteen years when he was a young man and he looked more like a peace officer or an honest gambler than a storekeeper. He had owned good saloons in his time and run them well. But when the country had been lumbered off he had stayed and bought farming land. Finally when the county had gone local option he had bought this store. He already owned the hotel. But he said he didn't like a hotel without a bar and so he almost never went near it. Mrs. Packard ran the hotel. She was more ambitious than Mr. John and Mr. John said he didn't want to waste time with people who had enough money to take a vacation anywhere in the country they wanted and then came to a hotel without a bar and spent their time sitting on the porch in rocking chairs. He called the resorters "change-of-lifers" and he made fun of them to Mrs. Packard but she loved him and never minded when he teased her.

"I don't mind if you call them change-of-lifers," she told him one night in bed. "I had the damn thing but I'm still all the woman you can handle, aren't I?"

She liked the resorters because some of them brought culture and Mr. John said she loved culture like a lumberjack loved Peerless, the great chewing tobacco. He really respected her love of culture because she said she loved it just like he loved good bonded whiskey and she said, "Packard, you don't have to care about culture. I won't bother you with it. But it makes me feel wonderful."

Mr. John said she could have culture until hell wouldn't hold it just so long as he never had to go to a Chautauqua or a Self-Betterment Course. He had been to camp meetings and a revival but he had never been to a Chautauqua. He said a camp meeting or a revival was bad enough but at least there was some sexual intercourse afterward by those who got really aroused although he never knew anyone to pay their bills after a camp meeting or a revival. Mrs. Packard, he told Nick Adams, would get worried about the salvation of his immortal soul after she had been to a big revival by somebody like Gypsy Smith, that great evangelist, but finally it would turn out that he, Packard, looked like Gypsy Smith and everything would be fine finally. But a Chautauqua was something strange. Culture maybe was better than religion, Mr. John thought.

But it was a cold proposition. Still they were crazy for it. He could see it was more than a fad, though.

"It's sure got a hold on them," he had told Nick Adams. "It must be sort of like the Holy Rollers only in the brain. You study it sometime and tell me what you think. You going to be a writer you ought to get in on it early. Don't let them get too far ahead of you."

Mr. John liked Nick Adams because he said he had original sin. Nick did not understand this but he was proud.

"You're going to have things to repent, boy," Mr. John had told Nick. "That's one of the best things there is. You can always decide whether to repent them or not. But the thing is to have them."

"I don't want to do anything bad," Nick had said.

"I don't want you to," Mr. John had said. "But you're alive and you're going to do things. Don't you lie and don't you steal. Everybody has to lie. But you pick out somebody you never lie to."

"I'll pick out you."

"That's right. Don't you ever lie to me no matter what and I won't lie to you."

"I'll try," Nick had said.

"That isn't it," Mr. John said. "It has to be absolute."

"All right," Nick said. "I'll never lie to you."

"What became of your girl?"

"Somebody said she was working up at the Soo."

"She was a beautiful girl and I always liked her," Mr. John had said.

"So did I," Nick said.

"Try and not feel too bad about it."

"I can't help it," Nick said. "None of it was her fault. She's just built that way. If I ran into her again I guess I'd get mixed up with her again."

"Maybe not."

"Maybe too. I'd try not to."

Mr. John was thinking about Nick when he went out to the back counter where the two men were waiting for him. He looked them over as he stood there and he didn't like either of them. He had always disliked the local man Evans and had no respect for him but he sensed that the down-state man was dangerous. He had not analyzed it yet but he saw the man had very flat eyes and a mouth that was tighter than a simple tobacco chewer's mouth needed to be. He had a real elk's tooth too on his watch chain. It was a really fine tusk from about a five-year-old bull. It was a beautiful tusk and Mr. John looked at it again and at the over-large bulge the man's shoulder holster made under his coat.

"Did you kill that bull with that cannon you're carrying around under your arm?" Mr. John asked the down-state man.

The down-state man looked at Mr. John unappreciatively.

"No," he said. "I killed that bull out in the thoroughfare country in Wyoming with a Winchester 45–70."

"You're a big-gun man, eh?" Mr. John said. He looked under the counter. "Have big feet, too. Do you need that big a cannon when you go out hunting kids?"

"What do you mean, kids," the down-state man said. He was one ahead.

"I mean the kid you're looking for."

"You said, kids," the down-state man said.

Mr. John moved in. It was necessary. "What's Evans carry when he goes after a boy who's licked his own boy twice? You must be heavily armed, Evans. That boy could lick you, too."

"Why don't you produce him and we could try it," Evans said.

[101]

"You said, kids, Mr. Jackson," the down-state man said. "What made you say that?"

"Looking at you, you cock-sucker," Mr. John said. "You splayfooted bastard."

"Why don't you come out from behind that counter if you want to talk like that?" the down-state man said.

"You're talking to the United States Postmaster," Mr. John said. "You're talking without witnesses except for Turd-face Evans. I suppose you know why they call him Turd-face. You can figure it out. You're a detective."

He was happy now. He had drawn the attack and he felt now as he used to feel in the old days before he made a living from feeding and bedding resorters who rocked in rustic chairs on the front porch of his hotel while they looked out over the lake.

"Listen, Splayfoot, I remember you very well now. Don't you remember me, Splayzey?"

The down-state man looked at him. But he did not remember him.

"I remember you in Cheyenne the day Tom Horn was hanged," Mr. John told him. "You were one of the ones that framed him with promises from the association. Do you remember now? Who owned the saloon in Medicine Bow when you worked for the people that gave it to Tom? Is that why you ended up doing what you're doing? Haven't you got any memory?"

"When did you come back here?"

"Two years after they dropped Tom."

"I'll be goddamned."

"Do you remember when I gave you that bull tusk when we were packing out from Greybull?"

"Sure. Listen, Jim, I got to get this kid."

"My name's John," Mr. John said. "John Packard. Come on in back and have a drink. You want to get to know this other character. His name is Crut-Face Evans. We used to call him Turd-Face. I just changed it now out of kindness."

"Mr. John," said Mr. Evans. "Why don't you be friendly and cooperative."

"I just changed your name, didn't I"? said Mr. John. "What kind of cooperation do you boys want?"

In the back of the store Mr. John took a bottle off a low shelf in the corner and handed it to the down-state man.

"Drink up, Splayzey," he said. "You look like you need it."

They each took a drink and then Mr. John asked, "What are you after this kid for?"

"Violation of the game laws," the down-state man said.

"What particular violation?"

"He killed a buck deer the twelfth of last month."

"Two men with guns out after a boy because he killed a deer the twelfth of last month," Mr. John said.

"There've been other violations."

"But this is the one you've got proof of."

"That's about it."

"What were the other violations?"

"Plenty."

"But you haven't got proof."

"I didn't say that," Evans said. "But we've got proof on this."

"And the date was the twelfth?"

"That's right," said Evans.

"Why don't you ask some questions instead of answering them?" the down-state man said to his partner. Mr. John laughed. "Let him alone, Splayzey," he said. "I like to see that great brain work."

"How well do you know the boy?" the down-state man asked.

"Pretty well."

"Ever do any business with him?"

[103]

"He buys a little stuff here once in a while. Pays cash."

"Do you have any idea where he'd head for?"

"He's got folks in Oklahoma."

"When did you see him last?" Evans asked.

"Come on, Evans," the down-state man said. "You're wasting our time. Thanks for the drink, Jim."

"John," Mr. John said. "What's your name, Splayzey?"

"Porter. Henry J. Porter."

"Splayzey, you're not going to do any shooting at that boy."

"I'm going to bring him in."

"You always were a murderous bastard."

"Come on, Evans," the down-state man said. "We're wasting time in here."

"You remember what I said about the shooting," Mr. John said very quietly.

"I heard you," the down-state man said.

The two men went out through the store and unhitched their light wagon and drove off. Mr. John watched them go up the road. Evans was driving and the down-state man was talking to him.

"Henry J. Porter," Mr. John thought. "The only name I can remember for him is Splayzey. He had such big feet he had to have made to order boots. Splayfoot they called him. Then Splayzey. It was his tracks by the spring where that Nester's boy was shot that they hung Tom for. Splayzey. Splayzey what? Maybe I never did know. Splayfoot Splayzey. Splayfoot Porter? No it wasn't Porter."

"I'm sorry about those baskets, Mrs. Tabeshaw," he said. "It's too late in the season now and they don't carry over. But if you'd be patient with them down at the hotel you'd get rid of them."

"You buy them, sell at the hotel," Mrs. Tabeshaw suggested.

"No. They'd buy them better from you," Mr. John told her. "You're a fine-looking woman."

"Long time ago," Mrs. Tabeshaw said.

"Suzy, I'd like to see you," Mr. John said.

In the back of the store he said, "Tell me about it."

"I told you already. They came for Nickie and they waited for him to come home. His youngest sister let him know they were waiting for him. When they were sleeping drunk Nickie got his stuff and pulled out. He's got grub for two weeks easy and he's got his rifle and young Littless went with him."

"Why did she go?"

"I don't know, Mr. John. I guess she wanted to look after him and keep him from doing anything bad. You know him."

"You live up by Evans's. How much do you think he knows about the country Nick uses?"

"All he can. But I don't know how much."

"Where do you think they went?"

"I wouldn't know, Mr. John. Nickie knows a lot of country."

"That man with Evans is no good. He's really bad."

"He isn't very smart."

"He's smarter than he acts. The booze has him down. But he's smart and he's bad. I used to know him."

"What do you want me to do."

"Nothing, Suzy. Let me know about anything."

"I'll add up my stuff, Mr. John, and you can check it."

"How are you going home?"

"I can get the boat up to Henry's Dock and then get a rowboat from the cottage and row down and get the stuff. Mr. John, what will they do with Nickie?"

"That's what I'm worried about."

"They were talking about getting him put in the reform school."

"I wish he hadn't killed that buck."

"So does he. He told me he was reading in a book about how you could crease something with a bullet and it wouldn't do it any harm. It would just stun it and Nickie wanted to try it. He said it was a damn fool thing to do. But he wanted to try it. Then he hit the buck and broke his neck. He felt awful about it. He felt awful about trying to crease it in the first place."

"I know."

"Then it must have been Evans found the meat where he had it hung up in the old springhouse. Anyway somebody took it."

"Who could have told Evans?"

"I think it was just that boy of his found it. He trails around after Nick all the time. You never see him. He could have seen Nickie kill the buck. That boy's no good, Mr. John. But he sure can trail around after anybody. He's liable to be in this room right now."

"No," said Mr. John. "But he could be listening outside."

"I think he's after Nick by now," the girl said.

"Did you hear them say anything about him at the house?"

"They never mentioned him," Suzy said.

"Evans must have left him home to do the chores. I don't think we have to worry about him till they get home to Evans's."

"I can row up the lake to home this afternoon and get one of our kids to let me know if Evans hires anyone to do the chores. That will mean he's turned that boy loose."

"Both the men are too old to trail anybody."

"But that boy's terrible, Mr. John, and he knows too much about Nickie and where he would go. He'd find them and then bring the men up to them."

"Come in back of the post office," Mr. John said.

Back of the filing slits and the lockboxes and the registry book and the flat stamp books in place along with the can-

cellation stamps and their pads, with the General Delivery
window down, so that Suzy felt again the glory of office that
had been hers when she had helped out in the store, Mr. John
said, "Where do you think they went, Suzy?"

"I wouldn't know, true. Somewhere not too far or he
wouldn't take Littless. Somewhere that's really good or he
wouldn't take her. They know about the trout for trout dinners, too, Mr. John."

"That boy?"

"Sure."

"Maybe we better do something about the Evans boy."

"I'd kill him. I'm pretty sure that's why Littless went
along. So Nickie wouldn't kill him."

"You fix it up so we keep track of them."

"I will. But you have to think out something, Mr. John.
Mrs. Adams, she's just broke down. She just gets a sick headache like always. Here. You better take this letter."

"You drop it in the box," Mr. John said. "That's United
States mail."

"I wanted to kill them both last night when they were
asleep."

"No," Mr. John told her. "Don't talk that way and don't
think that way."

"Didn't you ever want to kill anybody, Mr. John?"

"Yes. But it's wrong and it doesn't work out."

"My father killed a man."

"It didn't do him any good."

"He couldn't help it."

"You have to learn to help it," Mr. John said. "You get
along now, Suzy."

"I'll see you tonight or in the morning," Suzy said. "I wish
I still worked here, Mr. John."

"So do I, Suzy. But Mrs. Packard doesn't see it that way."

"I know," said Suzy. "That's the way everything is."

Nick and his sister were lying on a browse bed under a lean-to that they had built together on the edge of the hemlock forest looking out over the slope of the hill to the cedar swamp and the blue hills beyond.

"If it isn't comfortable, Littless, we can feather in some more balsam on that hemlock. We'll be tired tonight and this will do. But we can fix it up really good tomorrow."

"It feels lovely," his sister said. "Lie loose and really feel it, Nickie."

"It's a pretty good camp," Nick said. "And it doesn't show. We'll only use little fires."

"Would a fire show across to the hills?"

"It might," Nick said. "A fire shows a long way at night. But I'll stake out a blanket behind it. That way it won't show."

"Nickie, wouldn't it be nice if there wasn't anyone after us and we were just here for fun?"

"Don't start thinking that way so soon," Nick said. "We just started. Anyway if we were just here for fun we wouldn't be here."

"I'm sorry, Nickie."

"You don't need to be," Nick told her. "Look, Littless, I'm going down to get a few trout for supper."

"Can I come?"

"No. You stay here and take a rest. You had a tough day. You read a while or just be quiet."

"It was tough in the slashings, wasn't it? I thought it was really hard. Did I do all right?"

"You did wonderfully and you were wonderful making camp. But you take it easy now."

"Have we got a name for this camp?"

"Let's call it Camp Number One," Nick said.

He went down the hill toward the creek and when he had come almost to the bank he stopped and cut himself a willow stick about four feet long and trimmed it, leaving the bark on. He could see the clear fast water of the stream. It was narrow and deep and the banks were mossy here before the stream entered the swamp. The dark clear water flowed fast and its rushing made bulges on the surface. Nick did not go close to it as he knew it flowed under the banks and he did not want to frighten a fish by walking on the bank.

There must be quite a few up here in the open now, he thought. It's pretty late in the summer.

He took a coil of silk line out of a tobacco pouch he carried in the left breast pocket of his shirt and cut a length that was not quite as long as the willow stick and fastened it to the tip where he had notched it lightly. Then he fastened on a hook that he took from the pouch; then holding the shank of the hook he tested the pull of the line and the bend of the willow. He laid his rod down now and went back to where the trunk of a small birch tree, dead for several years, lay on its side in the grove of birches that bordered the cedars by the stream. He rolled the log over and found several earthworms under it. They were not big. But they were red and lively and he put them in a flat round tin with holes punched in the top that had once held Copenhagen snuff. He put some dirt over them and rolled the log back. This was the third year he had found bait at this same place and he had always replaced the log so that it was as he had found it.

Nobody knows how big this creek is, he thought. It picks up an awful volume of water in that bad swamp up above. Now he looked up the creek and down it and up the hill to the hemlock forest where the camp was. Then he walked to where he had left the pole with the line and the hook and baited the hook carefully and spat on it for good luck. Holding the pole and the line with the baited hook in his right hand he walked very carefully and gently toward the bank of the narrow, heavy-flowing stream.

It was so narrow here that his willow pole would have spanned it and as he came close to the bank he heard the turbulent rush of the water. He stopped by the bank, out of sight of anything in the stream, and took two lead shot, split down one side, out of the tobacco pouch and bent them on the line about a foot above the hook, clinching them with his teeth.

He swung the hook on which the two worms curled out over the water and dropped it gently in so that it sank, swirling in the fast water, and he lowered the tip of the willow pole to let the current take the line and the baited hook under the bank. He felt the line straighten and a sudden heavy firmness. He swung up on the pole and it bent almost double in his hand. He felt the throbbing, jerking pull that did not yield as he pulled. Then it yielded, rising in the water with the line. There was a heavy wildness of movement in the narrow, deep current, and the trout was torn out of the water and, flopping in the air, sailed over Nick's shoulder and onto the bank behind him. Nick saw him shine in the sun and then he found him where he was tumbling in the ferns. He was strong and heavy in Nick's hands and he had a pleasant smell and Nick saw how dark his back was and how brilliant his spots were colored and how bright the edges of his fins were. They were white on the edge with a black line behind and then there was the lovely golden sunset color of his belly. Nick held him in his right hand and he could just reach around him.

He's pretty big for the skillet, he thought. But I've hurt him and I have to kill him.

He knocked the trout's head sharply against the handle of his hunting knife and laid him against the trunk of a birch tree.

"Damn," he said. "He's a perfect size for Mrs. Packard and her trout dinners. But he's pretty big for Littless and me."

I better go upstream and find a shallow and try to get a couple of small ones, he thought. Damn, didn't he feel like something when I horsed him out though? They can talk all they want about playing them but people that have never horsed them out don't know what they can make you feel. What if it only lasts that long? It's the time when there's no give at all and then they start to come and what they do to you on the way up and into the air.

This is a strange creek, he thought. It's funny when you have to hunt for small ones.

He found his pole where he had thrown it. The hook was bent and he straightened it. Then he picked up the heavy fish and started up the stream.

There's one shallow, pebbly part just after she comes out of the upper swamp, he thought. I can get a couple of small ones there. Littless might not like this big one. If she gets homesick I'll have to take her back. I wonder what those old boys are doing now? I don't think that goddam Evans kid knows about this place. That son of a bitch. I don't think anybody fished in here but Indians. You should have been an Indian, he thought. It would have saved you a lot of trouble.

He made his way up the creek, keeping back from the stream but once stepping onto a piece of bank where the stream flowed underground. A big trout broke out in a violence that made a slashing wake in the water. He was a trout so big that it hardly seemed he could turn in the stream.

"When did you come up?" Nick said when the fish had gone under the bank again further upstream. "Boy, what a trout."

At the pebbly shallow stretch he caught two small trout. They were beautiful fish, too, firm and hard and he gutted the three fish and tossed the guts into the stream, then washed the trout carefully in the cold water and then wrapped them in a small faded sugar sack from his pocket.

It's a good thing that girl likes fish, he thought. I wish we could have picked some berries. I know where I can always get some, though. He started back up the hill slope toward their camp. The sun was down behind the hill and the weather was good. He looked out across the swamp and up in the sky, above where the arm of the lake would be, he saw a fish hawk flying.

He came up to the lean-to very quietly and his sister did not hear him. She was lying on her side, reading. Seeing her, he spoke softly not to startle her.

"What did you do, you monkey?"

She turned and looked at him and smiled and shook her head.

"I cut it off," she said.

"How?"

"With a scissors. How did you think?"

"How did you see to do it?"

"I just held it out and cut it. It's easy. Do I look like a boy?"

"Like a wild boy of Borneo."

"I couldn't cut it like a Sunday-school boy. Does it look too wild?"

"No."

"It's very exciting," she said. "Now I'm your sister but I'm a boy, too. Do you think it will change me into a boy?"

"No."

"I wish it would."

"You're crazy, Littless."

"Maybe I am. Do I look like an idiot boy?"

"A little."

"You can make it neater. You can see to cut it with a comb."

"I'll have to make it a little better but not much. Are you hungry, idiot brother?"

"Can't I just be an un-idiot brother?"

"I don't want to trade you for a brother."

"You have to now, Nickie, don't you see? It was something we had to do. I should have asked you but I knew it was something we had to do so I did it for a surprise."

"I like it," Nick said. "The hell with everything. I like it very much."

"Thank you, Nickie, so much. I was laying trying to rest like you said. But all I could do was imagine things to do for you. I was going to get you a chewing tobacco can full of knockout drops from some big saloon in some place like Sheboygan."

"Who did you get them from?"

Nick was sitting down now and his sister sat on his lap and held her arms around his neck and rubbed her cropped head against his cheek.

"I got them from the Queen of the Whores," she said. "And you know the name of the saloon?"

"No."

"The Royal Ten Dollar Gold Piece Inn and Emporium."

"What did you do there?"

"I was a whore's assistant."

"What's a whore's assistant do?"

"Oh she carries the whore's train when she walks and opens her carriage door and shows her to the right room. It's like a lady in waiting I guess."

"What's she say to the whore?"

"She'll say anything that comes into her mind as long as it's polite."

"Like what, brother?"

"Like, 'Well ma'am, it must be pretty tiring on a hot day

[113]

like today to be just a bird in a gilded cage.' Things like that."

"What's the whore say?"

"She says, 'Yes, indeedy. It sure is sweetness.' Because this whore I was whore's assistant to is of humble origin."

"What kind of origin are you?"

"I'm the sister or the brother of a morbid writer and I'm delicately brought up. This makes me intensely desirable to the main whore and to all of her circle."

"Did you get the knockout drops?"

"Of course. She said, 'Hon, take these little old drops.' 'Thank you,' I said. 'Give my regards to your morbid brother and ask him to stop by the Emporium anytime he is at She-boygan.' "

"Get off my lap," Nick said.

"That's just the way they talk in the Emporium," Littless said.

"I have to get supper. Aren't you hungry?"

"I'll get supper."

"No," Nick said. "You keep on talking."

"Don't you think we're going to have fun, Nickie?"

"We're having fun now."

"Do you want me to tell you about the other thing I did for you?"

"You mean before you decided to do something practical and cut off your hair?"

"This was practical enough. Wait till you hear it. Can I kiss you while you're making supper?"

"Wait a while and I'll tell you. What was it you were going to do?"

"Well, I guess I was ruined morally last night when I stole the whiskey. Do you think you can be ruined morally by just one thing like that?"

"No. Anyway the bottle was open."

"Yes. But I took the empty pint bottle and the quart bottle with the whiskey in it out to the kitchen and I poured the pint bottle full and some spilled on my hand and I licked it off and I thought that probably ruined me morally."

"How'd it taste?"

"Awfully strong and funny and a little sick-making."

"That wouldn't ruin you morally."

"Well, I'm glad because if I was ruined morally how could I exercise a good influence on you?"

"I don't know," Nick said. "What was it you were going to do?"

He had his fire made and the skillet resting on it and he was laying strips of bacon in the skillet. His sister was watching and she had her hands folded across her knees and he watched her unclasp her hands and put one arm down and lean on it and put her legs out straight. She was practicing being a boy.

"I've got to learn to put my hands right."

"Keep them away from your head."

"I know. It would be easy if there was some boy my own age to copy."

"Copy me."

"That would be natural, wouldn't it? You won't laugh, though?"

"Maybe."

"Gee, I hope I won't start to be a girl while we're on the trip."

"Don't worry."

"We have the same shoulders and the same kind of legs."

"What was the other thing you were going to do?"

Nick was cooking the trout now. The bacon was curled brown on a fresh-cut chip of wood from the piece of fallen timber they were using for the fire and they both smelled the trout cooking in the bacon fat. Nick basted them and then turned them and basted them again. It was getting dark and he had rigged a piece of canvas behind the little fire so that it would not be seen.

"What were you going to do?" he asked again. Littless leaned forward and spat toward the fire.

"How was that?"

"You missed the skillet anyway."

"Oh, it's pretty bad. I got it out of the Bible. I was going to take three spikes, one for each of them, and drive them into the temples of those two and that boy while they slept."

"What were you going to drive them in with?"

"A muffled hammer."

"How do you muffle a hammer?"

"I'd muffle it all right."

"That nail thing's pretty rough to try."

"Well, that girl did it in the Bible and since I've seen armed men drunk and asleep and circulated among them at night and stolen their whiskey why shouldn't I go the whole way, especially if I learned it in the Bible?"

"They didn't have a muffled hammer in the Bible."

"I guess I mixed it up with muffled oars."

"Maybe. And we don't want to kill anybody. That's why you came along."

"I know. But crime comes easy for you and me, Nickie. We're different from the others. Then I thought if I was ruined morally I might as well be useful."

"You're crazy, Littless," he said. "Listen, does tea keep you awake?"

"I don't know. I never had it at night. Only peppermint tea."

"I'll make it very weak and put canned cream in it."

"I don't need it, Nickie, if we're short."

"It will just give the milk a little taste."

They were eating now. Nick had cut them each two slices of rye bread and he soaked one slice for each in the bacon fat in the skillet. They ate that and the trout that were crisp outside and cooked well and very tender inside. Then they put the trout skeletons in the fire and ate the bacon made in a sandwich with the other piece of bread, and then Littless drank the weak tea with the condensed milk in it and Nick tapped two slivers of wood into the holes he had punched in the can.

"Did you have enough?"

"Plenty. The trout was wonderful and the bacon, too. Weren't we lucky they had rye bread?"

"Eat an apple," he said. "Maybe we'll have something good tomorrow. Maybe I should have made a bigger supper, Littless."

"No. I had plenty."

"You're sure you're not hungry?"

"No. I'm full. I've got some chocolate if you'd like some."

"Where'd you get it?"

"From my savior."

"Where?"

"My savior. Where I save everything."

"Oh."

"This is fresh. Some is the hard kind from the kitchen. We can start on that and save the other for sometime special. Look, my savior's got a drawstring like a tobacco pouch. We can use it for nuggets and things like that. Do you think we'll get out west, Nickie, on this trip?"

"I haven't got it figured yet."

"I'd like to get my savior packed full of nuggets worth sixteen dollars an ounce."

Nick cleaned up the skillet and put the pack in at the head of the lean-to. One blanket was spread over the browse bed and he put the other one on it and tucked it under on Littless's side. He cleaned out the two-quart tin pail he'd made tea in and filled it with cold water from the spring. When he came back from the spring his sister was in the bed asleep, her head on the pillow she had made by rolling her blue jeans around her moccasins. He kissed her but she did not wake and he put on his old Mackinaw coat and felt in the packsack until he found the pint bottle of whiskey.

He opened it and smelled it and it smelled very good. He dipped a half a cup of water out of the small pail he had brought from the spring and poured a little of the whiskey in it. Then he sat and sipped this very slowly, letting it stay under his tongue before he brought it slowly back over his tongue and swallowed it.

He watched the small coals of the fire brighten with the light evening breeze and he tasted the whiskey and cold water and looked at the coals and thought. Then he finished the cup, dipped up some cold water and drank it and went to bed. The rifle was under his left leg and his head was on the good hard pillow his moccasins and the rolled trousers made and he pulled his side of the blanket tight around him and said his prayers and went to sleep.

In the night he was cold and he spread his Mackinaw coat over his sister and rolled his back over closer to her so that there was more of his side of the blanket under him. He felt for the gun and tucked it under his leg again. The air was cold and sharp to breathe and he smelled the cut hemlock and balsam boughs. He had not realized how tired he was until the cold had waked him. Now he lay comfortable again feeling the warmth of his sister's body against his back and he thought, I must take good care of her and keep her happy and get her back safely. He listened to her breathing and to the quiet of the night and then he was asleep again.

It was just light enough to see the far hills beyond the swamp when he woke. He lay quietly and stretched the stiffness from his body. Then he sat up and pulled on his khaki trousers and put on his moccasins. He watched his sister sleeping with the collar of the warm Mackinaw coat under her chin and her high cheekbones and brown freckled skin light rose under the brown, her chopped-off hair showing the beautiful line of her head and emphasizing her straight nose and her close-set ears. He wished he could draw her face and he watched the way her long lashes lay on her cheeks.

She looks like a small wild animal, he thought, and she sleeps like one. How would you say her head looks, he thought. I guess the nearest is that it looks as though someone had cut her hair off on a wooden block with an ax. It has a sort of a carved look.

He loved his sister very much and she loved him too much. But, he thought, I guess those things straighten out. At least I hope so.

There's no sense waking anyone up, he thought. She must have been really tired if I'm as tired as I am. If we are all right here we are doing just what we should do: staying out of sight until things quiet down and that down-state man pulls out. I've got to feed her better, though. It's a shame I couldn't have outfitted really good.

We've got a lot of things, though. The pack was heavy enough. But what we want to get today is berries. I better get a partridge or a couple if I can. We can get good mushrooms, too. We'll have to be careful about the bacon but we won't need it with the shortening. Maybe I fed her too light last night. She's used to lots of milk, too, and sweet things. Don't worry about it. We'll feed good. It's a good thing she likes trout. They were really good. Don't worry about her. She'll eat wonderfully. But, Nick, boy, you certainly didn't feed her too much yesterday. Better to let her sleep than to wake her up now. There's plenty for you to do.

He started to get some things out of the pack very carefully and his sister smiled in her sleep. The brown skin came taut over her cheekbones when she smiled and the undercolor showed. She did not wake and he started to prepare to make breakfast and get the fire ready. There was plenty of wood cut and he built a very small fire and made tea while he waited to start breakfast. He drank his tea straight and ate three dried apricots and he tried to read in Lorna Doone. But he had read it and it did not have magic any more and he knew it was a loss on this trip.

Late in the afternoon, when they had made camp, he had put some prunes in a tin pail to soak and he put them on the fire now to stew. In the pack he found the prepared buckwheat flour and he put it out with an enameled saucepan and a tin cup to mix the flour with water to make a batter. He had the tin of vegetable shortening and he cut a piece off the top of an empty flour sack and wrapped it around a cut stick and tied it tight with a piece of fish line. Littless had brought four old flour sacks and he was proud of her.

He mixed the batter and put the skillet on the fire, greasing it with the shortening which he spread with the cloth on the stick. First it made the skillet shine darkly, then it sizzled and spat and he greased again and poured the batter smoothly and watched it bubble and then start to firm around the edges. He watched the rising and the forming of the texture and the gray color of the cake. He loosened it from the pan with a fresh clean chip and flipped it and caught it, the beautiful browned side up, the other sizzling. He could feel its weight but see it growing in buoyancy in the skillet.

"Good morning," his sister said. "Did I sleep awfully late?"

"No, devil."

She stood up with her shirt hanging down over her brown legs.

"You've done everything."

"No. I just started the cakes."

"Doesn't that one smell wonderful? I'll go to the spring and wash and come and help."

"Don't wash in the spring."

"I'm not white man," she said. She was gone behind the lean-to.

"Where did you leave the soap?" she asked.

"It's by the spring. There's an empty lard bucket. Bring the butter, will you. It's in the spring."

"I'll be right back."

There was a half a pound of butter and she brought it wrapped in the oiled paper in the empty lard bucket.

They ate the buckwheat cakes with butter and Log Cabin syrup out of a tin Log Cabin can. The top of the chimney unscrewed and the syrup poured from the chimney. They were both very hungry and the cakes were delicious with the butter melting on them and running down into the cut places with the syrup. They ate the prunes out of the tin cups and drank the juice. Then they drank tea from the same cups.

"Prunes taste like a celebration," Littless said. "Think of that. How did you sleep, Nickie?"

"Good."

"Thank you for putting the Mackinaw on me. Wasn't it a lovely night, though?"

"Yes. Did you sleep all night?"

"I'm still asleep. Nickie, can we stay here always?"

"I don't think so. You'd grow up and have to get married."

"I'm going to get married to you anyway. I want to be your common-law wife. I read about it in the paper."

"That's where you read about the Unwritten Law."

"Sure. I'm going to be your common-law wife under the Unwritten Law. Can't I, Nickie?"

"No."

"I will. I'll surprise you. All you have to do is live a certain time as man and wife. I'll get them to count this time now. It's just like homesteading."

"I won't let you file."

"You can't help yourself. That's the Unwritten Law. I've thought it out lots of times. I'll get cards printed Mrs. Nick Adams, Cross Village, Michigan—common-law wife. I'll hand these out to a few people openly each year until the time's up."

"I don't think it would work."

"I've got another scheme. We'll have a couple of children while I'm a minor. Then you have to marry me under the Unwritten Law."

"That's not the Unwritten Law."

"I get mixed up on it."

"Anyway, nobody knows yet if it works."

"It must," she said. "Mr. Thaw is counting on it."

"Mr. Thaw might make a mistake."

"Why Nickie, Mr. Thaw practically invented the Unwritten Law."

"I thought it was his lawyer."

"Well, Mr. Thaw put it in action anyway."

"I don't like Mr. Thaw," Nick Adams said.

"That's good. There's things about him I don't like either. But he certainly made the paper more interesting reading, didn't he?"

"He gives the others something new to hate."

"They hate Mr. Stanford White, too."

"I think they're jealous of both of them."

"I believe that's true, Nickie. Just like they're jealous of us."

"Think anybody is jealous of us now?"

"Not right now maybe. Our mother will think we're fugitives from justice steeped in sin and iniquity. It's a good thing she doesn't know I got you that whiskey."

"I tried it last night. It's very good."

"Oh, I'm glad. That's the first whiskey I ever stole anywhere. Isn't it wonderful that it's good? I didn't think anything about those people could be good."

"I've got to think about them too much. Let's not talk about them," Nick said.

"All right. What are we going to do today?"

"What would you like to do?"

"I'd like to go to Mr. John's store and get everything we need."

"We can't do that."

"I know it. What do you plan to really do?"

"We ought to get some berries and I ought to get a partridge or some partridges. We've always got trout. But I don't want you to get tired of trout."

"Were you ever tired of trout?"

"No. But they say people get tired of them."

"I wouldn't get tired of them," Littless said. "You get tired of pike right away. But you never get tired of trout nor of perch. I know, Nickie. True."

"You don't get tired of walleyed pike either," Nick said. "Only of shovelnose. Boy, you sure get tired of them."

"I don't like the pitchfork bones," his sister said. "It's a fish that surfeits you."

"We'll clean up here and I'll find a place to cache the shells and we'll make a trip for berries and try to get some birds."

"I'll bring two lard pails and a couple of the sacks," his sister said.

"Littless," Nick said. "You remember about going to the bathroom, will you please?"

"Of course."

"That's important."

"I know it. You remember, too."

"I will."

Nick went back into the timber and buried the carton of .22 long-rifles and the loose boxes of .22 shorts under the brown-needled floor at the base of a big hemlock. He put back the packed needles he had cut with his knife and made a small cut as far up as he could reach on the heavy bark of the tree. He took a bearing on the tree and then came out onto the hillside and walked down to the lean-to.

It was a lovely morning now. The sky was high and clear blue and no clouds had come yet. Nick was happy with his sister and he thought, no matter how this thing comes out we might as well have a good happy time. He had already learned there was only one day at a time and that it was always the day you were in. It would be today until it was tonight and tomorrow would be today again. This was the main thing he had learned so far.

Today was a good day and coming down to the camp with his rifle he was happy although their trouble was like a fish-hook caught in his pocket that pricked him occasionally as he walked. They left the pack inside the lean-to. There were great odds against a bear bothering it in the daytime because any bear would be down below feeding on berries around the swamp. But Nick buried the bottle of whiskey up behind the spring. Littless was not back yet and Nick sat down on the log of the fallen tree they were using for firewood and checked his rifle. They were going after partridges so he pulled out the tube of the magazine and poured the long-rifle cartridges into his hand and then put them into a chamois pouch and filled the magazine with .22 shorts. They made less noise and would not tear the meat up if he could not get head shots.

He was all ready now and wanted to start. Where's that girl

anyway, he thought. Then he thought, don't get excited. You told her to take her time. Don't get nervous. But he was nervous and it made him angry at himself.

"Here I am," his sister said. "I'm sorry that I took so long. I went too far away, I guess."

"You're fine," Nick said. "Let's go. You have the pails?"

"Uh huh, and covers, too."

They started down across the hill to the creek. Nick looked carefully up the stream and along the hillside. His sister watched him. She had the pails in one of the sacks and carried it slung over her shoulder by the other sack.

"Aren't you taking a pole, Nickie?" she asked him.

"No. I'll cut one if we fish."

He moved ahead of his sister, holding the rifle in one hand, keeping a little way away from the stream. He was hunting now.

"It's a strange creek," his sister said.

"It's the biggest small stream I've ever known," Nick told her.

"It's deep and scary for a little stream."

"It keeps having new springs," Nick said. "And it digs under the bank and it digs down. It's awful cold water, Littless. Feel it."

"Gee," she said. It was numbing cold.

"The sun warms it a little," Nick said. "But not much. We'll hunt along easy. There's a berry patch down below."

They went along down the creek. Nick was studying the banks. He had seen a mink's track and shown it to his sister and they had seen tiny ruby-crowned kinglets that were hunting insects and let the boy and girl come close as they moved sharply and delicately in the cedars. They had seen cedar waxwings so calm and gentle and distinguished moving in their lovely elegance with the magic wax touches on their wing coverts and their tails, and Littless had said, "They're the most beautiful, Nickie. There couldn't be more simply beautiful birds."

"They're built like your face," he said.

"No, Nickie. Don't make fun. Cedar waxwings make me so proud and happy that I cry."

"When they wheel and light and then move so proud and friendly and gently," Nick said.

They had gone on and suddenly Nick had raised the rifle and shot before his sister could see what he was looking at. Then she heard the sound of a big bird tossing and beating its wings on the ground. She saw Nick pumping the gun and shoot twice more and each time she heard another pounding of wings in the willow brush. Then there was the whirring noise of wings as large brown birds burst out of the willows and one bird flew only a little way and lit in the willows and with its crested head on one side looked down, bending the collar of feathers on his neck where the other birds were still thumping. The bird looking down from the red willow brush was beautiful, plump, heavy and looked so stupid with his head turned down and as Nick raised his rifle slowly, his sister whispered, "No, Nickie. Please no. We've got plenty."

"All right," Nick said. "You want to take him?"

"No, Nickie. No."

Nick went forward into the willows and picked up the three grouse and batted their heads against the butt of the rifle stock and laid them out on the moss. His sister felt them, warm and full-breasted and beautifully feathered.

"Wait till we eat them," Nick said. He was very happy.

"I'm sorry for them now," his sister said. "They were enjoying the morning just like we were."

She looked up at the grouse still in the tree.

"It does look a little silly still staring down," she said.

[126]

"This time of year the Indians call them fool hens. After they've been hunted they get smart. They're not the real fool hens. Those never get smart. They're willow grouse. These are ruffed grouse."

"I hope we'll get smart," his sister said. "Tell him to go away, Nickie."

"You tell him."

"Go away, partridge."

The grouse did not move.

Nick raised the rifle and the grouse looked at him. Nick knew he could not shoot the bird without making his sister sad and he made a noise blowing out so his tongue rattled and lips shook like a grouse bursting from cover and the bird looked at him fascinated.

"We better not annoy him," Nick said.

"I'm sorry, Nickie," his sister said. "He is stupid."

"Wait till we eat them," Nick told her. "You'll see why we hunt them."

"Are they out of season, too?"

"Sure. But they are full grown and nobody but us would ever hunt them. I kill plenty of great horned owls and a great horned owl will kill a partridge every day if he can. They hunt all the time and they kill all the good birds."

"He certainly could kill that one easy," his sister said. "I don't feel bad any more. Do you want a bag to carry them in?"

"I'll draw them and then pack them in the bag with some ferns. It isn't so far to the berries now."

They sat against one of the cedars and Nick opened the birds and took out their warm entrails and feeling the inside of the birds hot on his right hand he found the edible parts of the giblets and cleaned them and then washed them in the stream. When the birds were cleaned he smoothed their feathers and wrapped them in ferns and put them in the flour

sack. He tied the mouth of the flour sack and two corners
with a piece of fish line and slung it over his shoulder and then
went back to the stream and dropped the entrails in and
tossed some bright pieces of lung in to see the trout rise in
the rapid heavy flow of the water.

"They'd make good bait but we don't need bait now," he
said. "Our trout are all in the stream and we'll take them
when we need them."

"This stream would make us rich if it was near home," his
sister said.

"It would be fished out then. This is the last really wild
stream there is except in another awful country to get to
beyond the foot of the lake. I never brought anybody here to
fish."

"Who ever fishes it?"

"Nobody I know."

"Is it a virgin stream?"

"No. Indians fish it. But they're gone now since they quit
cutting hemlock bark and the camps closed down."

"Does the Evans boy know?"

"Not him," Nick said. But then he thought about it and
it made him feel sick. He could see the Evans boy.

"What're you thinking, Nickie?"

"I wasn't thinking."

"You were thinking. You tell me. We're partners."

"He might know," Nick said. "Goddam it. He might
know."

"But you don't know that he knows?"

"No. That's the trouble. If I did I'd get out."

"Maybe he's back at camp now," his sister said.

"Don't talk that way. Do you want to bring him?"

"No," she said. "Please, Nickie, I'm sorry I brought it up."

"I'm not," Nick said. "I'm grateful. I knew it anyway. Only

I'd stopped thinking about it. I have to think about things now the rest of my life."

"You always thought about things."

"Not like this."

"Let's go down and get the berries anyway," Littless said. "There isn't anything we can do now to help is there?"

"No," Nick said. "We'll pick the berries and get back to camp."

But Nick was trying to accept it now and think his way all the way through it. He must not get in a panic about it. Nothing had changed. Things were just as they were when he had decided to come here and let things blow over. The Evans boy could have followed him here before. But it was very unlikely. He could have followed him one time when he had gone in from the road through the Hodges' place, but it was doubtful. Nobody had been fishing the stream. He could be sure of that. But the Evans boy did not care about fishing.

"All that bastard cares about is trailing me," he said.

"I know it, Nickie."

"This is three times he's made us trouble."

"I know it, Nickie. But don't you kill him."

That's why she came along, Nick thought. That's why she's here. I can't do it while she's along.

"I know I mustn't kill him," he said. "There's nothing we can do now. Let's not talk about it."

"As long as you don't kill him," his sister said. "There's nothing we can't get out of and nothing that won't blow over."

"Let's get back to camp," Nick said.

"Without the berries?"

"We'll get the berries another day."

"Are you nervous, Nickie?"

"Yes. I'm sorry."

"But what good will we be back at camp?"

[129]

"We'll know quicker."

"Can't we just go along the way we were going?"

"Not now. I'm not scared, Littless. And don't you be scared. But something's made me nervous."

Nick had cut up away from the stream into the edge of the timber and they were walking in the shade of the trees. They would come onto the camp now from above.

From the timber they approached the camp carefully. Nick went ahead with the rifle. The camp had not been visited.

"You stay here," Nick told his sister. "I'm going to have a look beyond." He left the sack with the birds and the berry pails with Littless and went well upstream. As soon as he was out of sight of his sister he changed the .22 shorts in the rifle for the long rifles. I won't kill him, he thought, but anyway it's the right thing to do. He made a careful search of the country. He saw no sign of anyone and he went down to the stream and then downstream and back up to the camp.

"I'm sorry I was nervous, Littless," he said. "We might as well have a good lunch and then we won't have to worry about a fire showing at night."

"I'm worried now, too," she said.

"Don't you be worried. It's just like it was before."

"But he drove us back from getting the berries without him even being here."

"I know. But he's not been here. Maybe he's never even been to this creek ever. Maybe we'll never see him again."

"He makes me scared, Nickie, worse when he's not here than when he's here."

"I know. But there isn't any use being scared."

"What are we going to do?"

"Well, we better wait to cook until night."

"Why did you change?"

"He won't be around here at night. He can't come through

[130]

the swamp in the dark. We don't have to worry about him early in the mornings and late in the evening nor in the dark. We'll have to be like the deer and only be out then. We'll lay up in the daytime."

"Maybe he'll never come."

"Sure. Maybe."

"But I can stay though, can't I?"

"I ought to get you home."

"No. Please, Nickie. Who's going to keep you from killing him then?"

"Listen, Littless, don't ever talk about killing and remember I never talked about killing. There isn't any killing nor ever going to be any."

"True?"

"True."

"I'm so glad."

"Don't even be that. Nobody ever talked about it."

"All right. I never thought about it nor spoke about it."

"Me either."

"Of course you didn't."

"I never even thought about it."

No, he thought. You never even thought about it. Only all day and all night. But you mustn't think about it in front of her because she can feel it because she is your sister and you love each other.

"Are you hungry, Littless?"

"Not really."

"Eat some of the hard chocolate and I'll get some fresh water from the spring."

"I don't have to have anything."

They looked across to where the big white clouds of the eleven o'clock breeze were coming up over the blue hills beyond the swamp. The sky was a high clear blue and the clouds

[131]

came up white and detached themselves from behind the hills and moved high in the sky as the breeze freshened and the shadows of the clouds moved over the swamp and across the hillside. The wind blew in the trees now and was cool as they lay in the shade. The water from the spring was cold and fresh in the tin pail and the chocolate was not quite bitter but was hard and crunched as they chewed it.

"It's as good as the water in the spring where we were when we first saw them," his sister said. "It tastes even better after the chocolate."

"We can cook if you're hungry."

"I'm not if you're not."

"I'm always hungry. I was a fool not to go on and get the berries."

"No. You came back to find out."

"Look, Littless. I know a place back by the slashing we came through where we can get berries. I'll cache everything and we can go in there through the timber all the way and pick a couple of pails full and then we'll have them ahead for tomorrow. It isn't a bad walk."

"All right. But I'm fine."

"Aren't you hungry?"

"No. Not at all now after the chocolate. I'd love to just stay and read. We had a nice walk when we were hunting."

"All right," Nick said. "Are you tired from yesterday?"

"Maybe a little."

"We'll take it easy. I'll read Wuthering Heights."

"Is it too old to read out loud to me?"

"No."

"Will you read it?"

"Sure."

Crossing the Mississippi

The Kansas City train stopped at a siding just east of the Mississippi River and Nick looked out at the road that was half a foot deep with dust. There was nothing in sight but the road and a few dust-grayed trees. A wagon lurched along through the ruts, the driver slouching with the jolts of his spring seat and letting the reins hang slack on the horses' backs.

Nick looked at the wagon and wondered where it was going, whether the driver lived near the Mississippi and whether he ever went fishing. The wagon lurched out of sight up the road and Nick thought of the World Series game going on in New York. He thought of Happy Felsch's home run in the first game he had watched at the White Sox Park, Slim Solee swinging far forward, his knee nearly touching the ground and the white dot of the ball on its far trajectory toward the green fence at center field, Felsch, his head down, tearing for the stuffed white square at first base and then the exulting roar from the spectators as the ball landed in a knot of scrambling fans in the open bleachers.

As the train started and the dusty trees and brown road commenced to move past, the magazine vendor came swaying down the aisle.

"Got any dope on the Series?" Nick asked him.

"White Sox won the final game," the news butcher answered, making his way down the aisle of the chair car with the sea-legs roll of a sailor. His answer gave Nick a comfortable glow. The White Sox had licked them. It was a fine feeling. Nick opened his Saturday Evening Post and commenced reading, occasionally looking out of the window to watch for any glimpse of the Mississippi. Crossing the Mississippi would be a big event he thought, and he wanted to enjoy every minute of it.

The scenery seemed to flow past in a stream of road, telegraph poles, occasional houses and flat brown fields. Nick had expected bluffs for the Mississippi shore but finally, after an endless seeming bayou had poured past the window, he could see out of the window the engine of the train curving out onto a long bridge above a broad, muddy brown stretch of water. Desolate hills were on the far side that Nick could now see and on the near side a flat mud bank. The river seemed to move solidly downstream, not to flow but to move like a solid, shifting lake, swirling a little where the abutments of the bridge jutted out. Mark Twain, Huck Finn, Tom Sawyer, and LaSalle crowded each other in Nick's mind as he looked up the flat, brown plain of slow-moving water. Anyhow I've seen the Mississippi, he thought happily to himself.

WAR

Night Before Landing

Walking around the deck in the dark Nick passed the Polish officers sitting in a row of deck chairs. Someone was playing the mandolin. Leon Chocianowicz put out his foot in the dark.

"Hey, Nick," he said, "where you going?"

"Nowhere. Just walking."

"Sit here. There's a chair."

Nick sat in the empty chair and looked out at the men passing against the light from the sea. It was a warm night in June. Nick leaned back in the chair.

"Tomorrow we get in," Leon said. "I heard it from the wireless man."

"I heard it from the barber," Nick said.

Leon laughed and spoke in Polish to the man in the next deck chair. He leaned forward and smiled at Nick.

"He doesn't speak English," Leon said. "He says he heard it from Gaby."

"Where's Gaby?"

"Up in a lifeboat with somebody."

"Where's Galinski?"

"Maybe with Gaby."

"No," said Nick. "She told me she couldn't stand him."

Gaby was the only girl on the boat. She had blonde hair which was always coming down, a loud laugh, a good body, and a bad odor of some sort. An aunt, who had not left her cabin since the boat sailed, was taking her back to her family in Paris. Her father had something to do with the French Line and she dined at the captain's table.

"Why doesn't she like Galinski?" Leon asked.

"She said he looked like a porpoise."

Leon laughed again. "Come on," he said, "let's go find him and tell him."

They stood up and walked over to the rail. Overhead the lifeboats were swung out ready to be lowered. The ship was listed, the decks slanted and the lifeboats hung slanted and widely swinging. The water slipped softly, great patches of phosphorescent kelp churned out and sucked and bubbled under.

"She makes good time," Nick said, looking down at the water.

"We're in the Bay of Biscay," Leon said. "Tomorrow we ought to see the land."

They walked around the deck and down a ladder back to the stern to watch the wake phosphorescent and turning like plowed land in perspective. Above them was the gun platform with two sailors walking up and down beside the gun black against the faint glow from the water.

"They're zigzagging," Leon watched the wake.

"All day."

"They say these boats carry the German mails and that's why they're never sunk."

"Maybe," said Nick. "I don't believe it."

"I don't either. But it's a nice idea. Let's go find Galinski."

They found Galinski in his cabin with a bottle of cognac. He was drinking out of a tooth mug.

"Hello, Anton."

"Hello, Nick. Hello, Leon. Haff a drink."

"You tell him, Nick."

"Listen, Anton. We've got a message for you from a beautiful lady."

"I know your beautiful lady. You take that beautiful lady and stick her up a funnel."

Lying on his back he put his feet against the springs and mattress of the upper berth and pushed.

"Carper!" he shouted. "Hey, Carper! Wake up and drink."

Over the edge of the upper bunk looked a face. It was a round face with steel-rimmed spectacles.

"Don't ask me to drink when I'm drunk."

"Come on down and drink," Galinski bellowed.

"No," from the upper berth. "Give me the liquor up here."

He had rolled over against the wall again.

"He's been drunk for two weeks," Galinski said.

"I'm sorry," came the voice from the upper berth. "That can't be an accurate statement because I only met you ten days ago."

"Haven't you been drunk for two weeks, Carper," Nick said.

"Of course," the Carper said, talking to the wall. "But Galinski has no right to say so."

Galinski jogged him up and down by pushing with his feet.

"I take it back, Carper," he said. "I don't think you're drunk."

"Don't make ridiculous statements," the Carper said faintly.

"What are you doing, Anton," Leon asked.

"Thinking about my girl in Niagara Falls."

"Come on, Nick," said Leon. "We'll leave this porpoise."

"Did she tell you I was a porpoise?" Galinski asked. "She told me I was a porpoise. You know what I said to her in French. 'Mademoiselle Gaby, you have got nothing that has any interest for me.' Take a drink, Nick."

He reached out the bottle and Nick swallowed some of the brandy.

"Leon?"

"No. Come on, Nick. We'll leave him."

"I go on duty with the men at midnight," Galinski said.

"Don't get drunk," Nick said.

"I have never been drunk."

In the upper bunk the Carper muttered something.

"What you say, Carper?"

"I was calling on God to strike him."

"I have neffer been drunk," Galinski repeated and poured the tooth mug half full of cognac.

"Go on, God," the Carper said. "Strike him."

"I have neffer been drunk. I have neffer slept with a woman."

"Come on. Do your stuff, God. Strike him."

"Come on, Nick. Let's get out."

Galinski handed the bottle to Nick. He took a swallow and followed the tall Pole out.

Outside the door they heard Galinski's voice shouting, "I have neffer been drunk. I have neffer slept with a woman. I have neffer told a lie."

"Strike him," came the Carper's thin voice. "Don't take that stuff from him, God. Strike him."

"They're a fine pair," Nick said.

"What about this Carper? Where does he come from?"

"He was two years in the ambulance before. They sent him home. He got fired out of college and now he's going back."

"He drinks too much."

"He isn't happy."

"Let's get a bottle of wine and sleep out in a lifeboat."

"Come on."

They stopped at the smoking room bar and Nick bought a bottle of red wine. Leon stood at the bar, tall in his French uniform. Inside the smoking room two big poker games were going on. Nick would have liked to play but not on the last night. Everybody was playing. It was smoky and hot with all the portholes closed and shuttered. Nick looked at Leon. "Want to play?"

"No. Let's drink the wine and talk."

"Let's get two bottles then."

They went out of the hot room onto the deck carrying the bottles. It was not hard to climb out onto one of the lifeboats although it scared Nick to look down at the water as he climbed out on the davits. Inside the boat they made themselves comfortable with life belts to lie back against the thwarts. There was a feeling of being between the sea and the sky. It was not like being on the throbbing of the big boat.

"This is good," said Nick.

"I sleep in one of these every night."

"I'd be afraid I'd walk in my sleep," Nick said. He was uncorking the wine. "I sleep on the deck."

He handed the bottle to Leon. "Keep this and open the other bottle for me," the Pole said.

"You take it," Nick said. He drew the cork from the second bottle and clinked it across the dark with Leon. They drank.

"You'll get better wine than this in France," Leon said.

"I won't be in France."

"I forgot. I wish we were going to soldier together."

"I wouldn't be any good," Nick said. He looked over the gunwale of the boat at the dark water below. He had been frightened coming out on the davits.

"I wonder if I'll be scared," he said.

"No," Leon said. "I don't think so."

"It will be fun to see all the planes and that stuff."

"Yes," said Leon. "I am going to fly as soon as I can transfer."

"I couldn't do that."

"Why not?"

"I don't know."

"You mustn't think about being scared."

"I don't. Really I don't. I never worry about it. I just thought because it made me feel funny coming out onto the boat just now."

[141]

Leon lay on his side, the bottle straight up beside his head.

"We don't have to think about being scared," he said. "We're not that kind."

"The Carper's scared," Nick said.

"Yes. Galinski told me."

"That's what he was sent back for. That's why he's drunk all the time."

"He's not like us," Leon said. "Listen, Nick. You and me, we've got something in us."

"I know. I feel that way. Other people can get killed but not me. I feel that absolutely."

"That's it. That's what we've got."

"I wanted to get into the Canadian army but they wouldn't take me."

"I know. You told me."

They both drank. Nick lay back and looked at the cloud of smoke from the funnel against the sky. The sky was beginning to lighten. Maybe the moon was going to come up.

"Have you got a girl, Leon?"

"No."

"None at all?"

"No."

"I got one," Nick said.

"You live with her?"

"We're engaged."

"I never slept with a girl."

"I've been with them in houses."

Leon took a drink. The bottle angled blackly from his mouth against the sky.

"That isn't what I mean. I done that. I don't like it. I mean sleep all night with one you love."

"My girl would have slept with me."

"Sure. If she loved you she'd sleep with you."

"We're going to get married."

"Nick Sat Against the Wall ..."

Nick sat against the wall of the church where they had dragged him to be clear of machine-gun fire in the street. Both legs stuck out awkwardly. He had been hit in the spine. His face was sweaty and dirty. The sun shone on his face. The day was very hot. Rinaldi, big-backed, his equipment sprawling, lay face downward against the wall. Nick looked straight ahead brilliantly. The pink wall of the house opposite had fallen out from the roof, and an iron bedstead hung twisted toward the street. Two Austrian dead lay in the rubble in the shade of the house. Up the street were other dead. Things were getting forward in the town. It was going well. Stretcher-bearers would be along any time now. Nick turned his head and looked down at Rinaldi. "Senta, Rinaldi, senta. You and me, we've made a separate peace." Rinaldi lay still in the sun, breathing with difficulty. "We're not patriots." Nick turned his head away, smiling sweatily. Rinaldi was a disappointing audience.

Now I Lay Me

That night we lay on the floor in the room and I listened to the silkworms eating. The silkworms fed in racks of mulberry leaves and all night you could hear them eating and a dropping sound in the leaves. I myself did not want to sleep because I had been living for a long time with the knowledge that if I ever shut my eyes in the dark and let myself go, my soul would go out of my body. I had been that way for a long time, ever since I had been blown up at night and felt it go out of me and go off and then come back. I tried never to think about it, but it had started to go since, in the nights, just at the moment of going off to sleep, and I could only stop it by a very great effort. So while now I am fairly sure that it would not really have gone out, yet then, that summer, I was unwilling to make the experiment.

I had different ways of occupying myself while I lay awake. I would think of a trout stream I had fished along when I was a boy and fish its whole length very carefully in my mind, fishing very carefully under all the logs, all the turns of the bank, the deep holes and the clear shallow stretches, sometimes catching trout and sometimes losing them. I would stop fishing at noon to eat my lunch, sometimes on a log over the stream, sometimes on a high bank under a tree, and I always ate my lunch very slowly and watched the stream below me while I ate. Often I ran out of bait because I would take only ten worms with me in a tobacco tin when I started. When I had used them all I had to find more worms, and sometimes it was very difficult digging in the bank of the stream where the cedar trees kept out the sun and there was no grass but only the bare moist earth and often I could find no worms. Always, though, I found some kind of bait, but one time in the swamp I could find no bait at all and had to cut up one of the trout I had caught and use him for bait.

Sometimes I found insects in the swamp meadows, in the grass or under ferns, and used them. There were beetles and insects with legs like grass stems, and grubs in old rotten logs, white grubs with brown pinching heads that would not stay on the hook and emptied into nothing in the cold water, and wood ticks under logs where sometimes I found angleworms that slipped into the ground as soon as the log was raised. Once I used a salamander from under an old log. The salamander was very small and neat and agile and a lovely color. He had tiny feet that tried to hold on to the hook, and after that one time I never used a salamander, although I found them very often. Nor did I use crickets, because of the way they acted about the hook.

Sometimes the stream ran through an open meadow, and in the dry grass I would catch grasshoppers and use them for bait and sometimes I would catch grasshoppers and toss them into the stream and watch them float along, swimming on the stream and circling on the surface as the current took them, and then disappear as a trout rose. Sometimes I would fish four or five different streams in the night, starting as near as I could get to their source and fishing them downstream. When I had finished too quickly and the time did not go, I would fish the stream over again, starting where it emptied into the lake and fishing back upstream, trying for all the trout I had missed coming down. Some nights, too, I made up streams, and some of them were very exciting, and it was like being awake and dreaming. Some of those streams I still remember and think that I have fished in them, and they are confused with streams I really know. I gave them all names and went to them on the train and sometimes walked for miles to get to them.

But some nights I could not fish, and on those nights I was cold-awake and said my prayers over and over and tried to pray for all the people I had ever known. That took up a great amount of time, for if you try to remember all the people you have ever known, going back to the earliest thing you remember—which was, with me, the attic of the house where I was born and my mother and father's wedding cake in a tin box hanging from one of the rafters, and, in the attic, jars of snakes and other specimens that my father had collected as a boy and preserved in alcohol, the alcohol sunken in the jars so the backs of some of the snakes and specimens were exposed and had turned white—if you thought back that far, you remembered a great many people. If you prayed for all of them, saying a Hail Mary and an Our Father for each one, it took a long time and finally it would be light, and then you could go to sleep, if you were in a place where you could sleep in the daylight.

On those nights I tried to remember everything that had ever happened to me, starting with just before I went to the war and remembering back from one thing to another. I found I could only remember back to that attic in my grandfather's house. Then I would start there and remember this way again, until I reached the war.

I remembered after my grandfather died we moved away from that house and to a new house designed and built by my mother. Many things that were not to be moved were burned in the back yard and I remember those jars from the attic being thrown in the fire, and how they popped in the heat and the fire flamed up from the alcohol. I remember the snakes burning in the fire in the back yard. But there were no people in that, only things. I could not remember who burned the things even, and I would go on until I came to people and then stop and pray for them.

About the new house I remembered how my mother was always cleaning things out and making a good clearance. One time when my father was away on a hunting trip she made a good thorough cleaning-out in the basement and burned everything that should not have been there. When my father came home and got down from his buggy and hitched the horse, the fire was still burning in the road beside the house. I went out to meet him. He handed me his shotgun and looked at the fire. "What's this?" he asked.

"I've been cleaning out the basement, dear," my mother said from the porch. She was standing there smiling, to meet him. My father looked at the fire and kicked at something. Then he leaned over and picked something out of the ashes. "Get a rake, Nick," he said to me. I went to the basement and brought a rake and my father raked very carefully in the ashes. He raked out stone axes and stone skinning knives and tools for making arrowheads and pieces of pottery and many arrowheads. They had all been blackened and chipped by the fire. My father raked them all out very carefully and spread them on the grass by the road. His shotgun in its leather case and his gamebags were on the grass where he had left them when he stepped down from the buggy.

"Take the gun and the bags in the house, Nick, and bring me a paper," he said. My mother had gone inside the house. I took the shotgun, which was heavy to carry and banged against my legs, and the two gamebags and started toward the

[147]

house. "Take them one at a time," my father said. "Don't try and carry too much at once." I put down the gamebags and took in the shotgun and brought out a newspaper from the pile in my father's office. My father spread all the blackened, chipped stone implements on the paper and then wrapped them up. "The best arrowheads went all to pieces," he said. He walked into the house with the paper package and I stayed outside on the grass with the two gamebags. After a while I took them in. In remembering that, there were only two people, so I would pray for them both.

Some nights, though, I could not remember my prayers even. I could only get as far as "On earth as it is in heaven" and then have to start all over and be absolutely unable to get past that. Then I would have to recognize that I could not remember and give up saying my prayers that night and try something else. So on some nights I would try to remember all the animals in the world by name and then the birds and then fishes and then countries and cities and then kinds of food and the names of all the streets I could remember in Chicago, and when I could not remember anything at all any more I would just listen. And I do not remember a night on which you could not hear things. If I could have a light I was not afraid to sleep, because I knew my soul would only go out of me if it were dark. So, of course, many nights I was where I could have a light and then I slept because I was nearly always tired and often very sleepy. And I am sure many times, too, that I slept without knowing it—but I never slept knowing it, and on this night I listened to the silkworms. You can hear silkworms eating very clearly in the night and I lay with my eyes open and listened to them.

There was only one other person in the room and he was awake, too. I listened to him being awake, for a long time. He could not lie as quietly as I could because, perhaps, he had not had as much practice being awake. We were lying on blankets spread over straw and when he moved the straw was noisy, but the silkworms were not frightened by any noise we made and ate on steadily. There were the noises of night seven kilometres behind the lines outside but they were different from the small noises inside the room in the dark. The other man in the room tried lying quietly. Then he moved again. I moved, too, so he would know I was awake. He had lived ten years in Chicago. They had taken him for a soldier in nineteen fourteen when he had come back to visit his family, and they had given him to me for an orderly because he spoke English. I heard him listening, so I moved again in the blankets.

"Can't you sleep, Signor Tenente?" he asked.

"No."

"I can't sleep, either."

"What's the matter?"

"I don't know. I can't sleep."

"You feel all right?"

"Sure. I feel good. I just can't sleep."

"You want to talk a while?" I asked.

"Sure. What can you talk about in this damn place?"

"This place is pretty good," I said.

"Sure," he said. "It's all right."

"Tell me about out in Chicago," I said.

"Oh," he said, "I told you all that once."

"Tell me about how you got married."

"I told you that."

"Was the letter you got Monday—from her?"

"Sure. She writes me all the time. She's making good money with the place."

"You'll have a nice place when you go back."

"Sure. She runs it fine. She's making a lot of money."

"Don't you think we'll wake them up, talking?" I asked.

"No. They can't hear. Anyway, they sleep like pigs. I'm different," he said. "I'm nervous."

"Talk quiet," I said. "Want a smoke?"

We smoked skillfully in the dark.

"You don't smoke much, Signor Tenente."

"No. I've just about cut it out."

"Well," he said, "it don't do you any good and I suppose you get so you don't miss it. Did you ever hear a blind man won't smoke because he can't see the smoke come out?"

"I don't believe it."

"I think it's all bull, myself," he said. "I just heard it somewhere. You know how you hear things."

We were both quiet and I listened to the silkworms.

"You hear those damn silkworms?" he asked. "You can hear them chew."

"It's funny," I said.

"Say, Signor Tenente, is there something really the matter that you can't sleep? I never see you sleep. You haven't slept nights ever since I been with you."

"I don't know, John," I said. "I got in pretty bad shape along early last spring and at night it bothers me."

"Just like I am," he said. "I shouldn't have ever got in this war. I'm too nervous."

"Maybe it will get better."

"Say, Signor Tenente, what did you get in this war for, anyway?"

"I don't know, John. I wanted to, then."

"Wanted to," he said. "That's a hell of a reason."

"We oughtn't to talk out loud," I said.

"They sleep just like pigs," he said. "They can't understand the English language, anyway. They don't know a damn thing. What are you going to do when it's over and we go back to the States?"

"I'll get a job on a paper."

"In Chicago?"

"Maybe."

"Do you ever read what this fellow Brisbane writes? My wife cuts it out for me and sends it to me."

"Sure."

"Did you ever meet him?"

"No, but I've seen him."

"I'd like to meet that fellow. He's a fine writer. My wife don't read English but she takes the paper just like when I was home and she cuts out the editorials and the sport page and sends them to me."

"How are your kids?"

"They're fine. One of the girls is in the fourth grade now. You know, Signor Tenente, if I didn't have the kids I wouldn't be your orderly now. They'd have made me stay in the line all the time."

"I'm glad you've got them."

"So am I. They're fine kids but I want a boy. Three girls and no boy. That's a hell of a note."

"Why don't you try and go to sleep."

"No, I can't sleep now. I'm wide awake now, Signor Tenente. Say, I'm worried about you not sleeping, though."

"It'll be all right, John."

"Imagine a young fellow like you not to sleep."

"I'll get all right. It just takes a while."

"You got to get all right. A man can't get along that don't sleep. Do you worry about anything? You got anything on your mind?"

"No, John, I don't think so."

"You ought to get married, Signor Tenente. Then you wouldn't worry."

"I don't know."

"You ought to get married. Why don't you pick out some nice Italian girl with plenty of money. You could get any one you want. You're young and you got good decorations and you look nice. You been wounded a couple of times."

"I can't talk the language well enough."

"You talk it fine. To hell with talking the language. You don't have to talk to them. Marry them."

"I'll think about it."

"You know some girls, don't you?"

"Sure."

"Well, you marry the one with the most money. Over here, the way they're brought up, they'll all make you a good wife."

"I'll think about it."

"Don't think about it, Signor Tenente. Do it."

"All right."

"A man ought to be married. You'll never regret it. Every man ought to be married."

"All right," I said. "Let's try and sleep a while."

"All right, Signor Tenente. I'll try it again. But you remember what I said."

"I'll remember it," I said. "Now let's sleep a while, John."

"All right," he said. "I hope you sleep, Signor Tenente."

I heard him roll in his blankets on the straw and then he was very quiet and I listened to him breathing regularly. Then he started to snore. I listened to him snore for a long time and then I stopped listening to him snore and listened to the silkworms eating. They ate steadily, making a dropping in the leaves. I had a new thing to think about and I lay in the dark with my eyes open and thought of all the girls I had ever known and what kind of wives they would make. It was a very interesting thing to think about and for a while it killed off trout fishing and interfered with my prayers. Finally, though, I went back to trout fishing, because I found that I could remember all the streams and there was always something new about them, while the girls, after I had thought about them a few times, blurred and I could not call them into my mind and finally they all blurred and all became rather the same and I gave up thinking about them almost altogether. But I kept on with my prayers and I prayed very often for John in the nights and his class was removed from active service before the October offensive. I was glad he was not there, because he would have been a great worry to me. He came to the hospital in Milan to see me several months after and was very disappointed that I had not yet married, and I know he would feel very badly if he knew that, so far, I have never married. He was going back to America and he was very certain about marriage and knew it would fix up everything.

A Way You'll Never Be

The attack had gone across the field, been held up by machine-gun fire from the sunken road and from the group of farmhouses, encountered no resistance in the town, and reached the bank of the river. Coming along the road on a bicycle, getting off to push the machine when the surface of the road became too broken, Nicholas Adams saw what had happened by the position of the dead.

They lay alone or in clumps in the high grass of the field and along the road, their pockets out, and over them were flies and around each body or group of bodies were the scattered papers.

In the grass and the grain, beside the road, and in some places scattered over the road, there was much material: a field kitchen, it must have come over when things were going well; many of the calfskin-covered haversacks, stick bombs, helmets, rifles, sometimes one butt up, the bayonet stuck in the dirt, they had dug quite a little at the last; stick bombs, helmets, rifles, intrenching tools, ammunition boxes, star-shell pistols, their shells scattered about, medical kits, gas masks, empty gas-mask cans, a squat, tripodded machine gun in a nest of empty shells, full belts protruding from the boxes, the water-cooling can empty and on its side, the breechblock gone, the crew in odd positions, and around them, in the grass, more of the typical papers.

There were mass prayer books, group postcards showing the machine-gun unit standing in ranked and ruddy cheerfulness as in a football picture for a college annual; now they were humped and swollen in the grass; propaganda postcards showing a soldier in Austrian uniform bending a woman backward over a bed; the figures were impressionistically drawn, very attractively depicted and had nothing in common with actual rape in which the woman's skirts are pulled over her head to smother her, one comrade sometimes sitting upon the head. There were many of these inciting cards which had evidently been issued just before the offensive. Now they were scattered with the smutty postcards, photographic; the small photographs of village girls by village photographers, the occasional pictures of children, and the letters, letters, letters. There was always much paper about the dead and the debris of this attack was no exception.

These were new dead and no one had bothered with anything but their pockets. Our own dead, or what he thought of, still, as our own dead, were surprisingly few, Nick noticed. Their coats had been opened too and their pockets were out, and they showed, by their positions, the manner and the skill of the attack. The hot weather had swollen them all alike regardless of nationality.

The town had evidently been defended, at the last, from the line of the sunken road and there had been few or no Austrians to fall back into it. There were only three bodies in the street and they looked to have been killed running. The houses of the town were broken by the shelling and the street had much rubble of plaster and mortar and there were broken beams, broken tiles, and many holes, some of them yellow-edged from the mustard gas. There were many pieces of shell, and shrapnel balls were scattered in the rubble. There was no one in the town at all.

Nick Adams had seen no one since he had left Fornaci,

although, riding along the road through the over-foliaged country, he had seen guns hidden under screens of mulberry leaves to the left of the road, noticing them by the heat waves in the air above the leaves where the sun hit the metal. Now he went on through the town, surprised to find it deserted, and came out on the low road beneath the bank of the river. Leaving the town there was a bare open space where the road slanted down and he could see the placid reach of the river and the low curve of the opposite bank and the whitened, sun-baked mud where the Austrians had dug. It was all very lush and over-green since he had seen it last and becoming historical had made no change in this, the lower river.

The battalion was along the bank to the left. There was a series of holes in the top of the bank with a few men in them. Nick noticed where the machine guns were posted and the signal rockets in their racks. The men in the holes in the side of the bank were sleeping. No one challenged. He went on and as he came around a turn in the mud bank a young second lieutenant with a stubble of beard and red-rimmed, very blood-shot eyes pointed a pistol at him.

"Who are you?"

Nick told him.

"How do I know this?"

Nick showed him the tessera with photograph and identification and the seal of the Third Army. He took hold of it.

"I will keep this."

"You will not," Nick said. "Give me back the card and put your gun away. There. In the holster."

"How am I to know who you are?"

"The tessera tells you."

"And if the tessera is false? Give me that card."

"Don't be a fool," Nick said cheerfully. "Take me to your company commander."

[156]

"I should send you to battalion headquarters."

"All right," said Nick. "Listen, do you know the Captain Paravicini? The tall one with the small mustache who was an architect and speaks English?"

"You know him?"

"A little."

"What company does he command?"

"The second."

"He is commanding the battalion."

"Good," said Nick. He was relieved to know that Para was all right. "Let us go to the battalion."

As Nick had left the edge of the town three shrapnel had burst high and to the right over one of the wrecked houses and since then there had been no shelling. But the face of this officer looked like the face of a man during a bombardment. There was the same tightness and the voice did not sound natural. His pistol made Nick nervous.

"Put it away," he said. "There's the whole river between them and you."

"If I thought you were a spy I would shoot you now," the second lieutenant said.

"Come on," said Nick. "Let us go to the battalion." This officer made him very nervous.

The Captain Paravicini, acting major, thinner and more English-looking than ever, rose when Nick saluted from behind the table in the dugout that was battalion headquarters.

"Hello," he said. "I didn't know you. What are you doing in that uniform?"

"They've put me in it."

"I am very glad to see you, Nicolo."

"Right. You look well. How was the show?"

"We made a very fine attack. Truly. A very fine attack. I will show you. Look."

[157]

He showed on the map how the attack had gone.

"I came from Fornaci," Nick said. "I could see how it had been. It was very good."

"It was extraordinary. Altogether extraordinary. Are you attached to the regiment?"

"No. I am supposed to move around and let them see the uniform."

"How odd."

"If they see one American uniform that is supposed to make them believe others are coming."

"But how will they know it is an American uniform?"

"You will tell them."

"Oh. Yes, I see. I will send a corporal with you to show you about and you will make a tour of the lines."

"Like a bloody politician," Nick said.

"You would be much more distinguished in civilian clothes. They are what is really distinguished."

"With a homburg hat," said Nick.

"Or with a very furry fedora."

"I'm supposed to have my pockets full of cigarettes and postal cards and such things," Nick said. "I should have a musette full of chocolate. These I should distribute with a kind word and a pat on the back. But there weren't any cigarettes and postcards and no chocolate. So they said to circulate around anyway."

"I'm sure your appearance will be very heartening to the troops."

"I wish you wouldn't," Nick said. "I feel badly enough about it as it is. In principle, I would have brought you a bottle of brandy."

"In principle," Para said and smiled, for the first time, showing yellowed teeth. "Such a beautiful expression. Would you like some Grappa?"

"No, thank you," Nick said.

"It hasn't any ether in it."

"I can taste that still," Nick remembered suddenly and completely.

"You know I never knew you were drunk until you started talking coming back in the camions."

"I was stinking in every attack," Nick said.

"I can't do it," Para said. "I took it in the first show, the very first show, and it only made me very upset and then frightfully thirsty."

"You don't need it."

"You're much braver in an attack than I am."

"No," Nick said. "I know how I am and I prefer to get stinking. I'm not ashamed of it."

"I've never seen you drunk."

"No?" said Nick. "Never? Not when we rode from Mestre to Portogrande that night and I wanted to go to sleep and used the bicycle for a blanket and pulled it up under my chin?"

"That wasn't in the lines."

"Let's not talk about how I am," Nick said. "It's a subject I know too much about to want to think about it any more."

"You might as well stay here a while," Paravicini said. "You can take a nap if you like. They didn't do much to this in the bombardment. It's too hot to go out yet."

"I suppose there is no hurry."

"How are you really?"

"I'm fine. I'm perfectly all right."

"No. I mean really."

"I'm all right. I can't sleep without a light of some sort. That's all I have now."

"I said it should have been trepanned. I'm no doctor but I know that."

"Well, they thought it was better to have it absorb, and that's what I got. What's the matter? I don't seem crazy to you, do I?"

"You seem in top-hole shape."

"It's a hell of a nuisance once they've had you certified as nutty," Nick said. "No one ever has any confidence in you again."

"I would take a nap, Nicolo," Paravicini said. "This isn't battalion headquarters as we used to know it. We're just waiting to be pulled out. You oughtn't to go out in the heat now— it's silly. Use that bunk."

"I might just lie down," Nick said.

Nick lay on the bunk. He was very disappointed that he felt this way and more disappointed, even, that it was so obvious to Captain Paravicini. This was not as large a dugout as the one where that platoon of the class of 1899, just out at the front, got hysterics during the bombardment before the attack, and Para had had him walk them two at a time outside to show them nothing would happen, he wearing his own chin strap tight across his mouth to keep his lips quiet. Knowing they could not hold it when they took it. Knowing it was all a bloody balls—. If he can't stop crying, break his nose to give him something else to think about. I'd shoot one but it's too late now. They'd all be worse. Break his nose. They've put it back to five-twenty. We've only got four minutes more. Break that other silly bugger's nose and kick his silly ass out of here. Do you think they'll go over? If they don't, shoot two and try to scoop the others out some way. Keep behind them, sergeant. It's no use to walk ahead and find there's nothing coming behind you. Bail them out as you go. What a bloody balls. All right. That's right. Then, looking at the watch, in that quiet tone, that valuable quiet tone, "Savoia." Making it cold, no time to get it, he couldn't find his own after the cave-in, one whole end had caved in; it was that started them; making it cold up that slope the only time he hadn't done it stinking. And after they came back the teleferica house burned, it seemed, and some of the wounded got down four days later and some did not get down, but we went up and we went back and we came down—we always came down. And there was Gaby Delys, oddly enough, with feathers on; you called me baby doll a year ago tadada you said that I was rather nice to know tadada with feathers on, with feathers off, the great Gaby, and my name's Harry Pilcer, too, we used to step out of the far side of the taxis when it got steep going up the hill and he could see that hill every night when he dreamed with Sacré Coeur, blown white, like a soap bubble. Sometimes his girl was there and sometimes she was with someone else and he could not understand that, but those were the nights the river ran so much wider and stiller than it should and outside of Fossalta there was a low house painted yellow with willows all around it and a low stable and there was a canal, and he had been there a thousand times and never seen it, but there it was every night as plain as the hill, only it frightened him. That house meant more than anything and every night he had it. That was what he needed but it frightened him especially when the boat lay there quietly in the willows on the canal, but the banks weren't like this river. It was all lower, as it was at Portogrande, where they had seen them come wallowing across the flooded ground holding the rifles high until they fell with them in the water. Who ordered that one? If it didn't get so damned mixed up he could follow it all right. That was why he noticed everything in such detail to keep it all straight so he would know just where he was, but suddenly it confused without reason as now, he lying in a bunk at battalion headquarters, with Para commanding a battalion and he in a bloody American uniform. He sat up and looked around; they all watching him. Para was gone out. He lay down again.

The Paris part came earlier and he was not frightened of it except when she had gone off with someone else and the fear that they might take the same driver twice. That was what frightened about that. Never about the front. He never dreamed about the front now any more but what frightened him so that he could not get rid of it was that long yellow house and the different width of the river. Now he was back here at the river, he had gone through that same town, and there was no house. Nor was the river that way. Then where did he go each night and what was the peril, and why would he wake, soaking wet, more frightened than he had ever been in a bombardment, because of a house and a long stable and a canal?

He sat up, swung his legs carefully down; they stiffened any time they were out straight for long; returned the stares of the adjutant, the signallers and the two runners by the door and put on his cloth-covered trench helmet.

"I regret the absence of the chocolate, the postal cards and cigarettes," he said. "I am, however, wearing the uniform."

"The major is coming back at once," the adjutant said. In that army an adjutant is not a commissioned officer.

"The uniform is not very correct," Nick told them. "But it gives you the idea. There will be several millions of Americans here shortly."

"Do you think they will send Americans down here?" asked the adjutant.

"Oh, absolutely. Americans twice as large as myself, healthy, with clean hearts, sleep at night, never been wounded, never been blown up, never had their heads caved in, never been scared, don't drink, faithful to the girls they left behind them, many of them never had crabs, wonderful chaps. You'll see."

"Are you an Italian?" asked the adjutant.

"No, American. Look at the uniform. Spagnolini made it but it's not quite correct."

"A North or South American?"

"North," said Nick. He felt it coming on now. He would quiet down.

"But you speak Italian."

"Why not? Do you mind if I speak Italian? Haven't I a right to speak Italian?"

"You have Italian medals."

"Just the ribbons and the papers. The medals come later. Or you give them to people to keep and the people go away, or they are lost with your baggage. You can purchase others in Milan. It is the papers that are of importance. You must not feel badly about them. You will have some yourself if you stay at the front long enough."

"I am a veteran of the Eritrea campaign," said the adjutant stiffly. "I fought in Tripoli."

"It's quite something to have met you," Nick put out his hand. "Those must have been trying days. I noticed the ribbons. Were you, by any chance, on the Carso?"

"I have just been called up for this war. My class was too old."

"At one time I was under the age limit," Nick said. "But now I am reformed out of the war."

"But why are you here now?"

"I am demonstrating the American uniform," Nick said. "Don't you think it is very significant? It is a little tight in the collar but soon you will see untold millions wearing this uniform swarming like locusts. The grasshopper, you know, what we call the grasshopper in America, is really a locust. The true grasshopper is small and green and comparatively feeble. You must not, however, make a confusion with the seven-year locust or cicada which emits a peculiar sustained sound which at the moment I cannot recall. I try to recall it but I cannot. I can almost hear it and then it is quite gone. You will pardon me if I break off our conversation?"

"See if you can find the major," the adjutant said to one of the two runners. "I can see you have been wounded," he said to Nick.

"In various places," Nick said. "If you are interested in scars

[163]

I can show you some very interesting ones but I would rather talk about grasshoppers. What we call grasshoppers, that is, and what are, really, locusts. These insects at one time played a very important part in my life. It might interest you and you can look at the uniform while I am talking."

The adjutant made a motion with his hand to the second runner, who went out.

"Fix your eyes on the uniform. Spagnolini made it, you know. You might as well look, too," Nick said to the signallers. "I really have no rank. We're under the American consul. It's perfectly all right for you to look. You can stare, if you like. I will tell you about the American locust. We always preferred one that we called the medium-brown. They last the best in the water and fish prefer them. The larger ones that fly, making a noise somewhat similar to that produced by a rattlesnake rattling his rattlers, a very dry sound, have vivid-colored wings, some are bright red, others yellow barred with black, but their wings go to pieces in the water and they make a very blowsy bait, while the medium-brown is a plump, compact, succulent hopper that I can recommend as far as one may well recommend something you gentlemen will probably never encounter. But I must insist that you will never gather a sufficient supply of these insects for a day's fishing by pursuing them with your hands or trying to hit them with a hat. That is sheer nonsense and a useless waste of time. I repeat, gentlemen, that you will get nowhere at it. The correct procedure, and one which should be taught all young officers at every small-arms course if I had anything to say about it, and who knows but what I will have, is the employment of a seine or net made of common mosquito netting. Two officers holding this length of netting at alternate ends, or let us say one at each end, stoop, hold the bottom extremity of the net in one hand and the top extremity in the other and run into the wind. The hoppers, flying with the wind, fly against the length of netting and are imprisoned in its folds. It is no trick at all to catch a very great quantity indeed, and no officer, in my opinion, should be without a length of mosquito netting suitable for the improvisation of one of these grasshopper seines. I hope I have made myself clear, gentlemen. Are there any questions? If there is anything in the course you do not understand please ask questions. Speak up. None? Then I would like to close on this note. In the words of that great soldier and gentleman, Sir Henry Wilson: Gentlemen, either you must govern or you must be governed. Let me repeat it. Gentlemen, there is one thing I would like to have you remember. One thing I would like you to take with you as you leave this room. Gentlemen, either you must govern—or you must be governed. That is all, gentlemen. Good day."

He removed his cloth-covered helmet, put it on again and, stooping, went out the low entrance of the dugout. Para, accompanied by the two runners, was coming down the line of the sunken road. It was very hot in the sun and Nick removed the helmet.

"There ought to be a system for wetting these things," he said. "I shall wet this one in the river." He started up the bank.

"Nicolo," Paravicini called. "Nicolo. Where are you going?"

"I don't really have to go." Nick came down the slope, holding the helmet in his hands. "They're a damned nuisance wet or dry. Do you wear yours all the time?"

"All the time," said Para. "It's making me bald. Come inside."

Inside Para told him to sit down.

"You know they're absolutely no damned good," Nick said. "I remember when they were a comfort when we first had them, but I've seen them full of brains too many times."

"Nicolo," Para said. "I think you should go back. I think

it would be better if you didn't come up to the line until you had those supplies. There's nothing here for you to do. If you move around, even with something worth giving away, the men will group and that invites shelling. I won't have it."

"I know it's silly," Nick said. "It wasn't my idea. I heard the brigade was here so I thought I would see you or someone else I knew. I could have gone to Zenzon or to San Dona. I'd like to go to San Dona to see the bridge again."

"I won't have you circulating around to no purpose," Captain Paravicini said.

"All right," said Nick. He felt it coming on again.

"You understand?"

"Of course," said Nick. He was trying to hold it in.

"Anything of that sort should be done at night."

"Naturally," said Nick. He knew he could not stop it now.

"You see, I am commanding the battalion," Para said.

"And why shouldn't you be?" Nick said. Here it came. "You can read and write, can't you?"

"Yes," said Para gently.

"The trouble is you have a damned small battalion to command. As soon as it gets to strength again they'll give you back your company. Why don't they bury the dead? I've seen them now. I don't care about seeing them again. They can bury them any time as far as I'm concerned and it would be much better for you. You'll all get bloody sick."

"Where did you leave your bicycle?"

"Inside the last house."

"Do you think it will be all right?"

"Don't worry," Nick said. "I'll go in a little while."

"Lie down a little while, Nicolo."

"All right."

He shut his eyes, and in place of the man with the beard who looked at him over the sights of the rifle, quite calmly before squeezing off, the white flash and clublike impact, on his knees, hot-sweet choking, coughing it onto the rock while they went past him, he saw a long, yellow house with a low stable and the river much wider than it was and stiller. "Christ," he said, "I might as well go."

He stood up.

"I'm going, Para," he said. "I'll ride back now in the afternoon. If any supplies have come I'll bring them down tonight. If not I'll come at night when I have something to bring."

"It is still hot to ride," Captain Paravicini said.

"You don't need to worry," Nick said. "I'm all right now for quite a while. I had one then but it was easy. They're getting much better. I can tell when I'm going to have one because I talk so much."

"I'll send a runner with you."

"I'd rather you didn't. I know the way."

"You'll be back soon?"

"Absolutely."

"Let me send——"

"No," said Nick. "As a mark of confidence."

"Well, ciao, then."

"Ciao," said Nick. He started back along the sunken road toward where he had left the bicycle. In the afternoon the road would be shady once he had passed the canal. Beyond that there were trees on both sides that had not been shelled at all. It was on that stretch that, marching, they had once passed the Terza Savoia cavalry regiment riding in the snow with their lances. The horses' breath made plumes in the cold air. No, that was somewhere else. Where was that?

"I'd better get to that damned bicycle," Nick said to himself. "I don't want to lose the way to Fornaci."

In Another Country

In the fall the war was always there, but we did not go to it any more. It was cold in the fall in Milan and the dark came very early. Then the electric lights came on, and it was pleasant along the streets looking in the windows. There was much game hanging outside the shops, and the snow powdered in the fur of the foxes and the wind blew their tails. The deer hung stiff and heavy and empty, and small birds blew in the wind and the wind turned their feathers. It was a cold fall and the wind came down from the mountains.

We were all at the hospital every afternoon, and there were different ways of walking across the town through the dusk to the hospital. Two of the ways were alongside canals, but they were long. Always, though, you crossed a bridge across a canal to enter the hospital. There was a choice of three bridges. On one of them a woman sold roasted chestnuts. It was warm, standing in front of her charcoal fire, and the chestnuts were warm afterward in your pocket. The hospital was very old and very beautiful, and you entered through a gate and walked across a courtyard and out a gate on the other side. There were usually funerals starting from the courtyard. Beyond the old hospital were the new brick pavilions, and there we met every afternoon and were all very polite and interested in what was the matter, and sat in the machines that were to make so much difference.

The doctor came up to the machine where I was sitting and said: "What did you like best to do before the war? Did you practice a sport?"

I said: "Yes, football."

"Good," he said. "You will be able to play football again better than ever."

My knee did not bend and the leg dropped straight from the knee to the ankle without a calf, and the machine was to bend the knee and make it move as in riding a tricycle. But it did not bend yet, and instead the machine lurched when it came to the bending part. The doctor said: "That will all pass. You are a fortunate young man. You will play football again like a champion."

In the next machine was a major who had a little hand like a baby's. He winked at me when the doctor examined his hand, which was between two leather straps that bounced up and down and flapped the stiff fingers, and said: "And will I, too, play football, captain-doctor?" He had been a very great fencer, and before the war the greatest fencer in Italy.

The doctor went to his office in a back room and brought a photograph which showed a hand that had been withered almost as small as the major's, before it had taken a machine course, and after was a little larger. The major held the photograph with his good hand and looked at it very carefully. "A wound?" he asked.

"An industrial accident," the doctor said.

"Very interesting, very interesting," the major said, and handed it back to the doctor.

"You have confidence?"

"No," said the major.

There were three boys who came each day who were about the same age I was. They were all three from Milan, and one of them was to be a lawyer, and one was to be a painter, and one had intended to be a soldier, and after we were finished with the machines, sometimes we walked back together to the Café Cova, which was next door to the Scala. We walked the short way through the Communist quarter because we were four together. The people hated us because we were officers, and from a wineshop someone would call out, "*A basso gli ufficiali!*" as we passed. Another boy who walked with us sometimes and made us five wore a black silk handkerchief across his face because he had no nose then and his face was to be rebuilt. He had gone out to the front from the military academy and been wounded within an hour after he had gone into the front line for the first time. They rebuilt his face, but he came from a very old family and they could never get the nose exactly right. He went to South America and worked in a bank. But this was a long time ago, and then we did not any of us know how it was going to be afterward. We only knew then that there was always the war, but that we were not going to it any more.

We all had the same medals, except the boy with the black silk bandage across his face, and he had not been at the front long enough to get any medals. The tall boy with a very pale face who was to be a lawyer had been a lieutenant of Arditi and had three medals of the sort we each had only one of. He had lived a very long time with death and was a little detached. We were all a little detached, and there was nothing that held us together except that we met every afternoon at the hospital. Although, as we walked to the Cova through the tough part of town, walking in the dark, with light and singing coming out of the wineshops, and sometimes having to walk into the street when the men and women would crowd together on the sidewalk so that we would have had to jostle them to get by, we felt held together by there being something that had happened that they, the people who disliked us, did not understand.

We ourselves all understood the Cova, where it was rich and warm and not too brightly lighted, and noisy and smoky at certain hours, and there were always girls at the tables and the illustrated papers on a rack on the wall. The girls at the Cova were very patriotic, and I found that the most patriotic people in Italy were the café girls—and I believe they are still patriotic.

The boys at first were very polite about my medals and asked me what I had done to get them. I showed them the papers, which were written in very beautiful language and full of *fratellanza* and *abnegazione*, but which really said, with the adjectives removed, that I had been given the medals because I was an American. After that their manner changed a little toward me, although I was their friend against outsiders. I was a friend, but I was never really one of them after they had read the citations, because it had been different with them and they had done very different things to get their medals. I had been wounded, it was true; but we all knew that being wounded, after all, was really an accident. I was never ashamed of the ribbons, though, and sometimes, after the cocktail hour, I would imagine myself having done all the things they had done to get their medals; but walking home at night through the empty streets with the cold wind and all the shops closed, trying to keep near the streetlights, I knew that I would never have done such things, and I was very much afraid to die, and often lay in bed at night by myself, afraid to die and wondering how I would be when I went back to the front again.

The three with the medals were like hunting-hawks; and I was not a hawk, although I might seem a hawk to those who had never hunted; they, the three, knew better and so we drifted apart. But I stayed good friends with the boy who had been wounded his first day at the front, because he would never know now how he would have turned out; so he could never be accepted either, and I liked him because I thought perhaps he would not have turned out to be a hawk either.

The major, who had been the great fencer, did not believe in bravery and spent much time while we sat in the machines correcting my grammar. He had complimented me on how I spoke Italian, and we talked together very easily. One day I had said that Italian seemed such an easy language to me that I could not take a great interest in it; everything was so easy to say. "Ah, yes," the major said. "Why, then, do you not take up the use of grammar?" So we took up the use of grammar, and soon Italian was such a difficult language that I was afraid to talk to him until I had the grammar straight in my mind.

The major came very regularly to the hospital. I do not think he ever missed a day, although I am sure he did not believe in the machines. There was a time when none of us believed in the machines, and one day the major said it was all nonsense. The machines were new then and it was we who were to prove them. It was an idiotic idea, he said, "a theory, like another." I had not learned my grammar, and he said I was a stupid impossible disgrace, and he was a fool to have bothered with me. He was a small man and he sat straight up in his chair with his right hand thrust into the machine and looked straight ahead at the wall while the straps thumped up and down with his fingers in them.

"What will you do when the war is over if it is over?" he asked me. "Speak grammatically!"

"I will go to the States."

"Are you married?"

"No, but I hope to be."

"The more of a fool you are," he said. He seemed very angry. "A man must not marry."

"Why, Signor Maggiore?"

"Don't call me 'Signor Maggiore.'"

"Why must not a man marry?"

"He cannot marry. He cannot marry," he said angrily. "If he is to lose everything, he should not place himself in a position to lose that. He should not place himself in a position to lose. He should find things he cannot lose."

He spoke very angrily and bitterly, and looked straight ahead while he talked.

"But why should he necessarily lose it?"

"He'll lose it," the major said. He was looking at the wall. Then he looked down at the machine and jerked his little hand out from between the straps and slapped it hard against his thigh. "He'll lose it," he almost shouted. "Don't argue with me!" Then he called to the attendant who ran the machines. "Come and turn this damned thing off."

He went back into the other room for the light treatment and the massage. Then I heard him ask the doctor if he might use his telephone and he shut the door. When he came back into the room, I was sitting in another machine. He was wearing his cape and had his cap on, and he came directly toward my machine and put his arm on my shoulder.

"I am so sorry," he said, and patted me on the shoulder with his good hand. "I would not be rude. My wife has just died. You must forgive me."

"Oh—" I said, feeling sick for him. "I am so sorry."

He stood there, biting his lower lip. "It is very difficult," he said. "I cannot resign myself."

He looked straight past me and out through the window. Then he began to cry. "I am utterly unable to resign myself," he said and choked. And then crying, his head up looking at nothing, carrying himself straight and soldierly, with tears on both his cheeks and biting his lips, he walked past the machines and out the door.

The doctor told me that the major's wife, who was very

[173]

young and whom he had not married until he was definitely invalided out of the war, had died of pneumonia. She had been sick only a few days. No one expected her to die. The major did not come to the hospital for three days. Then he came at the usual hour, wearing a black band on the sleeve of his uniform. When he came back, there were large framed photographs around the wall, of all sorts of wounds before and after they had been cured by the machines. In front of the machine the major used were three photographs of hands like his that were completely restored. I do not know where the doctor got them. I always understood we were the first to use the machines. The photographs did not make much difference to the major because he only looked out of the window.

A SOLDIER HOME

Big Two-Hearted River

I

The train went on up the track out of sight, around one of the hills of burnt timber. Nick sat down on the bundle of canvas and bedding the baggage man had pitched out of the door of the baggage car. There was no town, nothing but the rails and the burned-over country. The thirteen saloons that had lined the one street of Seney had not left a trace. The foundations of the Mansion House hotel stuck up above the ground. The stone was chipped and split by the fire. It was all that was left of the town of Seney. Even the surface had been burned off the ground.

Nick looked at the burned-over stretch of hillside, where he had expected to find the scattered houses of the town and then walked down the railroad track to the bridge over the river. The river was there. It swirled against the log spiles of the bridge. Nick looked down into the clear, brown water, colored from the pebbly bottom, and watched the trout keeping themselves steady in the current with wavering fins. As he watched them they changed their positions by quick angles, only to hold steady in the fast water again. Nick watched them a long time.

He watched them holding themselves with their noses into

the current, many trout in deep, fast-moving water, slightly distorted as he watched far down through the glassy convex surface of the pool, its surface pushing and swelling smooth against the resistance of the log-driven spiles of the bridge. At the bottom of the pool were the big trout. Nick did not see them at first. Then he saw them at the bottom of the pool, big trout looking to hold themselves on the gravel bottom in a varying mist of gravel and sand, raised in spurts by the current.

Nick looked down into the pool from the bridge. It was a hot day. A kingfisher flew up the stream. It was a long time since Nick had looked into a stream and seen trout. They were very satisfactory. As the shadow of the kingfisher moved up the stream, a big trout shot upstream in a long angle, only his shadow marking the angle, then lost his shadow as he came through the surface of the water, caught the sun, and then, as he went back into the stream under the surface, his shadow seemed to float down the stream with the current, unresisting, to his post under the bridge, where he tightened, facing up into the current.

Nick's heart tightened as the trout moved. He felt all the old feeling.

He turned and looked down the stream. It stretched away, pebbly-bottomed with shallows and big boulders and a deep pool as it curved away around the foot of a bluff.

Nick walked back up the ties to where his pack lay in the cinders beside the railway track. He was happy. He adjusted the pack harness around the bundle, pulling straps tight, slung the pack on his back, got his arms through the shoulder straps and took some of the pull off his shoulders by leaning his forehead against the wide band of the tumpline. Still, it was too heavy. It was much too heavy. He had his leather rod-case in his hand and leaning forward to keep the weight of the pack high on his shoulders he walked along the road that paralleled the railway track, leaving the burned town behind in the heat, and then turned off around a hill with a high, fire-scarred hill on either side onto a road that went back into the country. He walked along the road feeling the ache from the pull of the heavy pack. The road climbed steadily. It was hard work walking uphill. His muscles ached and the day was hot, but Nick felt happy. He felt he had left everything behind, the need for thinking, the need to write, other needs. It was all back of him.

From the time he had gotten down off the train and the baggage man had thrown his pack out of the open car door things had been different. Seney was burned, the country was burned over and changed, but it did not matter. It could not all be burned. He knew that. He hiked along the road, sweating in the sun, climbing to cross the range of hills that separated the railway from the pine plains.

The road ran on, dipping occasionally, but always climbing. Nick went on up. Finally the road, after going parallel to the burnt hillside, reached the top. Nick leaned back against a stump and slipped out of the pack harness. Ahead of him, as far as he could see, was the pine plain. The burned country stopped off at the left with the range of hills. On ahead islands of dark pine trees rose out of the plain. Far off to the left was the line of the river. Nick followed it with his eye and caught glints of the water in the sun.

There was nothing but the pine plain ahead of him, until the far blue hills that marked the Lake Superior height of land. He could hardly see them, faint and far away in the heat-light over the plain. If he looked too steadily they were gone. But if he only half-looked they were there, the far-off hills of the height of land.

Nick sat down against the charred stump and smoked a cigarette. His pack balanced on the top of the stump, harness holding ready, a hollow molded in it from his back. Nick sat smoking, looking out over the country. He did not need to get his map out. He knew where he was from the position of the river.

As he smoked, his legs stretched out in front of him, he noticed a grasshopper walk along the ground and up onto his woolen sock. The grasshopper was black. As he had walked along the road, climbing, he had started many grasshoppers from the dust. They were all black. They were not the big grasshoppers with yellow and black or red and black wings whirring out from their black wing sheathing as they fly up. These were just ordinary hoppers, but all a sooty black in color. Nick had wondered about them as he walked, without really thinking about them. Now, as he watched the black hopper that was nibbling at the wool of his sock with its four-way lip, he realized that they had all turned black from living in the burned-over land. He realized that the fire must have come the year before, but the grasshoppers were all black now. He wondered how long they would stay that way.

Carefully he reached his hand down and took hold of the hopper by the wings. He turned him up, all his legs walking in the air, and looked at his jointed belly. Yes, it was black too, iridescent where the back and head were dusty.

"Go on, hopper," Nick said, speaking out loud for the first time. "Fly away somewhere."

He tossed the grasshopper up into the air and watched him sail away to a charcoal stump across the road.

Nick stood up. He leaned his back against the weight of his pack where it rested upright on the stump and got his arms through the shoulder straps. He stood with the pack on his back on the brow of the hill looking out across the country, toward the distant river and then struck down the hillside away from the road. Underfoot the ground was good walking. Two hundred yards down the hillside the fire line stopped.

Then it was sweet fern, growing ankle-high, to walk through, and clumps of jack pines; a long undulating country with frequent rises and descents, sandy underfoot and the country alive again.

Nick kept his direction by the sun. He knew where he wanted to strike the river and he kept on through the pine plain, mounting small rises to see other rises ahead of him and sometimes from the top of a rise a great solid island of pines off to his right or his left. He broke off some sprigs of the heathery sweet fern and put them under his pack straps. The chafing crushed it and he smelled it as he walked.

He was tired and very hot, walking across the uneven, shadeless pine plain. At any time he knew he could strike the river by turning off to his left. It could not be more than a mile away. But he kept on toward the north to hit the river as far upstream as he could go in one day's walking.

For some time as he walked Nick had been in sight of one of the big islands of pine standing out above the rolling high ground he was crossing. He dipped down and then as he came slowly up to the crest of the ridge he turned and made toward the pine trees.

There was no underbrush in the island of pine trees. The trunks of the trees went straight up or slanted toward each other. The trunks were straight and brown without branches. The branches were high above. Some interlocked to make a solid shadow on the brown forest floor. Around the grove of trees was a bare space. It was brown and soft underfoot as Nick walked on it. This was the overlapping of the pine needle floor, extending out beyond the width of the high branches. The trees had grown tall and the branches moved high, leaving in the sun this bare space they had once covered with shadow. Sharp at the edge of this extension of the forest floor commenced the sweet fern.

Nick slipped off his pack and lay down in the shade. He lay on his back and looked up into the pine trees. His neck and back and the small of his back rested as he stretched. The earth felt good against his back. He looked up at the sky, through the branches, and then shut his eyes. He opened them and looked up again. There was a wind high up in the branches. He shut his eyes again and went to sleep.

Nick woke stiff and cramped. The sun was nearly down. His pack was heavy and the straps painful as he lifted it on. He leaned over with the pack on and picked up the leather rod-case and started out from the pine trees across the sweet fern swale, toward the river. He knew it could not be more than a mile.

He came down a hillside covered with stumps into a meadow. At the edge of the meadow flowed the river. Nick was glad to get to the river. He walked upstream through the meadow. His trousers were soaked with the dew as he walked. After the hot day, the dew had come quickly and heavily. The river made no sound. It was too fast and smooth. At the edge of the meadow, before he mounted to a piece of high ground to make camp, Nick looked down the river at the trout rising. They were rising to insects come from the swamp on the other side of the stream when the sun went down. The trout jumped out of water to take them. While Nick walked through the little stretch of meadow alongside the stream, trout had jumped high out of water. Now as he looked down the river, the insects must be settling on the surface, for the trout were feeding steadily all down the stream. As far down the long stretch as he could see, the trout were rising, making circles all down the surface of the water, as though it were starting to rain.

The ground rose, wooded and sandy, to overlook the meadow, the stretch of river and the swamp. Nick dropped his pack and rod-case and looked for a level piece of ground. He was very hungry and he wanted to make his camp before he cooked. Between two jack pines, the ground was quite level. He took the ax out of the pack and chopped out two projecting roots. That leveled a piece of ground large enough to sleep on. He smoothed out the sandy soil with his hand and pulled all the sweet fern bushes by their roots. His hands smelled good from the sweet fern. He smoothed the uprooted earth. He did not want anything making lumps under the blankets. When he had the ground smooth, he spread his three blankets. One he folded double, next to the ground. The other two he spread on top.

With the ax he slit off a bright slab of pine from one of the stumps and split it into pegs for the tent. He wanted them long and solid to hold in the ground. With the tent unpacked and spread on the ground, the pack, leaning against a jack pine, looked much smaller. Nick tied the rope that served the tent for a ridgepole to the trunk of one of the pine trees and pulled the tent up off the ground with the other end of the rope and tied it to the other pine. The tent hung on the rope like a canvas blanket on a clothesline. Nick poked a pole he had cut up under the back peak of the canvas and then made it a tent by pegging out the sides. He pegged the sides out taut and drove the pegs deep, hitting them down into the ground with the flat of the ax until the rope loops were buried and the canvas was drum tight.

Across the open mouth of the tent Nick fixed cheesecloth to keep out mosquitoes. He crawled inside under the mosquito bar with various things from the pack to put at the head of the bed under the slant of the canvas. Inside the tent the light came through the brown canvas. It smelled pleasantly of canvas. Already there was something mysterious and home-like. Nick was happy as he crawled inside the tent. He had not been unhappy all day. This was different though. Now things were done. There had been this to do. Now it was done. It had been a hard trip. He was very tired. That was done. He had made his camp. He was settled. Nothing could touch him. It was a good place to camp. He was there, in the good place. He was in his home where he had made it. Now he was hungry.

He came out, crawling under the cheesecloth. It was quite dark outside. It was lighter in the tent.

Nick went over to the pack and found, with his fingers, a long nail in a paper sack of nails, in the bottom of the pack. He drove it into the pine tree, holding it close and hitting it gently with the flat of the ax. He hung the pack up on the nail. All his supplies were in the pack. They were off the ground and sheltered now.

Nick was hungry. He did not believe he had ever been hungrier. He opened and emptied a can of pork and beans and a can of spaghetti into the frying pan.

"I've got a right to eat this kind of stuff, if I'm willing to carry it," Nick said. His voice sounded strange in the darkening woods. He did not speak again.

He started a fire with some chunks of pine he got with the ax from a stump. Over the fire he stuck a wire grill, pushing the four legs down into the ground with his boot. Nick put the frying pan on the grill over the flames. He was hungrier. The beans and spaghetti warmed. Nick stirred them and mixed them together. They began to bubble, making little bubbles that rose with difficulty to the surface. There was a good smell. Nick got out a bottle of tomato catchup and cut four slices of bread. The little bubbles were coming faster now. Nick sat down beside the fire and lifted the frying pan off. He poured about half the contents out into the tin plate. It spread slowly on the plate. Nick knew it was too hot. He poured on some tomato catchup. He knew the beans and spaghetti were still too hot. He looked at the fire, then at the tent, he was not going to spoil it all by burning his tongue. For years he had never enjoyed fried bananas because he had never been able to wait for them to cool. His tongue was very sensitive. He was very hungry. Across the river in the swamp, in the almost dark, he saw a mist rising. He looked at the tent once more. All right. He took a full spoonful from the plate.

"Chrise," Nick said, "Geezus Chrise," he said happily.

He ate the whole plateful before he remembered the bread. Nick finished the second plateful with the bread, mopping the plate shiny. He had not eaten since a cup of coffee and a ham sandwich in the station restaurant at St. Ignace. It had been a very fine experience. He had been that hungry before, but had not been able to satisfy it. He could have made camp hours before if he had wanted to. There were plenty of good places to camp on the river. But this was good.

Nick tucked two big chips of pine under the grill. The fire flared up. He had forgotten to get water for the coffee. Out of the pack he got a folding canvas bucket and walked down the hill, across the edge of the meadow, to the stream. The other bank was in the white mist. The grass was wet and cold as he knelt on the bank and dipped the canvas bucket into the stream. It bellied and pulled hard in the current. The water was ice cold. Nick rinsed the bucket and carried it full up to the camp. Up away from the stream it was not so cold.

Nick drove another big nail and hung up the bucket full of water. He dipped the coffeepot half full, put some more chips under the grill onto the fire and put the pot on. He could not remember which way he made coffee. He could remember an argument about it with Hopkins, but not which side he had taken. He decided to bring it to a boil. He remembered now that was Hopkins's way. He had once argued about everything with Hopkins. While he waited for the coffee to boil, he opened a small can of apricots. He liked to open cans. He emptied the can of apricots out into a tin cup. While he watched the coffee on the fire, he drank the juice syrup of the apricots, carefully at first to keep from spilling, then meditatively, sucking the apricots down. They were better than fresh apricots.

The coffee boiled as he watched. The lid came up and coffee and grounds ran down the side of the pot. Nick took it off the grill. It was a triumph for Hopkins. He put sugar in the empty apricot cup and poured some of the coffee out to cool. It was too hot to pour and he used his hat to hold the handle of the coffeepot. He would not let it steep in the pot at all. Not the first cup. It should be straight Hopkins all the way. Hop deserved that. He was a very serious coffee maker. He was the most serious man Nick had ever known. Not heavy, serious. That was a long time ago. Hopkins spoke without moving his lips. He had played polo. He made millions of dollars in Texas. He had borrowed carfare to go to Chicago, when the wire came that his first big well had come in. He could have wired for money. That would have been too slow. They called Hop's girl the Blonde Venus. Hop did not mind because she was not his real girl. Hopkins said very confidently that none of them would make fun of his real girl. He was right. Hopkins went away when the telegram came. That was on the Black River. It took eight days for the telegram to reach him. Hopkins gave away his .22 caliber Colt automatic pistol to Nick. He gave his camera to Bill. It was to remember him always by. They were all going fishing again next summer. The Hop Head was rich. He would get a yacht and they would all cruise along the north shore of Lake Superior. He was excited but serious. They said good-by and all felt bad. It broke up the trip. They never saw Hopkins again. That was a long time ago on the Black River.

Nick drank the coffee, the coffee according to Hopkins. The coffee was bitter. Nick laughed. It made a good ending to the story. His mind was starting to work. He knew he could choke it because he was tired enough. He spilled the coffee out of the pot and shook the grounds loose into the fire. He lit a cigarette and went inside the tent. He took off his shoes and trousers, sitting on the blankets, rolled the shoes up inside the trousers for a pillow and got in between the blankets.

Out through the front of the tent he watched the glow of the fire when the night wind blew on it. It was a quiet night. The swamp was perfectly quiet. Nick stretched under the blanket comfortably. A mosquito hummed close to his ear. Nick sat up and lit a match. The mosquito was on the canvas, over his head. Nick moved the match quickly up to it. The mosquito made a satisfactory hiss in the flame. The match went out. Nick lay down again under the blankets. He turned on his side and shut his eyes. He was sleepy. He felt sleep coming. He curled up under the blanket and went to sleep.

II

In the morning the sun was up and the tent was starting to get hot. Nick crawled out under the mosquito netting stretched across the mouth of the tent to look at the morning. The grass was wet on his hands as he came out. He held his trousers and his shoes in his hands. The sun was just up over the hill. There was the meadow, the river and the swamp. There were birch trees in the green of the swamp on the other side of the river.

The river was clear and smoothly fast in the early morning. Down about two hundred yards were three logs all the way across the stream. They made the water smooth and deep above them. As Nick watched, a mink crossed the river on the logs and went into the swamp. Nick was excited. He was excited by the early morning and the river. He was really too hurried to eat breakfast, but he knew he must. He built a little fire and put on the coffeepot. While the water was heating in the pot he took an empty bottle and went down over the edge of the high ground to the meadow. The meadow was wet with dew and Nick wanted to catch grasshoppers for bait before the sun dried the grass. He found plenty of good grasshoppers. They were at the base of the grass stems. Sometimes they clung to a grass stem. They were cold and wet with the dew and could not jump until the sun warmed them. Nick picked them up, taking only the medium-sized brown ones, and put them into the bottle. He turned over a log and just under the shelter of the edge were several hundred hoppers. It was a grasshopper lodging house. Nick put about fifty of the medium browns into the bottle. While he was picking up the hoppers the others warmed in the sun and commenced to hop away. They flew when they hopped. At first they made one flight and stayed stiff when they landed, as though they were dead.

Nick knew that by the time he was through with breakfast they would be as lively as ever. Without dew in the grass it would take him all day to catch a bottle full of good grasshoppers and he would have to crush many of them, slamming at them with his hat. He washed his hands at the stream. He was excited to be near it. Then he walked up to the tent. The hoppers were already jumping stiffly in the grass. In the bottle, warmed by the sun, they were jumping in a mass. Nick put in a pine stick as a cork. It plugged the mouth of the bottle enough so the hoppers could not get out, and left plenty of air passage.

He had rolled the log back and knew he could get grasshoppers there every morning.

Nick laid the bottle full of jumping grasshoppers against a pine trunk. Rapidly he mixed some buckwheat flour with water and stirred it smooth, one cup of flour, one cup of water. He put a handful of coffee in the pot and dipped a lump of grease out of a can and slid it sputtering across the hot skillet. On the smoking skillet he poured smoothly the buckwheat batter. It spread like lava, the grease spitting sharply. Around the edges the buckwheat cake began to firm, then brown, then crisp. The surface was bubbling slowly to porousness. Nick pushed under the browned undersurface with a fresh pine chip. He shook the skillet sideways and the cake was loose on the surface. I won't try and flop it, he thought. He slid the chip of clean wood all the way under the cake, and flopped it over onto its face. It sputtered in the pan.

When it was cooked Nick regreased the skillet. He used all the batter. It made another big flapjack and one smaller one.

Nick ate a big flapjack and a smaller one, covered with apple butter. He put apple butter on the third cake, folded it over twice, wrapped it in oiled paper and put it in his shirt pocket. He put the apple butter jar back in the pack and cut bread for two sandwiches.

In the pack he found a big onion. He sliced it in two and peeled the silky outer skin. Then he cut one half into slices and made onion sandwiches. He wrapped them in oiled paper and buttoned them in the other pocket of his khaki shirt. He turned the skillet upside down on the grill, drank the coffee, sweetened and yellow brown with the condensed milk in it, and tidied up the camp. It was a nice little camp.

Nick took his fly rod out of the leather rod-case, jointed it, and shoved the rod-case back into the tent. He put on the reel and threaded the line through the guides. He had to hold it from hand to hand, as he threaded it, or it would slip back through its own weight. It was a heavy, double-tapered fly line. Nick had paid eight dollars for it a long time ago. It was made heavy to lift back in the air and come forward flat and heavy and straight to make it possible to cast a fly which has no weight. Nick opened the aluminum leader box. The leaders were coiled between the damp flannel pads. Nick had wet the pads at the water cooler on the train up to St. Ignace. In the damp pads the gut leaders had softened and Nick unrolled one and tied it by a loop at the end to the heavy fly line. He fastened a hook on the end of the leader. It was a small hook, very thin and springy.

Nick took it from his hook book, sitting with the rod across his lap. He tested the knot and the spring of the rod by pulling the line taut. It was a good feeling. He was careful not to let the hook bite into his finger.

He started down to the stream, holding his rod, the bottle of grasshoppers hung from his neck by a thong tied in half hitches around the neck of the bottle. His landing net hung by a hook from his belt. Over his shoulder was a long flour sack tied at each corner into an ear. The cord went over his shoulder. The sack flapped against his legs.

Nick felt awkward and professionally happy with all his equipment hanging from him. The grasshopper bottle swung against his chest. In his shirt the breast pockets bulged against him with the lunch and his fly book.

He stepped into the stream. It was a shock. His trousers clung tight to his legs. His shoes felt the gravel. The water was a rising cold shock.

Rushing, the current sucked against his legs. Where he stepped in, the water was over his knees. He waded with the current. The gravel slid under his shoes. He looked down at the swirl of water below each leg and tipped up the bottle to get a grasshopper.

The first grasshopper gave a jump in the neck of the bottle and went out into the water. He was sucked under in the whirl by Nick's right leg and came to the surface a little way down stream. He floated rapidly, kicking. In a quick circle, breaking the smooth surface of the water, he disappeared. A trout had taken him.

Another hopper poked his head out of the bottle. His antennae wavered. He was getting his front legs out of the bottle to jump. Nick took him by the head and held him while he threaded the slim hook under his chin, down through his thorax and into the last segments of his abdomen. The grasshopper took hold of the hook with his front feet, spitting tobacco juice on it. Nick dropped him into the water.

Holding the rod in his right hand he let out line against the pull of the grasshopper in the current. He stripped off line from the reel with his left hand and let it run free. He could see the hopper in the little waves of the current. It went out of sight.

There was a tug on the line. Nick pulled against the taut line. It was his first strike. Holding the now living rod across the current, he brought in the line with his left hand. The rod bent in jerks, the trout pumping against the current. Nick knew it was a small one. He lifted the rod straight up in the air. It bowed with the pull.

He saw the trout in the water jerking with his head and body against the shifting tangent of the line in the stream.

Nick took the line in his left hand and pulled the trout, thumping tiredly against the current, to the surface. His back was mottled the clear, water-over-gravel color, his side flashing in the sun. The rod under his right arm, Nick stooped, dipping his right hand into the current. He held the trout, never still, with his moist right hand, while he unhooked the barb from his mouth, then dropped him back into the stream.

He hung unsteadily in the current, then settled to the bottom beside a stone. Nick reached down his hand to touch him, his arm to the elbow underwater. The trout was steady in the moving stream, resting on the gravel, beside a stone. As Nick's fingers touched him, touched his smooth, cool, underwater feeling, he was gone, gone in a shadow across the bottom of the stream.

He's all right, Nick thought. He was only tired.

He had wet his hand before he touched the trout, so he would not disturb the delicate mucus that covered him. If a trout was touched with a dry hand, a white fungus attacked the unprotected spot. Years before when he had fished crowded streams, with fly fishermen ahead of him and behind him, Nick had again and again come on dead trout, furry with white fungus, drifted against a rock, or floating belly up in some pool. Nick did not like to fish with other men on the river. Unless they were of your party, they spoiled it.

He wallowed down the stream, above his knees in the current, through the fifty yards of shallow water above the pile of logs that crossed the stream. He did not rebait his hook and held it in his hand as he waded. He was certain he could catch small trout in the shallows, but he did not want them. There would be no big trout in the shallows this time of day.

Now the water deepened up his thighs sharply and coldly. Ahead was the smooth dammed-back flood of water above the logs. The water was smooth and dark; on the left, the lower edge of the meadow; on the right, the swamp.

Nick leaned back against the current and took a hopper from the bottle. He threaded the hopper on the hook and spat on him for good luck. Then he pulled several yards of line from the reel and tossed the hopper out ahead onto the fast, dark water. It floated down toward the logs, then the weight of the line pulled the bait under the surface. Nick held the rod in his right hand, letting the line run out through his fingers.

There was a long tug. Nick struck and the rod came alive and dangerous, bent double, the line tightening, coming out of water, tightening, all in a heavy, dangerous, steady pull. Nick felt the moment when the leader would break if the strain increased and let the line go.

The reel ratcheted into a mechanical shriek as the line went out in a rush. Too fast. Nick could not check it, the line rushing out, the reel note rising as the line ran out.

With the core of the reel showing, his heart feeling stopped with the excitement, leaning back against the current that mounted icily his thighs, Nick thumbed the reel hard with his left hand. It was awkward getting his thumb inside the fly reel frame.

As he put on pressure the line tightened into sudden hardness and beyond the logs a huge trout went high out of water. As he jumped, Nick lowered the tip of the rod. But he felt, as he dropped the tip to ease the strain, the moment when the strain was too great, the hardness too tight. Of course, the leader had broken. There was no mistaking the feeling when all spring left the line and it became dry and hard. Then it went slack.

His mouth dry, his heart down, Nick reeled in. He had never seen so big a trout. There was a heaviness, a power not to be held, and then the bulk of him, as he jumped. He looked as broad as a salmon.

Nick's hand was shaky. He reeled in slowly. The thrill had been too much. He felt, vaguely, a little sick, as though it would be better to sit down.

The leader had broken where the hook was tied to it. Nick took it in his hand. He thought of the trout somewhere on the bottom, holding himself steady over the gravel, far down below the light, under the logs, with the hook in his jaw. Nick knew the trout's teeth would cut through the snell

[193]

of the hook. The hook would imbed itself in his jaw. He'd bet the trout was angry. Anything that size would be angry. That was a trout. He had been solidly hooked. Solid as a rock. He felt like a rock, too, before he started off. By God, he was a big one. By God, he was the biggest one I ever heard of.

Nick climbed out onto the meadow and stood, water running down his trousers and out of his shoes, his shoes squlchy. He went over and sat on the logs. He did not want to rush his sensations any.

He wriggled his toes in the water, in his shoes, and got out a cigarette from his breast pocket. He lit it and tossed the match into the fast water below the logs. A tiny trout rose at the match, as it swung around in the fast current. Nick laughed. He would finish the cigarette.

He sat on the logs, smoking, drying in the sun, the sun warm on his back, the river shallow ahead, entering the woods, curving into the woods, shallows, light glittering, big water-smooth rocks, cedars along the bank and white birches, the logs warm in the sun, smooth to sit on, without bark, gray to the touch; slowly the feeling of disappointment left him. It went away slowly, the feeling of disappointment that came sharply after the thrill that made his shoulders ache. It was all right now. His rod lying out on the logs, Nick tied a new hook on the leader, pulling the gut tight until it grimped into itself in a hard knot.

He baited up, then picked up the rod and walked to the far end of the logs to get into the water, where it was not too deep. Under and beyond the logs was a deep pool. Nick walked around the shallow shelf near the swamp shore until he came out on the shallow bed of the stream.

On the left, where the meadow ended and the woods began, a great elm tree was uprooted. Gone over in a storm, it lay back into the woods, its roots clotted with dirt, grass growing in them, rising a solid bank beside the stream. The river cut to the edge of the uprooted tree. From where Nick stood he could see deep channels, like ruts, cut in the shallow bed of the stream by the flow of the current. Pebbly where he stood and pebbly and full of boulders beyond; where it curved near the tree roots, the bed of the stream was marly and between the ruts of deep water green weed fronds swung in the current.

Nick swung the rod back over his shoulder and forward, and the line, curving forward, laid the grasshopper down on one of the deep channels in the weeds. A trout struck and Nick hooked him.

Holding the rod far out toward the uprooted tree and slosh-ing backward in the current, Nick worked the trout, plunging, the rod bending alive, out of the danger of the weeds into the open river. Holding the rod, pumping alive against the cur-rent, Nick brought the trout in. He rushed, but always came, the spring of the rod yielding to the rushes, sometimes jerking underwater, but always bringing him in. Nick eased down-stream with the rushes. The rod above his head, he led the trout over the net, then lifted.

The trout hung heavy in the net, mottled trout back and silver sides in the meshes. Nick unhooked him; heavy sides, good to hold, big undershot jaw; and slipped him, heaving and big, sliding, into the long sack that hung from his shoulders in the water.

Nick spread the mouth of the sack against the current and it filled, heavy with water. He held it up, the bottom in the stream, and the water poured out through the sides. Inside at the bottom was the big trout, alive in the water.

Nick moved downstream. The sack out ahead of him, sunk, heavy in the water, pulling from his shoulders.

It was getting hot, the sun hot on the back of his neck.

Nick had one good trout. He did not care about getting

many trout. Now the stream was shallow and wide. There were trees along both banks. The trees of the left bank made short shadows on the current in the forenoon sun. Nick knew there were trout in each shadow. In the afternoon, after the sun had crossed toward the hills, the trout would be in the cool shadows on the other side of the stream.

The very biggest ones would lie up close to the bank. You could always pick them up there on the Black. When the sun was down they all moved out into the current. Just when the sun made the water blinding in the glare before it went down, you were liable to strike a big trout anywhere in the current. It was almost impossible to fish then, the surface of the water was blinding as a mirror in the sun. Of course, you could fish upstream, but in a stream like the Black, or this, you had to wallow against the current and in a deep place, the water piled up on you. It was no fun to fish upstream with this much current.

Nick moved along through the shallow stretch, watching the banks for deep holes. A beech tree grew close beside the river, so that the branches hung down into the water. The stream went back in under the leaves. There were always trout in a place like that.

Nick did not care about fishing that hole. He was sure he would get hooked in the branches.

It looked deep, though. He dropped the grasshopper so the current took it underwater, back in under the overhanging branch. The line pulled hard and Nick struck. The trout threshed heavily, half out of water in the leaves and branches. The line was caught. Nick pulled hard and the trout was off. He reeled in and, holding the hook in his hand, walked down the stream.

Ahead, close to the left bank, was a big log. Nick saw it was hollow; pointing up river the current entered it smoothly, only a little ripple spread each side of the log. The water was deepening. The top of the hollow log was gray and dry. It was partly in the shadow.

Nick took the cork out of the grasshopper bottle and a hopper clung to it. He picked him off, hooked him and tossed him out. He held the rod far out so that the hopper on the water moved into the current flowing into the hollow log. Nick lowered the rod and the hopper floated in. There was a heavy strike. Nick swung the rod against the pull. It felt as though he were hooked into the log itself, except for the live feeling.

He tried to force the fish out into the current. It came, heavily.

The line went slack and Nick thought the trout was gone. Then he saw him, very near, in the current, shaking his head, trying to get the hook out. His mouth was clamped shut. He was fighting the hook in the clear flowing current.

Looping in the line with his left hand, Nick swung the rod to make the line taut and tried to lead the trout toward the net, but he was gone, out of sight, the line pumping. Nick fought him against the current, letting him thump in the water against the spring of the rod. He shifted the rod to his left hand, worked the trout upstream, holding his weight, fighting on the rod, and then let him down into the net. He lifted him clear of the water, a heavy half circle in the net, the net dripping, unhooked him and slid him into the sack.

He spread the mouth of the sack and looked down in at the two big trout alive in the water.

Through the deepening water, Nick waded over to the hollow log. He took the sack off, over his head, the trout flopping as it came out of water, and hung it so the trout were deep in the water. Then he pulled himself up on the log and sat, the water from his trousers and boots running down into the

[197]

stream. He laid his rod down, moved along to the shady end of the log and took the sandwiches out of his pocket. He dipped the sandwiches in the cold water. The current carried away the crumbs. He ate the sandwiches and dipped his hat full of water to drink, the water running out through his hat just ahead of his drinking.

It was cool in the shade, sitting on the log. He took a cigarette out and struck a match to light it. The match sunk into the gray wood, making a tiny furrow. Nick leaned over the side of the log, found a hard place and lit the match. He sat smoking and watching the river.

Ahead the river narrowed and went into a swamp. The river became smooth and deep and the swamp looked solid with cedar trees, their trunks close together, their branches solid. It would not be possible to walk through a swamp like that. The branches grew so low. You would have to keep almost level with the ground to move at all. You could not crash through the branches. That must be why the animals that lived in swamps were built the way they were, Nick thought.

He wished he had brought something to read. He felt like reading. He did not feel like going on into the swamp. He looked down the river. A big cedar slanted all the way across the stream. Beyond that the river went into the swamp.

Nick did not want to go in there now. He felt a reaction against deep wading with the water deepening up under his armpits, to hook big trout in places impossible to land them. In the swamp the banks were bare, the big cedars came together overhead, the sun did not come through, except in patches; in the fast deep water, in the half light, the fishing would be tragic. In the swamp fishing was a tragic adventure. Nick did not want it. He did not want to go down the stream any farther today.

He took out his knife, opened it and stuck it in the log.

Then he pulled up the sack, reached into it and brought out one of the trout. Holding him near the tail, hard to hold, alive, in his hand, he whacked him against the log. The trout quivered, rigid. Nick laid him on the log in the shade and broke the neck of the other fish the same way. He laid them side by side on the log. They were fine trout.

Nick cleaned them, slitting them from the vent to the tip of the jaw. All the insides and the gills and tongue came out in one piece. They were both males; long gray-white strips of milt, smooth and clean. All the insides clean and compact, coming out all together. Nick tossed the offal ashore for the minks to find.

He washed the trout in the stream. When he held them back up in the water they looked like live fish. Their color was not gone yet. He washed his hands and dried them on the log. Then he laid the trout on the sack spread out on the log, rolled them up in it, tied the bundle and put it in the landing net. His knife was still standing, blade stuck in the log. He cleaned it on the wood and put it in his pocket.

Nick stood up on the log, holding his rod, the landing net hanging heavy, then stepped into the water and splashed ashore. He climbed the bank and cut up into the woods, toward the high ground. He was going back to camp. He looked back. The river just showed through the trees. There were plenty of days coming when he could fish the swamp.

The End of Something

In the old days Hortons Bay was a lumbering town. No one who lived in it was out of sound of the big saws in the mill by the lake. Then one year there were no more logs to make lumber. The lumber schooners came into the bay and were loaded with the cut of the mill that stood stacked in the yard. All the piles of lumber were carried away. The big mill building had all its machinery that was removable taken out and hoisted on board one of the schooners by the men who had worked in the mill. The schooner moved out of the bay toward the open lake, carrying the two great saws, the traveling carriage that hurled the logs against the revolving, circular saws and all the rollers, wheels, belts and iron piled on a hull-deep load of lumber. Its open hold covered with canvas and lashed tight, the sails of the schooner filled and it moved out into the open lake, carrying with it everything that had made the mill a mill and Hortons Bay a town.

The one-story bunkhouses, the eating house, the company store, the mill offices, and the big mill itself stood deserted in the acres of sawdust that covered the swampy meadow by the shore of the bay.

Ten years later there was nothing of the mill left except the broken white limestone of its foundations showing through the swampy second growth as Nick and Marjorie rowed along the shore. They were trolling along the edge of the channel bank where the bottom dropped off suddenly from sandy shallows to twelve feet of dark water. They were trolling on their way to the point to set night lines for rainbow trout.

"There's our old ruin, Nick," Marjorie said.

Nick, rowing, looked at the white stone in the green trees. "There it is," he said.

"Can you remember when it was a mill?" Marjorie asked.

"I can just remember," Nick said.

"It seems more like a castle," Marjorie said.

Nick said nothing. They rowed on out of sight of the mill, following the shore line. Then Nick cut across the bay.

"They aren't striking," he said.

"No," Marjorie said. She was intent on the rod all the time they trolled, even when she talked. She loved to fish. She loved to fish with Nick.

Close beside the boat a big trout broke the surface of the water. Nick pulled hard on one oar so the boat would turn and the bait, spinning far behind, would pass where the trout was feeding. As the trout's back came up out of the water the minnows jumped wildly. They sprinkled the surface like a handful of shot thrown into the water. Another trout broke water, feeding on the other side of the boat.

"They're feeding," Marjorie said.

"But they won't strike," Nick said.

He rowed the boat around to troll past both the feeding fish, then headed it for the point. Marjorie did not reel in until the boat touched the shore.

They pulled the boat up the beach and Nick lifted out a pail of live perch. The perch swam in the water pail. Nick caught three of them with his hands and cut their heads off and skinned them while Marjorie chased with her hands in the bucket, finally caught a perch, cut its head off and skinned it. Nick looked at her fish.

"You don't want to take the ventral fin out," he said. "It'll be all right for bait but it's better with the ventral fin in."

He hooked each of the skinned perch through the tail. There were two hooks attached to a leader on each rod. Then Marjorie rowed the boat out over the channel-bank, holding the line in her teeth, and looking toward Nick, who stood on the shore holding the rod and letting the line run out from the reel.

"That's about right," he called.

"Should I let it drop?" Marjorie called back, holding the line in her hand.

"Sure. Let it go." Marjorie dropped the line overboard and watched the baits go down through the water.

She came in with the boat and ran the second line out the same way. Each time Nick set a heavy slab of driftwood across the butt of the rod to hold it solid and propped it up at an angle with a small slab. He reeled in the slack line so the line ran taut out to where the bait rested on the sandy floor of the channel and set the click on the reel. When a trout, feeding on the bottom, took the bait it would run with it, taking line out of the reel in a rush and making the reel sing with the click on.

Marjorie rowed up the point a little way so she would not disturb the line. She pulled hard on the oars and the boat went up the beach. Little waves came in with it. Marjorie stepped out of the boat and Nick pulled the boat high up the beach.

"What's the matter, Nick?" Marjorie asked.

"I don't know," Nick said, getting wood for a fire.

They made a fire with driftwood. Marjorie went to the boat and brought a blanket. The evening breeze blew the smoke toward the point, so Marjorie spread the blanket out between the fire and the lake.

Marjorie sat on the blanket with her back to the fire and waited for Nick. He came over and sat down beside her on the blanket. In back of them was the close second-growth timber of the point and in front was the bay with the mouth of Hortons Creek. It was not quite dark. The firelight went as far as the water. They could both see the two steel rods at an angle over the dark water. The fire glinted on the reels.

Marjorie unpacked the basket of supper.

"I don't feel like eating," said Nick.

"Come on and eat, Nick."

"All right."

They ate without talking and watched the two rods and the firelight in the water.

"There's going to be a moon tonight," said Nick. He looked across the bay to the hills that were beginning to sharpen against the sky. Beyond the hills he knew the moon was coming up.

"I know it," Marjorie said happily.

"You know everything," Nick said.

"Oh, Nick, please cut it out! Please, please don't be that way!"

"I can't help it," Nick said. "You do. You know everything. That's the trouble. You know you do."

Marjorie did not say anything.

"I've taught you everything. You know you do. What don't you know, anyway?"

"Oh, shut up," Marjorie said. "There comes the moon."

They sat on the blanket without touching each other and watched the moon rise.

"You don't have to talk silly," Marjorie said. "What's really the matter?"

"I don't know."

"Of course you know."

"No I don't."

[203]

"Go on and say it."

Nick looked on at the moon, coming up over the hills.

"It isn't fun any more."

He was afraid to look at Marjorie. Then he looked at her. She sat there with her back toward him. He looked at her back. "It isn't fun any more. Not any of it."

She didn't say anything. He went on. "I feel as though everything was gone to hell inside of me. I don't know, Marge. I don't know what to say."

He looked on at her back.

"Isn't love any fun?" Marjorie said.

"No," Nick said. Marjorie stood up. Nick sat there, his head in his hands.

"I'm going to take the boat," Marjorie called to him. "You can walk back around the point."

"All right," Nick said. "I'll push the boat off for you."

"You don't need to," she said. She was afloat in the boat on the water with the moonlight on it. Nick went back and lay down with his face in the blanket by the fire. He could hear Marjorie rowing on the water.

He lay there for a long time. He lay there while he heard Bill come into the clearing, walking around through the woods. He felt Bill coming up to the fire. Bill didn't touch him, either.

"Did she go all right?" Bill said.

"Oh, yes." Nick said, lying, his face on the blanket.

"Have a scene?"

"No, there wasn't any scene."

"How do you feel?"

"Oh, go away, Bill! Go away for a while." Bill selected a sandwich from the lunch basket and walked over to have a look at the rods.

The Three-Day Blow

The rain stopped as Nick turned into the road that went up through the orchard. The fruit had been picked and the fall wind blew through the bare trees. Nick stopped and picked up a Wagener apple from beside the road, shiny in the brown grass from the rain. He put the apple in the pocket of his Mackinaw coat.

The road came out of the orchard on to the top of the hill. There was the cottage, the porch bare, smoke coming from the chimney. In back were the garage, the chicken coop and the second-growth timber like a hedge against the woods behind. The big trees swayed far over in the wind as he watched. It was the first of the autumn storms.

As Nick crossed the open field above the orchard the door of the cottage opened and Bill came out. He stood on the porch looking out.

"Well, Wemedge," he said.

"Hey, Bill," Nick said, coming up the steps.

They stood together looking out across the country, down over the orchard, beyond the road, across the lower fields and the woods of the point of the lake. The wind was blowing straight down the lake. They could see the surf along Ten Mile point.

"She's blowing," Nick said.

"She'll blow like that for three days," Bill said.

"Is your dad in?" Nick asked.

"No. He's out with the gun. Come on in."

Nick went inside the cottage. There was a big fire in the fireplace. The wind made it roar. Bill shut the door.

"Have a drink?" he said.

He went out to the kitchen and came back with two glasses and a pitcher of water. Nick reached the whiskey bottle from the shelf above the fireplace.

"All right?" he said.

"Good," said Bill.

They sat in front of the fire and drank the Irish whiskey and water.

"It's got a swell, smoky taste," Nick said, and looked at the fire through the glass.

"That's the peat," Bill said.

"You can't get peat into liquor," Nick said.

"That doesn't make any difference," Bill said.

"You ever seen any peat?" Nick asked.

"No," said Bill.

"Neither have I," Nick said.

His shoes, stretched out on the hearth, began to steam in front of the fire.

"Better take your shoes off," Bill said.

"I haven't got any socks on."

"Take them off and dry them and I'll get you some," Bill said. He went upstairs into the loft and Nick heard him walking about overhead. Upstairs was open under the roof and was where Bill and his father and he, Nick, sometimes slept. In back was a dressing room. They moved the cots back out of the rain and covered them with rubber blankets.

Bill came down with a pair of heavy wool socks.

"It's getting too late to go around without socks," he said.

"I hate to start them again," Nick said. He pulled the socks on and slumped back in the chair, putting his feet up on the screen in front of the fire.

"You'll dent in the screen," Bill said. Nick swung his feet over to the side of the fireplace.

"Got anything to read?" he asked.

"Only the paper."

"What did the Cards do?"

"Dropped a double-header to the Giants."

"That ought to cinch it for them."

"It's a gift," Bill said. "As long as McGraw can buy every good ballplayer in the league there's nothing to it."

"He can't buy them all," Nick said.

"He buys all the ones he wants," Bill said. "Or he makes them discontented so they have to trade them to him."

"Like Heinie Zim," Nick agreed.

"That bonehead will do him a lot of good."

Bill stood up.

"He can hit," Nick offered. The heat from the fire was baking his legs.

"He's a sweet fielder, too," Bill said. "But he loses ball games."

"Maybe that's what McGraw wants him for," Nick suggested.

"Maybe," Bill agreed.

"There's always more to it than we know about," Nick said.

"Of course. But we've got pretty good dope for being so far away."

"Like how much better you can pick them if you don't see the horses."

"That's it."

Bill reached down the whiskey bottle. His big hand went all the way around it. He poured the whiskey into the glass Nick held out.

"How much water?"

"Just the same."

He sat down on the floor beside Nick's chair.

"It's good when the fall storms come, isn't it?" Nick said.

"It's swell."

"It's the best time of year," Nick said.

"Wouldn't it be hell to be in town?" Bill said.

"I'd like to see the World Series," Nick said.

"Well, they're always in New York or Philadelphia now," Bill said. "That doesn't do us any good."

"I wonder if the Cards will ever win a pennant?"

"Not in our lifetime," Bill said.

"Gee, they'd go crazy," Nick said.

"Do you remember when they got going that once before they had the train wreck?"

"Boy!" Nick said, remembering.

Bill reached over to the table under the window for the book that lay there, face down, where he had put it when he went to the door. He held his glass in one hand and the book in the other, leaning back against Nick's chair.

"What are you reading?"

"*Richard Feverel.*"

"I couldn't get into it."

"It's all right," Bill said. "It ain't a bad book, Wemedge."

"What else have you got I haven't read," Nick asked.

"Did you read the *Forest Lovers?*"

"Yup. That's the one where they go to bed every night with the naked sword between them."

"That's a good book, Wemedge."

"It's a swell book. What I couldn't ever understand was what good the sword would do. It would have to stay edge up all the time because if it went over flat you could roll right over it and it wouldn't make any trouble."

"It's a symbol," Bill said.

"Sure," said Nick, "but it isn't practical."

"Did you ever read *Fortitude?*"

"It's fine," Nick said. "That's a real book. That's where his old man is after him all the time. Have you got any more by Walpole?"

"*The Dark Forest,*" Bill said. "It's about Russia."

"What does he know about Russia?" Nick asked.

"I don't know. You can't ever tell about those guys. Maybe he was there when he was a boy. He's got a lot of dope on it."

"I'd like to meet him," Nick said.

"I'd like to meet Chesterton," Bill said.

"I wish he was here now," Nick said. "We'd take him fishing to the 'Voix tomorrow."

"I wonder if he'd like to go fishing," Bill said.

"Sure," said Nick. "He must be about the best guy there is. Do you remember the 'Flying Inn'?"

> If an angel out of heaven
> Gives you something else to drink,
> Thank him for his kind intentions;
> Go and pour them down the sink.

"That's right," said Nick. "I guess he's a better guy than Walpole."

"Oh, he's a better guy, all right," Bill said.

"But Walpole's a better writer."

"I don't know," Nick said. "Chesterton's a classic."

"Walpole's a classic, too," Bill insisted.

"I wish we had them both here," Nick said. "We'd take them both fishing to the 'Voix tomorrow."

"Let's get drunk," Bill said.

"All right," Nick agreed.

"My old man won't care," Bill said.

"Are you sure?" said Nick.

"I know it," Bill said.

"I'm a little drunk now," Nick said.

"You aren't drunk," Bill said.

He got up from the floor and reached for the whiskey bottle. Nick held out his glass. His eyes fixed on it while Bill poured.

Bill poured the glass half full of whiskey.

"Put in your own water," he said. "There's just one more shot."

"Got any more?" Nick asked.

"There's plenty more, but Dad only likes me to drink what's open."

"Sure," said Nick.

"He says opening bottles is what makes drunkards," Bill explained.

"That's right," said Nick. He was impressed. He had never thought of that before. He had always thought it was solitary drinking that made drunkards.

"How is your dad?" he asked respectfully.

"He's all right," Bill said. "He gets a little wild sometimes."

"He's a swell guy," Nick said. He poured water into his glass out of the pitcher. It mixed slowly with the whiskey. There was more whiskey than water.

"You bet your life he is," Bill said.

"My old man's all right," Nick said.

"You're damn right he is," said Bill.

"He claims he's never taken a drink in his life," Nick said, as though announcing a scientific fact.

"Well, he's a doctor. My old man's a painter. That's different."

"He's missed a lot," Nick said sadly.

"You can't tell," Bill said. "Everything's got its compensations."

"He says he's missed a lot himself," Nick confessed.

"Well, Dad's had a tough time," Bill said.

"It all evens up," Nick said.

They sat looking into the fire and thinking of this profound truth.

"I'll get a chunk from the back porch," Nick said. He had noticed while looking into the fire that the fire was dying down. Also he wished to show he could hold his liquor and be practical. Even if his father had never touched a drop Bill was not going to get him drunk before he himself was drunk.

"Bring one of the big beech chunks," Bill said. He was also being consciously practical.

Nick came in with the log through the kitchen and in passing knocked a pan off the kitchen table. He laid the log down and picked up the pan. It had contained dried apricots, soaking in water. He carefully picked up all the apricots off the floor, some of them had gone under the stove, and put them back in the pan. He dipped some more water onto them from the pail by the table. He felt quite proud of himself. He had been thoroughly practical.

He came in carrying the log and Bill got up from the chair and helped him put it on the fire.

"That's a swell log," Nick said.

"I'd been saving it for the bad weather," Bill said. "A log like that will burn all night."

"There'll be coals left to start the fire in the morning," Nick said.

"That's right," Bill agreed. They were conducting the conversation on a high plane.

"Let's have another drink," Nick said.

"I think there's another bottle open in the locker," Bill said.

He kneeled down in the corner in front of the locker and brought out a square-faced bottle.

"It's Scotch," he said.

"I'll get some more water," Nick said. He went out into the kitchen again. He filled the pitcher with the dipper, dipping cold spring water from the pail. On his way back to the living room he passed a mirror in the dining room and looked in it. His face looked strange. He smiled at the face in the mirror and it grinned back at him. He winked at it and went on. It was not his face but it didn't make any difference.

Bill poured out the drinks.

"That's an awfully big shot," Nick said.

"Not for us, Wemedge," Bill said.

"What'll we drink to?" Nick asked, holding up the glass.

"Let's drink to fishing," Bill said.

"All right," Nick said. "Gentlemen, I give you fishing."

"All fishing," Bill said. "Everywhere."

"Fishing," Nick said. "That's what we drink to."

"It's better than baseball," Bill said.

"There isn't any comparison," said Nick. "How did we ever get talking about baseball?"

"It was a mistake," Bill said. "Baseball is a game for louts."

They drank all that was in their glasses.

"Now let's drink to Chesterton."

"And Walpole," Nick interposed.

Nick poured out the liquor. Bill poured in the water. They looked at each other. They felt very fine.

"Gentlemen," Bill said, "I give you Chesterton and Walpole."

"Exactly, gentlemen," Nick said.

They drank. Bill filled up the glasses. They sat down in the big chairs in front of the fire.

"You were very wise, Wemedge," Bill said.

"What do you mean?" asked Nick.

"To bust off that Marge business," Bill said.

"I guess so," said Nick.

"It was the only thing to do. If you hadn't, by now you'd be back home working trying to get enough money to get married."

Nick said nothing.

"Once a man's married he's absolutely bitched," Bill went on. "He hasn't got anything more. Nothing. Not a damn thing. He's done for. You've seen the guys that get married."

Nick said nothing.

"You can tell them," Bill said. "They get this sort of fat married look. They're done for."

"Sure," said Nick.

"It was probably bad busting it off," Bill said. "But you always fall for somebody else and then it's all right. Fall for them but don't let them ruin you."

"Yes," said Nick.

"If you'd have married her you would have had to marry the whole family. Remember her mother and that guy she married."

Nick nodded.

"Imagine having them around the house all the time and going to Sunday dinners at their house and having them over to dinner and her telling Marge all the time what to do and how to act."

Nick sat quiet.

"You came out of it damned well," Bill said. "Now she can marry somebody of her own sort and settle down and be happy. You can't mix oil and water and you can't mix that sort of thing any more than if I'd marry Ida that works for Strattons. She'd probably like it, too."

Nick said nothing. The liquor had all died out of him and left him alone. Bill wasn't there. He wasn't sitting in front of the fire or going fishing tomorrow with Bill and his dad or anything. He wasn't drunk. It was all gone. All he knew was that he had once had Marjorie and that he had lost her. She was gone and he had sent her away. That was all that mattered. He might never see her again. Probably he never would. It was all gone, finished.

"Let's have another drink," Nick said.

Bill poured it out. Nick splashed in a little water.

"If you had gone on that way we wouldn't be here now," Bill said.

That was true. His original plan had been to go down home and get a job. Then he had planned to stay in Charlevoix all winter so he could be near Marge. Now he did not know what he was going to do.

"Probably we wouldn't even be going fishing tomorrow," Bill said. "You had the right dope, all right."

"I couldn't help it," Nick said.

"I know. That's the way it works out," Bill said.

"All of a sudden everything was over," Nick said. "I don't know why it was. I couldn't help it. Just like when the three-day blows come now and rip all the leaves off the trees."

"Well, it's over. That's the point," Bill said.

"It was my fault," Nick said.

"It doesn't make any difference whose fault it was," Bill said.

"No, I suppose not," Nick said.

The big thing was that Marjorie was gone and that probably he would never see her again. He had talked to her about how they would go to Italy together and the fun they would have. Places they would be together. It was all gone now. Something gone out of him.

"So long as it's over that's all that matters," Bill said. "I tell you, Wemedge, I was worried while it was going on. You played it right. I understand her mother is sore as hell. She told a lot of people you were engaged."

"We weren't engaged," Nick said.

"It was all around that you were."

"I can't help it," Nick said. "We weren't."

"Weren't you going to get married?" Bill asked.

"Yes. But we weren't engaged," Nick said.

"What's the difference?" Bill asked judicially.

"I don't know. There's a difference."

"I don't see it," said Bill.

"All right," said Nick. "Let's get drunk."

"All right," Bill said. "Let's get really drunk."

"Let's get drunk and then go swimming," Nick said.

He drank off his glass.

"I'm sorry as hell about her but what could I do?" he said. "You know what her mother was like!"

"She was terrible," Bill said.

"All of a sudden it was over," Nick said. "I oughtn't to talk about it."

"You aren't," Bill said. "I talked about it and now I'm through. We won't ever speak about it again. You don't want to think about it. You might get back into it again."

Nick had not thought about that. It had seemed so absolute. That was a thought. That made him feel better.

"Sure," he said. "There's always that danger."

He felt happy now. There was not anything that was irrevocable. He might go into town Saturday night. Today was Thursday.

"There's always a chance," he said.

"You'll have to watch yourself," Bill said.

"I'll watch myself," he said.

He felt happy. Nothing was finished. Nothing was ever lost. He would go into town on Saturday. He felt lighter, as he had felt before Bill started to talk about it. There was always a way out.

"Let's take the guns and go down to the point and look for your dad," Nick said.

"All right."

Bill took down the two shotguns from the rack on the wall. He opened a box of shells. Nick put on his Mackinaw coat and his shoes. His shoes were stiff from the drying. He was still quite drunk but his head was clear.

"How do you feel?" Nick asked.

"Swell. I've just got a good edge on." Bill was buttoning up his sweater.

"There's no use getting drunk."

"No. We ought to get outdoors."

They stepped out the door. The wind was blowing a gale.

"The birds will lie right down in the grass with this," Nick said.

They struck down toward the orchard.

"I saw a woodcock this morning," Bill said.

"Maybe we'll jump him," Nick said.

"You can't shoot in this wind," Bill said.

Outside now the Marge business was no longer so tragic. It was not even very important. The wind blew everything like that away.

"It's coming right off the big lake," Nick said.

Against the wind they heard the thud of a shotgun.

"That's Dad," Bill said. "He's down in the swamp."

"Let's cut down that way," Nick said.

"Let's cut across the lower meadow and see if we jump anything," Bill said.

"All right," Nick said.

None of it was important now. The wind blew it out of his head. Still he could always go into town Saturday night. It was a good thing to have in reserve.

Summer People

Halfway down the gravel road from Hortons Bay, the town, to the lake there was a spring. The water came up in a tile sunk beside the road, lipping over the cracked edge of the tile and flowing away through the close-growing mint into the swamp. In the dark Nick put his arm down into the spring but could not hold it there because of the cold. He felt the featherings of the sand spouting up from the spring cones at the bottom against his fingers. Nick thought, I wish I could put all of myself in there. I bet that would fix me. He pulled his arm out and sat down at the edge of the road. It was a hot night.

Down the road through the trees he could see the white of the Bean house on its piles over the water. He did not want to go down to the dock. Everybody was down there swimming. He did not want Kate with Odgar around. He could see the car on the road beside the warehouse. Odgar and Kate were down there. Odgar with that fried-fish look in his eye everytime he looked at Kate. Didn't Odgar know anything? Kate wouldn't ever marry him. She wouldn't ever marry anybody that didn't make her. And if they tried to make her she would curl up inside of herself and be hard and slip away. He could make her do it all right. Instead of curling up hard and slipping away she would open out smoothly, relaxing, untightening, easy to hold. Odgar thought it was love that did it. His eyes got walleyed and red at the edges of the lids. She couldn't bear to have him touch her. It was all in his eyes. Then Odgar would want them to be just the same friends as ever. Play in the sand. Make mud images. Take all-day trips in the boat together. Kate always in her bathing suit. Odgar looking at her.

Odgar was thirty-two and had been twice operated on for varicocele. He was ugly to look at and everybody liked his face. Odgar could never get it and it meant everything in the world to him. Every summer he was worse about it. It was pitiful. Odgar was awfully nice. He had been nicer to Nick than anybody ever had. Now Nick could get it if he wanted it. Odgar would kill himself, Nick thought, if he knew it. I wonder how he'd kill himself. He couldn't think of Odgar dead. He probably wouldn't do it. Still people did. It wasn't just love. Odgar thought just love would do it. Odgar loved her enough, God knows. It was liking, and liking the body, and introducing the body, and persuading, and taking chances, and never frightening, and assuming about the other person, and always taking never asking, and gentleness and liking, and making liking and happiness, and joking and making people not afraid. And making it all right afterwards. It wasn't loving. Loving was frightening. He, Nicholas Adams, could have what he wanted because of something in him. Maybe it did not last. Maybe he would lose it. He wished he could give it to Odgar, or tell Odgar about it. You couldn't ever tell anybody about anything. Especially Odgar. No, not especially Odgar. Anybody, anywhere. That had always been his big mistake, talking. He had talked himself out of too many things. There ought to be something you could do for the Princeton, Yale and Harvard virgins, though. Why weren't there any virgins in state universities? Coeducation maybe. They met girls who were out to marry and the girls helped them along and married them. What would become of fellows like Odgar and Harvey and Mike and all the rest? He didn't know. He hadn't lived long enough. They were the best people in the world. What became of them? How the hell could he know. How could he write like Hardy and Hamsun when he only knew ten years of life. He couldn't. Wait till he was fifty.

In the dark he kneeled down and took a drink from the spring. He felt all right. He knew he was going to be a great writer. He knew things and they couldn't touch him. Nobody could. Only he did not know enough things. That would come all right. He knew. The water was cold and made his eyes ache. He had swallowed too big a gulp. Like ice cream. That's the way with drinking with your nose underwater. He'd better go swimming. Thinking was no good. It started and went on so. He walked down the road, past the car and the big warehouse on the left where apples and potatoes were loaded onto the boats in the fall, past the white-painted Bean house where they danced by lantern light sometimes on the hardwood floor, out on the dock to where they were swimming.

They were all swimming off the end of the dock. As Nick walked along the rough boards high above the water he heard the double protest of the long springboard and a splash. The water lapped below in the piles. That must be the Ghee, he thought. Kate came up out of the water like a seal and pulled herself up the ladder.

"It's Wemedge," she shouted to the others. "Come on in, Wemedge. It's wonderful."

"Hi, Wemedge," said Odgar. "Boy it's great."

"Where's Wemedge?" It was the Ghee, swimming far out.

"Is this man Wemedge a nonswimmer?" Bill's voice very deep and bass over the water.

Nick felt good. It was fun to have people yell at you like that. He scuffed off his canvas shoes, pulled his shirt over his head and stepped out of his trousers. His bare feet felt the sandy planks of the dock. He ran very quickly out the yielding plank of the springboard, his toes shoved against the end of the board, he tightened and he was in the water, smoothly and deeply, with no conciousness of the dive. He had breathed in deeply as he took off and now went on and on through the water, holding his back arched, feet straight and trailing. Then he was on the surface, floating face down. He rolled over and opened his eyes. He did not care anything about swimming, only to dive and be underwater.

"How is it, Wemedge?" The Ghee was just behind him.

"Warm as piss," Nick said.

He took a deep breath, took hold of his ankles with his hands, his knees under his chin, and sank slowly down into the water. It was warm at the top but he dropped quickly into cool, then cold. As he neared the bottom it was quite cold. Nick floated down gently against the bottom. It was marly and his toes hated it as he uncurled and shoved hard against it to come up to the air. It was strange coming up from underwater into the dark. Nick rested in the water, barely paddling and comfortable. Odgar and Kate were talking together up on the dock.

"Have you ever swum in a sea where it was phosphorescent, Carl?"

"No." Odgar's voice was unnatural talking to Kate.

We might rub ourselves all over with matches, Nick thought. He took a deep breath, drew his knees up, clasped tight and sank, this time with his eyes open. He sank gently, first going off to one side, then sinking head first. It was no good. He could not see underwater in the dark. He was right to keep his eyes shut when he first dove in. It was funny about reactions like that. They weren't always right, though. He did not go all the way down but straightened out and swam along and up through the cool, keeping just below the warm surface water. It was funny how much fun it was to swim underwater and how little real fun there was in plain swimming. It was fun to swim on the surface in the ocean. That was the buoyancy. But there was the taste of the brine and the way it made you thirsty. Fresh water was better. Just like this on a hot night. He came up for air just under the projecting edge of the dock and climbed up the ladder.

"Oh, dive, Wemedge, will you?" Kate said. "Do a good dive." They were sitting together on the dock leaning back against one of the big piles.

"Do a noiseless one, Wemedge," Odgar said.

"All right."

Nick, dripping, walked out on the springboard, remembering how to do the dive. Odgar and Kate watched him, black in the dark, standing at the end of the board, poise and dive as he had learned from watching a sea otter. In the water as he turned to come up to the air Nick thought, Gosh, if I could only have Kate down here. He came up in a rush to the surface, feeling water in his eyes and ears. He must have started to take a breath.

"It was perfect. Absolutely perfect," Kate shouted from the dock.

Nick came up the ladder.

"Where are the men?" he asked.

"They're swimming way out in the bay," Odgar said.

Nick lay down on the dock beside Kate and Odgar. He could hear the Ghee and Bill swimming way out in the dark.

"You're the most wonderful diver, Wemedge," Kate said, touching his back with her foot. Nick tightened under the contact.

"No," he said.

"You're a wonder, Wemedge," Odgar said.

"Nope," Nick said. He was thinking, thinking if it was possible to be with somebody underwater, he could hold his breath three minutes, against the sand on the bottom, they could float up together, take a breath and go down, it was easy to sink if you knew how. He had once drunk a bottle of milk and peeled and eaten a banana underwater to show off, had to have weights, though, to hold him down, if there was a ring at the bottom, something he could get his arm through, he could do it all right. Gee, how it would be, you couldn't ever get a girl though, a girl couldn't go through with it, she'd swallow water, it would drown Kate, Kate wasn't really any good underwater, he wished there was a girl like that, maybe he'd get a girl like that, probably never, there wasn't anybody but him that was that way underwater. Swimmers, hell, swimmers were slobs, nobody knew about the water but him, there was a fellow up at Evanston that could hold his breath six minutes but he was crazy. He wished he was a fish, no he didn't. He laughed.

"What's the joke, Wemedge?" Odgar said in his husky, near-to-Kate voice.

"I wished I was a fish," Nick said.

"That's a good joke," said Odgar.

"Sure," said Nick.

"Don't be an ass, Wemedge," said Kate.

"Would you like to be a fish, Butstein?" he said, lying with his head on the planks, facing away from them.

"No," said Kate. "Not tonight."

Nick pressed his back hard against her foot.

"What animal would you like to be, Odgar?" Nick said.

"J. P. Morgan," Odgar said.

"You're nice, Odgar," Kate said. Nick felt Odgar glow.

"I'd like to be Wemedge," Kate said.

"You could always be Mrs. Wemedge," Odgar said.

"There isn't going to be any Mrs. Wemedge," Nick said. He tightened his back muscles. Kate had both her legs stretched out against his back as though she were resting them on a log in front of a fire.

"Don't be too sure," Odgar said.

"I'm awful sure," Nick said. "I'm going to marry a mermaid."

"She'd be Mrs. Wemedge," Kate said.

"No she wouldn't," Nick said. "I wouldn't let her."

"How would you stop her?"

"I'd stop her all right. Just let her try it."

"Mermaids don't marry," Kate said.

"That'd be all right with me," Nick said.

"The Mann Act would get you," said Odgar.

"We'd stay outside the four-mile limit," Nick said. "We'd get food from the rumrunners. You could get a diving suit and come and visit us, Odgar. Bring Butstein if she wants to come. We'll be at home every Thursday afternoon."

"What are we going to do tomorrow?" Odgar said, his voice becoming husky, near to Kate again.

"Oh, hell, let's not talk about tomorrow," Nick said. "Let's talk about my mermaid."

"We're through with your mermaid."

"All right," Nick said. "You and Odgar go on and talk. I'm going to think about her."

"You're immoral, Wemedge. You're disgustingly immoral."

"No, I'm not. I'm honest." Then, lying with his eyes shut, he said, "Don't bother me. I'm thinking about her."

He lay there thinking of his mermaid while Kate's insteps pressed against his back and she and Odgar talked.

Odgar and Kate talked but he did not hear them. He lay, no longer thinking, quite happy.

Bill and the Ghee had come out of the water farther down the shore, walked down the beach to the car and then backed it out onto the dock. Nick stood up and put on his clothes. Bill and the Ghee were in the front seat, tired from the long swim. Nick got in behind with Kate and Odgar. They leaned back. Bill drove roaring up the hill and turned onto the main road. On the main highway Nick could see the lights of other cars up ahead, going out of sight, then blinding as they mounted a hill, blinking as they came near, then dimmed as Bill passed. The road was high along the shore of the lake. Big cars out from Charlevoix, rich slobs riding behind their chauffeurs, came up and passed, hogging the road and not dimming their lights. They passed like railway trains. Bill flashed the spotlight on cars alongside the road in the trees, making the occupants change their positions. Nobody passed Bill from behind, although a spotlight played on the back of their heads for some time until Bill drew away. Bill slowed, then turned abruptly into the sandy road that ran up through the orchard to the farmhouse. The car, in low gear, moved steadily up through the orchard. Kate put her lips to Nick's ear.

"In about an hour, Wemedge," she said. Nick pressed his thigh hard against hers. The car circled at the top of the hill above the orchard and stopped in front of the house.

"Aunty's asleep. We've got to be quiet," Kate said.

"Good night, men," Bill whispered. "We'll stop by in the morning."

"Good night, Smith," whispered the Ghee. "Good night, Butstein."

"Good night, Ghee," Kate said.

Odgar was staying at the house.

"Good night, men," Nick said. "See you, Morgen."

"Night, Wemedge," Odgar said from the porch.

Nick and the Ghee walked down the road into the orchard. Nick reached up and took an apple from one of the Duchess trees. It was still green but he sucked the acid juice from the bite and spat out the pulp.

"You and the Bird took a long swim, Ghee," he said.

"Not so long, Wemedge," the Ghee answered.

They came out from the orchard past the mailbox onto the hard state highway. There was a cold mist in the hollow where the road crossed the creek. Nick stopped on the bridge.

"Come on, Wemedge," the Ghee said.

"All right," Nick agreed.

They went on up the hill to where the road turned into the grove of trees around the church. There were no lights in any of the houses they passed. Hortons Bay was asleep. No motor cars had passed them.

"I don't feel like turning in yet," Nick said.

"Want me to walk with you?"

"No, Ghee. Don't bother."

"All right."

"I'll walk up as far as the cottage with you," Nick said. They unhooked the screen door and went into the kitchen. Nick opened the meat safe and looked around.

"Want some of this, Ghee?" he said.

"I want a piece of pie," the Ghee said.

"So do I," Nick said. He wrapped up some fried chicken and two pieces of cherry pie in oiled paper from the top of the icebox.

"I'll take this with me," he said. The Ghee washed down his pie with a dipper full of water from the bucket.

"If you want anything to read, Ghee, get it out of my room," Nick said. The Ghee had been looking at the lunch Nick had wrapped up.

"Don't be a damn fool, Wemedge," he said.

"That's all right, Ghee."

"All right. Only don't be a damn fool," the Ghee said. He opened the screen door and went out across the grass to the cottage. Nick turned off the light and went out, hooking the screen door shut. He had the lunch wrapped up in a newspaper and crossed the wet grass, climbed the fence and went up the road through the town under the big elm trees, past the last cluster of R.F.D. mailboxes at the crossroads and out onto the Charlevoix highway. After crossing the creek he cut across a field, skirted the edge of the orchard, keeping to the edge of the clearing, and climbed the rail fence into the wood lot. In the center of the wood lot four hemlock trees grew close together. The ground was soft with pine needles and there was no dew. The wood lot had never been cut over and the forest floor was dry and warm without underbrush. Nick put the package of lunch by the base of one of the hemlocks and lay down to wait. He saw Kate coming through the trees in the dark but did not move. She did not see him and stood a moment, holding the two blankets in her arms. In the dark it looked like some enormous pregnancy. Nick was shocked. Then it was funny.

"Hello, Butstein," he said. She dropped the blankets.

"Oh, Wemedge. You shouldn't have frightened me like that. I was afraid you hadn't come."

"Dear Butstein," Nick said. He held her close against him, feeling her body against his, all the sweet body against his body. She pressed close against him.

"I love you so, Wemedge."

"Dear, dear old Butstein," Nick said.

They spread the blankets, Kate smoothing them flat.

"It was awfully dangerous to bring the blankets," Kate said.

"I know," Nick said. "Let's undress."

"Oh, Wemedge."

"It's more fun." They undressed sitting on the blankets. Nick was a little embarrassed to sit there like that.

"Do you like me with my clothes off, Wemedge?"

"Gee, let's get under," Nick said. They lay between the rough blankets. He was hot against her cool body, hunting for it, then it was all right.

"Is it all right?"

Kate pressed all the way up for answer.

"Is it fun?"

"Oh, Wemedge. I've wanted it so. I've needed it so."

They lay together in the blankets. Wemedge slid his head down, his nose touching along the line of the neck, down between her breasts. It was like piano keys.

"You smell so cool," he said.

He touched one of her small breasts with his lips gently. It came alive between his lips, his tongue pressing against it. He felt the whole feeling coming back again and, sliding his hands down, moved Kate over. He slid down and she fitted close in against him. She pressed tight in against the curve of his abdomen. She felt wonderful there. He searched, a little awkwardly, then found it. He put both hands over her breasts and held her to him. Nick kissed hard against her back. Kate's head dropped forward.

"Is it good this way?" he said.

"I love it. I love it. I love it. Oh come, Wemedge. Please come. Come, come. Please, Wemedge. Please, please, Wemedge."

"There it is," Nick said.

He was suddenly conscious of the blanket rough against his bare body.

"Was I bad, Wemedge?" Kate said.

"No, you were good," Nick said. His mind was working very hard and clear. He saw everything very sharp and clear. "I'm hungry," he said.

"I wish we could sleep here all night." Kate cuddled against him.

"It would be swell," Nick said. "But we can't. You've got to get back to the house."

"I don't want to go," Kate said.

[227]

Nick stood up, a little wind blowing on his body. He pulled on his shirt and was glad to have it on. He put on his trousers and shoes.

"You've got to get dressed, slut," he said. She lay there, the blankets pulled over her head.

"Just a minute," she said. Nick got the lunch from over by the hemlock. He opened it up.

"Come on, get dressed, slut," he said.

"I don't want to," Kate said. "I'm going to sleep here all night." She sat up in the blankets. "Hand me those things, Wemedge."

Nick gave her the clothes.

"I've just thought of it," Kate said. "If I sleep out here they'll just think that I'm an idiot and came out here with the blankets and it will be all right."

"You won't be comfortable," Nick said.

"If I'm uncomfortable I'll go in."

"Let's eat before I have to go," Nick said.

"I'll put something on," Kate said.

They sat together and ate the fried chicken and each ate a piece of cherry pie.

Nick stood up, then kneeled down and kissed Kate.

He came through the wet grass to the cottage and upstairs to his room, walking carefully not to creak. It was good to be in bed, sheets, stretching out full length, dipping his head in the pillow. Good in bed, comfortable, happy, fishing tomorrow, he prayed as he always prayed when he remembered it, for the family, himself, to be a great writer, Kate, the men, Odgar, for good fishing, poor old Odgar, poor old Odgar, sleeping up there at the cottage, maybe not sleeping, maybe not sleeping all night. Still there wasn't anything you could do, not a thing.

COMPANY
OF TWO

Wedding Day

He had been in swimming and was washing his feet in the wash bowl after having walked up the hill. The room was hot and Dutch and Luman were both standing around looking nervous. Nick got a clean suit of underwear, clean silk socks, new garters, a white shirt and collar out from the drawer of the bureau and put them on. He stood in front of the mirror and tied his tie. Dutch and Luman reminded him of dressing rooms before fights and football games. He enjoyed their nervousness. He wondered if it would be this way if he were going to be hanged. Probably. He could never realize anything until it happened. Dutch went out for a corkscrew and came in and opened the bottle.

"Take a good shot, Dutch."

"After you, Stein."

"No. What the hell. Go on and drink."

Dutch took a good long pull. Nick resented the length of it. After all, that was the only bottle of whiskey there was. Dutch passed the bottle to him. He handed it to Luman. Luman took a shot not quite as long as Dutch's.

"All right, Stein, old kid." He handed the bottle to Nick.

Nick took a couple of swallows. He loved whiskey. Nick pulled on his trousers. He wasn't thinking at all. Horny Bill, Art Meyer and the Ghee were dressing upstairs. They ought to have liquor. Christ, why wasn't there any more than one bottle.

After the wedding was over they got into John Kotesky's Ford and drove over the hill road to the lake. Nick paid John Kotesky five dollars and Kotesky helped him carry the bags down to the rowboat. They both shook hands with Kotesky and then his Ford went back up along the road. They could hear it for a long time. Nick could not find the oars where his father had hidden them for him in the plum trees back of the ice house and Helen waited for him down at the boat. Finally he found them and carried them down to the shore.

It was a long row across the lake in the dark. The night was hot and depressing. Neither of them talked much. A few people had spoiled the wedding. Nick rowed hard when they were near shore and shot the boat up on the sandy beach. He pulled it up and Helen stepped out. Nick kissed her. She kissed him back hard the way he had taught her with her mouth a little open so their tongues could play with each other. They held tight to each other and then walked up to the cottage. It was dark and long. Nick unlocked the door and then went back to the boat to get the bags. He lit the lamps and they looked through the cottage together.

On Writing

It was getting hot, the sun hot on the back of his neck.

Nick had one good trout. He did not care about getting many trout. Now the stream was shallow and wide. There were trees along both banks. The trees of the left bank made short shadows on the current in the forenoon sun. Nick knew there were trout in each shadow. He and Bill Smith had discovered that on the Black River one hot day. In the afternoon, after the sun had crossed toward the hills, the trout would be in the cool shadows on the other side of the stream.

The very biggest ones would lie up close to the bank. You could always pick them up there on the Black. Bill and he had discovered it. When the sun was down they all moved out into the current. Just when the sun made the water blinding in the glare before it went down you were liable to strike a big trout anywhere in the current. It was almost impossible to fish then, the surface of the water was blinding as a mirror in the sun. Of course you could fish upstream, but in a stream like the Black or this you had to wallow against the current and in a deep place the water piled up on you. It was no fun to fish upstream although all the books said it was the only way.

All the books. He and Bill had fun with the books in the old days. They all started with a fake premise. Like fox hunting. Bill Bird's dentist in Paris said, in fly fishing you pit your intelligence against that of the fish. That's the way I'd always thought of it, Ezra said. That was good for a laugh. There were so many things good for a laugh. In the States they thought bullfighting was a joke. Ezra thought fishing was a joke. Lots of people think poetry is a joke. Englishmen are a joke.

Remember when they pushed us over the barrera in front of the bull at Pamplona because they thought we were Frenchmen? Bill's dentist is as bad the other way about fishing. Bill Bird, that is. Once Bill meant Bill Smith. Now it means Bill Bird. Bill Bird was in Paris now.

When he married he lost Bill Smith, Odgar, the Ghee, all the old gang. Was it because they were virgins? The Ghee certainly was not. No, he lost them because he admitted by marrying that something was more important than the fishing.

He had built it all up. Bill had never fished before they met. Everyplace they had been together. The Black, the Sturgeon, the Pine Barrens, the Upper Minnie, all the little streams. Most about fishing he and Bill had discovered together. They worked on the farm and fished and took long trips in the woods from June to October. Bill always quit his job every spring. So did he. Ezra thought fishing was a joke.

Bill forgave him the fishing he had done before they met. He forgave him all the rivers. He was really proud of them. It was like a girl about other girls. If they were before they did not matter. But after was different.

That was why he lost them, he guessed.

They were all married to fishing. Ezra thought fishing was a joke. So did most everybody. He'd been married to it before he married Helen. Really married to it. It wasn't any joke.

So he lost them all. Helen thought it was because they didn't like her.

Nick sat down on a boulder in the shade and hung his sack

down into the river. The water swirled around both sides of the boulder. It was cool in the shade. The bank of the river was sandy under the edge of the trees. There were mink tracks in the sand.

He might as well be out of the heat. The rock was dry and cool. He sat letting the water run out of his boots down the side of the rock.

Helen thought it was because they did not like her. She really did. Gosh, he remembered the horror he used to have of people getting married. It was funny. Probably it was because he had always been with older people, nonmarrying people.

Odgar always wanted to marry Kate. Kate wouldn't ever marry anybody. She and Odgar always quarreled about it but Odgar did not want anybody else and Kate wouldn't have anybody. She wanted them to be just as good friends and Odgar wanted to be friends and they were always miserable and quarreling trying to be.

It was the Madame planted all that asceticism. The Ghee went with girls in houses in Cleveland but he had it, too. Nick had had it, too. It was all such a fake. You had this fake ideal planted in you and then you lived your life to it.

All the love went into fishing and the summer.

He had loved it more than anything. He had loved digging potatoes with Bill in the fall, the long trips in the car, fishing in the bay, reading in the hammock on hot days, swimming off the dock, playing baseball at Charlevoix and Petoskey, living at the Bay, the Madame's cooking, the way she had with servants, eating in the dining room looking out the window across the long fields and the point to the lake, talking with her, drinking with Bill's old man, the fishing trips away from the farm, just lying around.

He loved the long summer. It used to be that he felt sick

when the first of August came and he realized that there were only four more weeks before the trout season closed. Now sometimes he had it that way in dreams. He would dream that the summer was nearly gone and he hadn't been fishing. It made him feel sick in the dream, as though he had been in jail.

The hills at the foot of Walloon Lake, storms on the lake coming up in the motorboat, holding an umbrella over the engine to keep the waves that came in off the spark plug, pumping out, running the boat in big storms delivering vegetables around the lake, climbing up, sliding down, the wave following behind, coming up from the foot of the lake with the groceries, the mail and the Chicago paper under a tarpaulin, sitting on them to keep them dry, too rough to land, drying out in front of the fire, the wind in the hemlocks and the wet pine needles underfoot when he was barefoot going for the milk. Getting up at daylight to row across the lake and hike over the hills after a rain to fish in Hortons Creek.

Hortons always needed a rain. Shultz's was no good if it rained, running muddy and overflowing, running through the grass. Where were the trout when a stream was like that?

That was where a bull chased him over the fence and he lost his pocketbook with all the hooks in it.

If he knew then what he knew about bulls now. Where were Maera and Algabeno now? August the Feria at Valencia, Santander, bad fights at St. Sebastien. Sanchez Mejias killing six bulls. The way phrases from bullfight papers kept coming into his head all the time until he had to quit reading them. The corrida of the Miuras. In spite of his notorious defects in the execution of the pase natural. The flower of Andalucia. Chiquelín el camelista. Juan Terremoto. Belmonte Vuelve?

Maera's kid brother was a bullfighter now. That was the way it went.

His whole inner life had been bullfights all one year. Chink pale and miserable about the horses. Don never minded them, he said. "And then suddenly I knew I was going to love bull-fighting." That must have been Maera. Maera was the greatest man he'd ever known. Chink knew it, too. He followed him around in the encierro.

He, Nick, was the friend of Maera and Maera waved at them from Box 87 above their sobrepuerta and waited for Helen to see him and waved again and Helen worshipped him and there were three picadors in the box and all the other picadors did their stuff right down in front of the box and looked up and waved before and after and he said to Helen that picadors only worked for each other, and of course it was true. And it was the best pic-ing he ever saw and the three pics in the box with their Cordoba hats nodded at each good vara and the other pics waved up at them and then did their stuff. Like the time the Portuguese were in and the old pic threw his hat into the ring hanging on over the barrera watching young Da Veiga. That was the saddest thing he'd ever seen. That was what that fat pic wanted to be, a caballero en plaza. God, how that Da Veiga kid could ride. That was riding. It didn't show well in the movies.

The movies ruined everything. Like talking about something good. That was what had made the war unreal. Too much talking.

Talking about anything was bad. Writing about anything actual was bad. It always killed it.

The only writing that was any good was what you made up, what you imagined. That made everything come true. Like when he wrote "My Old Man" he'd never seen a jockey killed and the next week Georges Parfrement was killed at that very jump and that was the way it looked. Everything good he'd ever written he'd made up. None of it had ever happened. Other things had happened. Better things, maybe. That was what the family couldn't understand. They thought it all was experience.

That was the weakness of Joyce. Daedalus in Ulysses was Joyce himself, so he was terrible. Joyce was so damn romantic and intellectual about him. He'd made Bloom up, Bloom was wonderful. He'd made Mrs. Bloom up. She was the greatest in the world.

That was the way with Mac. Mac worked too close to life. You had to digest life and then create your own people. Mac had stuff, though.

Nick in the stories was never himself. He made him up. Of course he'd never seen an Indian woman having a baby. That was what made it good. Nobody knew that. He'd seen a woman have a baby on the road to Karagatch and tried to help her. That was the way it was.

He wished he could always write like that. He would sometime. He wanted to be a great writer. He was pretty sure he would be. He knew it in lots of ways. He would in spite of everything. It was hard, though.

It was hard to be a great writer if you loved the world and living in it and special people. It was hard when you loved so many places. Then you were healthy and felt good and were having a good time and what the hell.

He always worked best when Helen was unwell. Just that much discontent and friction. Then there were times when you had to write. Not conscience. Just peristaltic action. Then you felt sometimes like you could never write but after a while you knew sooner or later you would write another good story.

It was really more fun than anything. That was really why you did it. He had never realized that before. It wasn't conscience. It was simply that it was the greatest pleasure. It had more bite to it than anything else. It was so damn hard to write well, too.

There were so many tricks.

It was easy to write if you used the tricks. Everybody used them. Joyce had invented hundreds of new ones. Just because they were new didn't make them any better. They would all turn into clichés.

He wanted to write like Cezanne painted.

Cezanne started with all the tricks. Then he broke the whole thing down and built the real thing. It was hell to do. He was the greatest. The greatest for always. It wasn't a cult. He, Nick, wanted to write about country so it would be there like Cezanne had done it in painting. You had to do it from inside yourself. There wasn't any trick. Nobody had ever written about country like that. He felt almost holy about it. It was deadly serious. You could do it if you would fight it out. If you'd lived right with your eyes.

It was a thing you couldn't talk about. He was going to work on it until he got it. Maybe never, but he would know as he got near it. It was a job. Maybe for all his life.

People were easy to do. All this smart stuff was easy. Against this age, skyscraper primitives, Cummings when he was smart, it was automatic writing, not The Enormous Room, *that was a book, it was one of the great books. Cummings worked hard to get it.*

Was there anybody else? Young Asch had something but you couldn't tell. Jews go bad quickly. They all start well. Mac had something. Don Stewart had the most next to Cummings. Sometimes in the Haddocks. Ring Lardner, maybe. Very maybe. Old guys like Sherwood. Older guys like Dreiser. Was there anybody else? Young guys, maybe. Great unknowns. There are never any unknowns, though.

They weren't after what he was after.

He could see the Cezannes. The portrait at Gertrude Stein's. She'd know it if he ever got things right. The two good ones at the Luxembourg, the ones he'd seen every day at the loan exhibit at Bernheim's. The soldiers undressing to swim, the house through the trees, one of the trees with a house beyond, not the lake one, the other lake one. The portrait of the boy. Cezanne could do people, too. But that was easier, he used what he got from the country to do people with. Nick could do that, too. People were easy. Nobody knew anything about them. If it sounded good they took your word for it. They took Joyce's word for it.

He knew just how Cezanne would paint this stretch of river. God, if he were only here to do it. They died and that was the hell of it. They worked all their lives and then got old and died.

Nick, seeing how Cezanne would do the stretch of river and the swamp, stood up and stepped down into the stream. The water was cold and actual. He waded across the stream, moving in the picture. He kneeled down in the gravel on the bank and reached down into the trout sack. It lay in the stream where he had dragged it across the shallows. The old boy was alive. Nick opened the mouth of the sack and slid the trout into the shallow water and watched him move off through the shallows, his back out of water, threading between rocks toward the deep current.

"He was too big to eat," Nick said. "I'll get a couple of little ones in front of camp for supper."

He climbed the bank of the stream, reeling up his line and started through the brush. He ate a sandwich. He was in a hurry and the rod bothered him. He was not thinking. He was holding something in his head. He wanted to get back to camp and get to work.

He moved through the brush, holding the rod close to him. The line caught on a branch. Nick stopped and cut the leader and reeled the line up. He went through the brush now easily, holding the rod out before him.

Ahead of him he saw a rabbit, flat out on the trail. He stopped, grudging. The rabbit was barely breathing. There were two ticks on the rabbit's head, one behind each ear. They were gray, tight with blood, as big as grapes. Nick pulled them off, their heads tiny and hard, with moving feet. He stepped on them on the trail.

Nick picked up the rabbit, limp, with dull button eyes, and put it under a sweet fern bush beside the trail. He felt its heart beating as he laid it down. The rabbit lay quiet under the bush. It might come to, Nick thought. Probably the ticks had attached themselves to it as it crouched in the grass. Maybe after it had been dancing in the open. He did not know.

He went on up the trail to the camp. He was holding something in his head.

An Alpine Idyll

It was hot coming down into the valley even in the early morning. The sun melted the snow from the skis we were carrying and dried the wood. It was spring in the valley but the sun was very hot. We came along the road into Galtur carrying our skis and rucksacks. As we passed the churchyard a burial was just over. I said, "Grüss Gott," to the priest as he walked past us coming out of the churchyard. The priest bowed.

"It's funny a priest never speaks to you," John said.

"You'd think they'd like to say 'Grüss Gott.'"

"They never answer," John said.

We stopped in the road and watched the sexton shoveling in the new earth. A peasant with a black beard and high leather boots stood beside the grave. The sexton stopped shoveling and straightened his back. The peasant in the high boots took the spade from the sexton and went on filling in the grave—spreading the earth evenly as a man spreading manure in a garden. In the bright May morning the grave-filling looked unreal. I could not imagine anyone being dead.

"Imagine being buried on a day like this," I said to John.

"I wouldn't like it."

"Well," I said, "we don't have to do it."

We went on up the road past the houses of the town to the

inn. We had been skiing in the Silvretta for a month, and it was good to be down in the valley. In the Silvretta the skiing had been all right, but it was spring skiing, the snow was good only in the early morning and again in the evening. The rest of the time it was spoiled by the sun. We were both tired of the sun. You could not get away from the sun. The only shadows were made by rocks or by the hut that was built under the protection of a rock beside a glacier, and in the shade the sweat froze in your underclothing. You could not sit outside the hut without dark glasses. It was pleasant to be burned black but the sun had been very tiring. You could not rest in it. I was glad to be down away from snow. It was too late in the spring to be up in the Silvretta. I was a little tired of skiing. We had stayed too long. I could taste the snow water we had been drinking melted off the tin roof of the hut. The taste was a part of the way I felt about skiing. I was glad there were other things besides skiing, and I was glad to be down, away from the unnatural high mountain spring, into this May morning in the valley.

The innkeeper sat on the porch of the inn, his chair tipped back against the wall. Beside him sat the cook.

"Ski-heil!" said the innkeeper.

"Heil!" we said and leaned the skis against the wall and took off our packs.

"How was it up above?" asked the innkeeper.

"Schön. A little too much sun."

"Yes. There's too much sun this time of year."

The cook sat on in his chair. The innkeeper went in with us and unlocked his office and brought out our mail. There was a bundle of letters and some papers.

"Let's get some beer," John said.

"Good. We'll drink it inside."

The proprietor brought two bottles and we drank them while we read the letters.

"We better have some more beer," John said. A girl brought it this time. She smiled as she opened the bottles.

"Many letters," she said.

"Yes. Many."

"Prosit," she said and went out, taking the empty bottles.

"I'd forgotten what beer tasted like."

"I hadn't," John said. "Up in the hut I used to think about it a lot."

"Well," I said, "we've got it now."

"You oughtn't to ever do anything too long."

"No. We were up there too long."

"Too damn long," John said. "It's no good doing a thing too long."

The sun came through the open window and shone through the beer bottles on the table. The bottles were half full. There was a little froth on the beer in the bottles, not much because it was very cold. It collared up when you poured it into the tall glasses. I looked out of the open window at the white road. The trees beside the road were dusty. Beyond was a green field and a stream. There were trees along the stream and a mill with a water wheel. Through the open side of the mill I saw a long log and a saw in it rising and falling. No one seemed to be tending it. There were four crows walking in the green field. One crow sat in a tree watching. Outside on the porch the cook got off his chair and passed into the hall that led back into the kitchen. Inside, the sunlight shone through the empty glasses on the table. John was leaning forward with his head on his arms.

Through the window I saw two men come up the front steps. They came into the drinking room. One was the bearded peasant in the high boots. The other was the sexton. They sat down at the table under the window. The girl came in and stood by their table. The peasant did not seem to see her. He

[244]

sat with his hands on the table. He wore his old army clothes. There were patches on the elbows.

"What will it be?" asked the sexton. The peasant did not pay any attention.

"What will you drink?"

"Schnapps," the peasant said.

"And a quarter litre of red wine," the sexton told the girl.

The girl brought the drinks and the peasant drank the schnapps. He looked out of the window. The sexton watched him. John had his head forward on the table. He was asleep.

The innkeeper came in and went over to the table. He spoke in dialect and the sexton answered him. The peasant looked out of the window. The innkeeper went out of the room. The peasant stood up. He took a folded ten-thousand-kronen note out of a leather pocketbook and unfolded it. The girl came up.

"Alles?" she asked.

"Alles," he said.

"Let me buy the wine," the sexton said.

"Alles," the peasant repeated to the girl. She put her hand in the pocket of her apron, brought it out full of coins and counted out the change. The peasant went out the door. As soon as he was gone the innkeeper came into the room again and spoke to the sexton. He sat down at the table. They talked in dialect. The sexton was amused. The innkeeper was disgusted. The sexton stood up from the table. He was a little man with a mustache. He leaned out of the window and looked up the road.

"There he goes in," he said.

"In the Löwen?"

"Ja."

They talked again and then the innkeeper came over to our

table. The innkeeper was a tall man and old. He looked at
John asleep.

"He's pretty tired."

"Yes, we were up early."

"Will you want to eat soon?"

"Anytime," I said. "What is there to eat?"

"Anything you want. The girl will bring the eating-card."

The girl brought the menu. John woke up. The menu was
written in ink on a card and the card slipped into a wooden
paddle.

"There's the *Speisekarte*," I said to John. He looked at it.
He was still sleepy.

"Won't you have a drink with us?" I asked the innkeeper.
He sat down. "Those peasants are beasts," said the innkeeper.

"We saw that one at a funeral coming into town."

"That was his wife."

"Oh."

"He's a beast. All these peasants are beasts."

"How do you mean?"

"You wouldn't believe it. You wouldn't believe what just
happened about that one."

"Tell me."

"You wouldn't believe it." The innkeeper spoke to the sexton. "Franz, come over here." The sexton came, bringing his
little bottle of wine and his glass.

"The gentlemen are just come down from the *Wiesbadener-
hütte*," the innkeeper said. We shook hands.

"What will you drink?" I asked.

"Nothing," Franz shook his finger.

"Another quarter litre?"

"All right."

"Do you understand dialect?" the innkeeper asked.

"No."

"What's it all about?" John asked.

"He's going to tell us about the peasant we saw filling the grave, coming into town."

"I can't understand it, anyway," John said. "It goes too fast for me."

"That peasant," the innkeeper said, "today he brought his wife in to be buried. She died last November."

"December," said the sexton.

"That makes nothing. She died last December then, and he notified the commune."

"December eighteenth," said the sexton.

"Anyway, he couldn't bring her over to be buried until the snow was gone."

"He lives on the other side of the Paznaun," said the sexton. "But he belongs to this parish."

"He couldn't bring her out at all?" I asked.

"No. He can only come, from where he lives, on skis until the snow melts. So today he brought her in to be buried and the priest, when he looked at her face, didn't want to bury her. You go on and tell it," he said to the sexton. "Speak German, not dialect."

"It was very funny with the priest," said the sexton. "In the report to the commune she died of heart trouble. We knew she had heart trouble here. She used to faint in church sometimes. She did not come for a long time. She wasn't strong to climb. When the priest uncovered her face he asked Olz, 'Did your wife suffer much?' 'No,' said Olz. 'When I came in the house she was dead across the bed.'

"The priest looked at her again. He didn't like it.

" 'How did her face get that way?'

" 'I don't know,' Olz said.

" 'You'd better find out,' the priest said, and put the blanket back. Olz didn't say anything. The priest looked at him. Olz looked back at the priest. 'You want to know?'

" 'I must know,' the priest said."

"This is where it's good," the innkeeper said. "Listen to this. Go on Franz."

" 'Well,' said Olz, 'when she died I made the report to the commune and I put her in the shed across the top of the big wood. When I started to use the big wood she was stiff and I put her up against the wall. Her mouth was open and when I came into the shed at night to cut up the big wood, I hung the lantern from it.'

" 'Why did you do that?' asked the priest.

" 'I don't know,' said Olz.

" 'Did you do that many times?'

" 'Every time I went to work in the shed at night.'

" 'It was very wrong,' said the priest. 'Did you love your wife?'

" 'Ja, I loved her,' Olz said. 'I loved her fine.' "

"Did you understand it all?" asked the innkeeper. "You understand it all about his wife?"

"I heard it."

"How about eating?" John asked.

"You order," I said. "Do you think it's true?" I asked the innkeeper.

"Sure it's true," he said. "These peasants are beasts."

"Where did he go now?"

"He's gone to drink at my colleague's, the Löwen."

"He didn't want to drink with me," said the sexton.

"He didn't want to drink with me, after he knew about his wife," said the innkeeper.

"Say," said John. "How about eating?"

"All right," I said.

Cross-Country Snow

The funicular car bucked once more and then stopped. It could not go farther, the snow drifted solidly across the track. The gale scouring the exposed surface of the mountain had swept the snow surface into a wind-board crust. Nick, waxing his skis in the baggage car, pushed his boots into the toe irons and shut the clamp tight. He jumped from the car sideways onto the hard wind-board, made a jump turn and crouching and trailing his sticks slipped in a rush down the slope.

On the white below George dipped and rose and dipped out of sight. The rush and the sudden swoop as he dropped down a steep undulation in the mountainside plucked Nick's mind out and left him only the wonderful flying, dropping sensation in his body. He rose to a slight uprun and then the snow seemed to drop out from under him as he went down, down, faster and faster in a rush down the last, long steep slope. Crouching so he was almost sitting back on his skis, trying to keep the center of gravity low, the snow driving like a sandstorm, he knew the pace was too much. But he held it. He would not let go and spill. Then a patch of soft snow, left in a hollow by the wind, spilled him and he went over and over in a clashing of skis, feeling like a shot rabbit, then stuck, his legs crossed, his skis sticking straight up and his nose and ears jammed full of snow.

George stood a little farther down the slope, knocking the snow from his wind jacket with big slaps.

"You took a beauty, Mike," he called to Nick. "That's lousy soft snow. It bagged me the same way."

"What's it like over the khud?" Nick kicked his skis around as he lay on his back and stood up.

"You've got to keep to your left. It's a good fast drop with a Christy at the bottom on account of a fence."

"Wait a sec and we'll take it together."

"No, you come on and go first. I like to see you take the khuds."

Nick Adams came up past George, big back and blond head still faintly snowy, then his skis started slipping at the edge and he swooped down, hissing in the crystalline powder snow and seeming to float up and drop down as he went up and down the billowing khuds. He held to his left and at the end, as he rushed toward the fence, keeping his knees locked tight together and turning his body like tightening a screw, brought his skis sharply around to the right in a smother of snow and slowed into a loss of speed parallel to the hillside and the wire fence.

He looked up the hill. George was coming down in Telemark position, kneeling; one leg forward and bent, the other trailing; his sticks hanging like some insect's thin legs, kicking up puffs of snow as they touched the surface and finally the whole kneeling, trailing figure coming around in a beautiful right curve, crouching, the legs shot forward and back, the body leaning out against the swing, the sticks accenting the curve like points of light, all in a wild cloud of snow.

"I was afraid to Christy," George said, "the snow was too deep. You made a beauty."

"I can't Telemark with my leg," Nick said.

Nick held down the top strand of the wire fence with his

ski and George slid over. Nick followed him down to the
road. They thrust bent-kneed along the road into a pine forest.
The road became polished ice, stained orange and a tobacco
yellow from the teams hauling logs. The skiers kept to the
stretch of snow along the side. The road dipped sharply to a
stream and then ran straight uphill. Through the woods they
could see a long, low-eaved, weather-beaten building. Through
the trees it was a faded yellow. Closer the window frames were
painted green. The paint was peeling. Nick knocked his clamps
loose with one of his ski sticks and kicked off the skis.

"We might as well carry them up here," he said.

He climbed the steep road with the skis on his shoulder,
kicking his heel nails into the icy footing. He heard George
breathing and kicking in his heels just behind him. They
stacked the skis against the side of the inn and slapped the
snow off each other's trousers, stamped their boots clean, and
went in.

Inside it was quite dark. A big porcelain stove shone in the
corner of the room. There was a low ceiling. Smooth benches
back of dark, wine-stained tables were along each side of the
room. Two Swiss sat over their pipes and two decies of cloudy
new wine next to the stove. The boys took off their jackets
and sat against the wall on the other side of the stove. A voice
in the next room stopped singing and a girl in a blue apron
came in through the door to see what they wanted to drink.

"A bottle of Sion," Nick said. "Is that all right, Gidge?"

"Sure," said George. "You know more about wine than I do.
I like any of it."

The girl went out.

"There's nothing really can touch skiing, is there?" Nick
said. "The way it feels when you first drop off on a long run."

"Huh," said George. "It's too swell to talk about."

The girl brought the wine in and they had trouble with the

cork. Nick finally opened it. The girl went out and they heard her singing in German in the next room.

"Those specks of cork in it don't matter," said Nick.

"I wonder if she's got any cake."

"Let's find out."

The girl came in and Nick noticed that her apron covered swellingly her pregnancy. I wonder why I didn't see that when she first came in, he thought.

"What were you singing?" he asked her.

"Opera, German opera." She did not care to discuss the subject. "We have some apple strudel if you want it."

"She isn't so cordial, is she?" said George.

"Oh, well. She doesn't know us and she thought we were going to kid her about her singing, maybe. She's from up where they speak German probably and she's touchy about being here and then she's got that baby coming without being married and she's touchy."

"How do you know she isn't married?"

"No ring. Hell, no girls get married around here till they're knocked up."

The door came open and a gang of woodcutters from up the road came in, stamping their boots and steaming in the room. The waitress brought in three litres of new wine for the gang and they sat at the two tables, smoking and quiet, with their hats off, leaning back against the wall or forward on the table. Outside the horses on the wood sledges made an occasional sharp jangle of bells as they tossed their heads.

George and Nick were happy. They were fond of each other. They knew they had the run back home ahead of them.

"When have you got to go back to school?" Nick asked.

"Tonight," George answered. "I've got to get the ten-forty from Montreux."

"I wish you could stick over and we could do the Dent du Lys tomorrow."

"I got to get educated," George said. "Gee, Mike, don't you wish we could just bum together? Take our skis and go on the train to where there was good running and then go on and put up at pubs and go right across the Oberland and up the Valais and all through the Engadine and just take repair kit and extra sweaters and pajamas in our rucksacks and not give a damn about school or anything."

"Yes, and go through the Schwartzwald that way. Gee, the swell places."

"That's where you went fishing last summer, isn't it?"

"Yes."

They ate the strudel and drank the rest of the wine.

George leaned back against the wall and shut his eyes.

"Wine always makes me feel this way," he said.

"Feel bad?" Nick asked.

"No. I feel good, but funny."

"I know," Nick said.

"Sure," said George.

"Should we have another bottle?" Nick asked.

"Not for me," George said.

They sat there, Nick leaning his elbows on the table, George slumped back against the wall.

"Is Helen going to have a baby?" George said, coming down to the table from the wall.

"Yes."

"When?"

"Late next summer."

"Are you glad?"

"Yes. Now."

"Will you go back to the States?"

"I guess so."

"Do you want to?"

"No."

"Does Helen?"

"No."

George sat silent. He looked at the empty bottle and the empty glasses.

"It's hell, isn't it?" he said.

"No. Not exactly," Nick said.

"Why not?"

"I don't know," Nick said.

"Will you ever go skiing together in the States?" George said.

"I don't know," said Nick.

"The mountains aren't much," George said.

"No," said Nick. "They're too rocky. There's too much timber and they're too far away."

"Yes," said George, "that's the way it is in California."

"Yes," Nick said, "that's the way it is everywhere I've ever been."

"Yes," said George, "that's the way it is."

The Swiss got up and paid and went out.

"I wish we were Swiss," George said.

"They've all got goiter," said Nick.

"I don't believe it," George said.

"Neither do I," said Nick.

They laughed.

"Maybe we'll never go skiing again, Nick," George said.

"We've got to," said Nick. "It isn't worth while if you can't."

"We'll go, all right," George said.

"We've got to," Nick agreed.

"I wish we could make a promise about it," George said.

Nick stood up. He buckled his wind jacket tight. He leaned over George and picked up the two ski poles from against the wall. He stuck one of the ski poles into the floor.

"There isn't any good in promising," he said.

They opened the door and went out. It was very cold. The

snow had crusted hard. The road ran up the hill into the pine trees.

They took down their skis from where they leaned against the wall in the inn. Nick put on his gloves. George was already started up the road, his skis on his shoulder. Now they would have the run home together.

Fathers and Sons

There had been a sign to detour in the center of the main street of this town, but cars had obviously gone through, so, believing it was some repair which had been completed, Nicholas Adams drove on through the town along the empty, brick-paved street, stopped by traffic lights that flashed on and off on this trafficless Sunday, and would be gone next year when the payments on the system were not met; on under the heavy trees of the small town that are a part of your heart if it is your town and you have walked under them, but that are only too heavy, that shut out the sun and that dampen the houses for a stranger; out past the last house and onto the highway that rose and fell straight away ahead with banks of red dirt sliced cleanly away and the second-growth timber on both sides. It was not his country but it was the middle of fall and all of this country was good to drive through and to see. The cotton was picked and in the clearings there were patches of corn, some cut with streaks of red sorghum, and, driving easily, his son asleep on the seat by his side, the day's run made, knowing the town he would reach for the night, Nick noticed which corn fields had soy beans or peas in them, how the thickets and the cutover land lay, where the cabins and houses were in relation to the fields and the thickets, hunting the country in his mind as he went by, sizing up each clearing as to feed and cover and figuring where you would find a covey and which way they would fly.

In shooting quail you must not get between them and their habitual cover, once the dogs have found them, or when they flush they will come pouring at you, some rising steep, some skimming by your ears, whirring into a size you have never seen them in the air as they pass, the only way being to turn and take them over your shoulder as they go, before they set their wings and angle down into the thicket. Hunting this country for quail as his father had taught him, Nicholas Adams started thinking about his father. When he first thought about him it was always the eyes. The big frame, the quick movements, the wide shoulders, the hooked, hawk nose, the beard that covered the weak chin, you never thought about—it was always the eyes. They were protected in his head by the formation of the brows, set deep as though a special protection had been devised for some very valuable instrument. They saw much further and much quicker than the human eye sees and they were the great gift his father had. His father saw as a bighorn ram or as an eagle sees, literally.

He would be standing with his father on one shore of the lake, his own eyes were very good then, and his father would say, "They've run up the flag." Nick could not see the flag or the flagpole. "There," his father would say, "it's your sister Dorothy. She's got the flag up and she's walking out onto the dock."

Nick would look across the lake and he could see the long wooded shoreline, the higher timber behind, the point that guarded the bay, the clear hills of the farm and the white of their cottage in the trees but he could not see any flagpole, or any dock; only the white of the beach and the curve of the shore.

"Can you see the sheep on the hillside toward the point?"

"Yes."

They were a whitish patch on the gray-green of the hill.

"I can count them," his father said.

Like all men with a faculty that surpasses human requirements, his father was very nervous. Then, too, he was sentimental, and, like most sentimental people, he was both cruel and abused. Also, he had much bad luck, and it was not all of it his own. He had died in a trap that he had helped only a little to set, and they had all betrayed him in their various ways before he died. All sentimental people are betrayed so many times. Nick could not write about him yet, although he would, later, but the quail country made him remember him as he was when Nick was a boy and he was very grateful to him for two things, fishing and shooting. His father was as sound on those two things as he was unsound on sex, for instance, and Nick was glad that it had been that way; for someone has to give you your first gun or the opportunity to get it and use it, and you have to live where there is game or fish if you are to learn about them, and now, at thirty-eight, he loved to fish and to shoot exactly as much as when he first had gone with his father. It was a passion that had never slackened and he was very grateful to his father for bringing him to know it.

While for the other, that his father was not sound about, all the equipment you will ever have is provided and each man learns all there is for him to know about it without advice; and it makes no difference where you live. He remembered very clearly the only two pieces of information his father had given him about that. Once when they were out shooting together Nick shot a red squirrel out of a hemlock tree. The squirrel fell, wounded, and when Nick picked him up, bit the boy clean through the ball of the thumb.

"The dirty little bugger," Nick said and smacked the squirrel's head against the tree. "Look how he bit me."

[258]

His father looked and said, "Suck it out clean and put some iodine on when you get home."

"The little bugger," Nick said.

"Do you know what a bugger is?" his father asked him.

"We call anything a bugger," Nick said.

"A bugger is a man who has intercourse with animals."

"Why?" Nick said.

"I don't know," his father said. "But it is a heinous crime."

Nick's imagination was both stirred and horrified by this and he thought of various animals but none seemed attractive or practical and that was the sum total of direct sexual knowledge bequeathed him by his father except on one other subject. One morning he read in the paper that Enrico Caruso had been arrested for mashing.

"What is mashing?"

"It is one of the most heinous of crimes," his father answered. Nick's imagination pictured the great tenor doing something strange, bizarre, and heinous with a potato masher to a beautiful lady who looked like the pictures of Anna Held on the inside of cigar boxes. He resolved, with considerable horror, that when he was old enough he would try mashing at least once.

His father had summed up the whole matter by stating that masturbation produced blindness, insanity, and death, while a man who went with prostitutes would contract hideous venereal diseases and that the thing to do was to keep your hands off of people. On the other hand his father had the finest pair of eyes he had ever seen and Nick had loved him very much and for a long time. Now, knowing how it had all been, even remembering the earliest times before things had gone badly was not good remembering. If he wrote it he could get rid of it. He had gotten rid of many things by writing them. But it was still too early for that. There were still too many people. So he decided to think of something else. There was nothing to do about his father and he had thought it all through many times. The handsome job the undertaker had done on his father's face had not blurred in his mind and all the rest of it was quite clear, including the responsibilities. He had complimented the undertaker. The undertaker had been both proud and smugly pleased. But it was not the undertaker that had given him that last face. The undertaker had only made certain dashingly executed repairs of doubtful artistic merit. The face had been making itself and being made for a long time. It had modeled fast in the last three years. It was a good story but there were still too many people alive for him to write it.

Nick's own education in those earlier matters had been acquired in the hemlock woods behind the Indian camp. This was reached by a trail which ran from the cottage through the woods to the farm and then by a road which wound through the slashings to the camp. Now he could still feel all of that trail with bare feet. First there was the pine needle loam through the hemlock woods behind the cottage where the fallen logs crumbled into wood dust and long splintered pieces of wood hung like javelins in the tree that had been struck by lightning. You crossed the creek on a log and if you stepped off there was the black muck of the swamp. You climbed a fence out of the woods and the trail was hard in the sun across the field with cropped grass and sheep sorrel and mullen growing and to the left the quaky bog of the creek bottom where the killdeer plover fed. The springhouse was in that creek. Below the barn there was fresh warm manure and the other older manure that was caked dry on top. Then there was another fence and the hard, hot trail from the barn to the house and the hot sandy road that ran down to the woods, crossing the creek, on a bridge this time, where the cattails grew that you soaked in kerosene to make jack lights with for spearing fish at night.

Then the main road went off to the left, skirting the woods and climbing the hill, while you went into the woods on the wide clay and shale road, cool under the trees, and broadened for them to skid out the hemlock bark the Indians cut. The hemlock bark was piled in long rows of stacks, roofed over with more bark, like houses, and the peeled logs lay huge and yellow where the trees had been felled. They left the logs in the woods to rot, they did not even clear away or burn the tops. It was only the bark they wanted for the tannery at Boyne City; hauling it across the lake on the ice in winter, and each year there was less forest and more open, hot, shadeless, weed-grown slashing.

But there was still much forest then, virgin forest where the trees grew high before there were any branches and you walked on the brown, clean springy-needled ground with no undergrowth and it was cool on the hottest days and they three lay against the trunk of a hemlock wider than two beds are long, with the breeze high in the tops and the cool light that came in patches, and Billy said:

"You want Trudy again?"

"You want to?"

"Un huh."

"Come on."

"No, here."

"But Billy——"

"I no mind Billy. He my brother."

Then afterward they sat, the three of them, listening for a black squirrel that was in the top branches where they could not see him. They were waiting for him to bark again because when he barked he would jerk his tail and Nick would shoot where he saw any movement. His father gave him only three cartridges a day to hunt with and he had a single-barrel twenty-gauge shotgun with a very long barrel.

"Son of a bitch never move," Billy said.

"You shoot, Nickie. Scare him. We see him jump. Shoot him again," Trudy said. It was a long speech for her.

"I've only got two shells," Nick said.

"Son of a bitch," said Billy.

They sat against the tree and were quiet. Nick was feeling hollow and happy.

"Eddie says he going to come some night sleep in bed with you sister Dorothy."

"What?"

"He said."

Trudy nodded.

"That's all he want do," she said. Eddie was their older half brother. He was seventeen.

"If Eddie Gilby ever comes at night and even speaks to Dorothy you know what I'd do to him? I'd kill him like this." Nick cocked the gun and hardly taking aim pulled the trigger, blowing a hole as big as your hand in the head or belly of that half-breed bastard Eddie Gilby. "Like that. I'd kill him like that."

"He better not come then," Trudy said. She put her hand in Nick's pocket.

"He better watch out plenty," said Billy.

"He's big bluff," Trudy was exploring with her hand in Nick's pocket. "But don't you kill him. You get plenty trouble."

"I'd kill him like that," Nick said. Eddie Gilby lay on the ground with all his chest shot away. Nick put his foot on him proudly.

"I'd scalp him," he said happily.

"No," said Trudy. "That's dirty."

"I'd scalp him and send it to his mother."

"His mother dead," Trudy said. "Don't you kill him, Nickie. Don't you kill him for me."

"After I scalped him I'd throw him to the dogs."

Billy was very depressed. "He better watch out," he said gloomily.

"They'd tear him to pieces," Nick said, pleased with the picture. Then, having scalped that half-breed renegade and standing, watching the dogs tear him, his face unchanging, he fell backward against the tree, held tight around the neck, Trudy holding, choking him, and crying, "No kill him! No kill him! No kill him! No. No. No. Nickie. Nickie. Nickie!"

"What's the matter with you?"

"No kill him."

"I got to kill him."

"He just a big bluff."

"All right," Nickie said. "I won't kill him unless he comes around the house. Let go of me."

"That's good," Trudy said. "You want to do anything now? I feel good now."

"If Billy goes away." Nick had killed Eddie Gilby, then pardoned him his life, and he was a man now.

"You go, Billy. You hang around all the time. Go on."

"Son a bitch," Billy said. "I get tired this. What we come? Hunt or what?"

"You can take the gun. There's one shell."

"All right. I get a big black one all right."

"I'll holler," Nick said.

Then, later, it was a long time after and Billy was still away.

"You think we make a baby?" Trudy folded her brown

legs together happily and rubbed against him. Something inside Nick had gone a long way away.

"I don't think so," he said.

"Make plenty baby what the hell."

They heard Billy shoot.

"I wonder if he got one."

"Don't care," said Trudy.

Billy came through the trees. He had the gun over his shoulder and he held a black squirrel by the front paws.

"Look," he said. "Bigger than a cat. You all through?"

"Where'd you get him?"

"Over there. Saw him jump first."

"Got to go home," Nick said.

"No," said Trudy.

"I got to get there for supper."

"All right."

"Want to hunt tomorrow?"

"All right."

"You can have the squirrel."

"All right."

"Come out after supper?"

"No."

"How you feel?"

"Good."

"All right."

"Give me kiss on the face," said Trudy.

Now, as he rode along the highway in the car and it was getting dark, Nick was all through thinking about his father. The end of the day never made him think of him. The end of the day had always belonged to Nick alone and he never felt right unless he was alone at it. His father came back to him in the fall of the year, or in the early spring when there had been jacksnipe on the prairie, or when he saw shocks of corn, or when he saw a lake; or if he ever saw a horse and buggy, or when he saw, or heard, wild geese, or in a duck blind; remembering the time an eagle dropped through the whirling snow to strike a canvas-covered decoy rising, his wings beating, the talons caught in the canvas. His father was with him, suddenly, in deserted orchards and in new-plowed fields, in thickets, on small hills, or when going through dead grass, whenever splitting wood or hauling water, by grist mills, cider mills and dams and always with open fires. The towns he lived in were not towns his father knew. After he was fifteen he had shared nothing with him.

His father had frost in his beard in cold weather and in hot weather he sweated very much. He liked to work in the sun on the farm because he did not have to and he loved manual work, which Nick did not. Nick loved his father but hated the smell of him and once when he had to wear a suit of his father's underwear that had gotten too small for his father it made him feel sick and he took it off and put it under two stones in the creek and said that he had lost it. He had told his father how it was when his father had made him put it on but his father had said it was freshly washed. It had been, too. When Nick had asked him to smell of it his father sniffed at it indignantly and said that it was clean and fresh. When Nick came home from fishing without it and said he lost it he was whipped for lying.

Afterward he had sat inside the woodshed with the door open, his shotgun loaded and cocked, looking across at his father sitting on the screen porch reading the paper, and thought, "I can blow him to hell. I can kill him." Finally he felt his anger go out of him and he felt a little sick about it being the gun that his father had given him. Then he had gone to the Indian camp, walking there in the dark, to get rid of the smell. There was only one person in his family that he liked the smell of, one sister. All the others he avoided all contact with. That sense blunted when he started to smoke. It was a good thing. It was good for a bird dog but it did not help a man.

"What was it like, Papa, when you were a little boy and used to hunt with the Indians?"

"I don't know." Nick was startled. He had not even noticed the boy was awake. He looked at him sitting beside him on the seat. He had felt quite alone but this boy had been with him. He wondered for how long. "We used to go all day to hunt black squirrels," he said. "My father only gave me three shells a day because he said that would teach me to hunt and it wasn't good for a boy to go banging around. I went with a boy named Billy Gilby and his sister Trudy. We used to go out nearly every day all one summer."

"Those are funny names for Indians."

"Yes, aren't they," Nick said.

"But tell me what they were like."

"They were Ojibways," Nick said. "And they were very nice."

"But what were they like to be with?"

"It's hard to say," Nick Adams said. Could you say she did first what no one has ever done better and mention plump brown legs, flat belly, hard little breasts, well-holding arms, quick searching tongue, the flat eyes, the good taste of mouth, then uncomfortably, tightly, sweetly, moistly, lovely, tightly, achingly, fully, finally, unendingly, never-endingly, never-to-endingly, suddenly ended, the great bird flown like an owl in the twilight, only it daylight in the woods and hemlock needles stuck against your belly. So that when you go in a place where Indians have lived you smell them gone and all the empty painkiller bottles and the flies that buzz do not kill the sweet-grass smell, the smoke smell and that other like a fresh-cased marten skin. Nor any jokes about them nor old squaws take that away. Nor the sick sweet smell they get to have. Nor what they did finally. It wasn't how they ended. They all ended the same. Long time ago good. Now no good.

And about the other. When you have shot one bird flying you have shot all birds flying. They are all different and they fly in different ways but the sensation is the same and the last one is as good as the first. He could thank his father for that.

"You might not like them," Nick said to the boy. "But I think you would."

"And my grandfather lived with them, too, when he was a boy, didn't he?"

"Yes. When I asked him what they were like he said that he had many friends among them."

"Will I ever live with them?"

"I don't know," Nick said. "That's up to you."

"How old will I be when I get a shotgun and can hunt by myself."

"Twelve years old if I see you are careful."

"I wish I was twelve now."

"You will be, soon enough."

"What was my grandfather like? I can't remember him except that he gave me an air rifle and an American flag when I came over from France that time. What was he like?"

"He's hard to describe. He was a great hunter and fisherman and he had wonderful eyes."

"Was he greater than you?"

"He was a much better shot and his father was a great wing shot, too."

"I'll bet he wasn't better than you."

"Oh, yes he was. He shot very quickly and beautifully. I'd

rather see him shoot than any man I ever knew. He was always very disappointed in the way I shot."

"Why do we never go to pray at the tomb of my grandfather."

"We live in a different part of the country. It's a long way from here."

"In France that wouldn't make any difference. In France we'd go. I think I ought to go to pray at the tomb of my grandfather."

"Sometime we'll go."

"I hope we won't live somewhere so that I can never go to pray at your tomb when you are dead."

"We'll have to arrange it."

"Don't you think we might all be buried at a convenient place? We could all be buried in France. That would be fine."

"I don't want to be buried in France," Nick said.

"Well, then, we'll have to get some convenient place in America. Couldn't we all be buried out at the ranch?"

"That's an idea."

"Then I could stop and pray at the tomb of my grandfather on the way to the ranch."

"You're awfully practical."

"Well, I don't feel good never to have even visited the tomb of my grandfather."

"We'll have to go," Nick said. "I can see we'll have to go."

Hudson River Editions

New

DARKNESS AT NOON
by Arthur Koestler
0-02-565210-9 $25.00

HOW GREEN WAS
MY VALLEY
by Richard Llewellyn
0-02-573420-2 $30.00

THE NICK ADAMS
STORIES
by Ernest Hemingway
0-02-550780-X $25.00

THE SNOWS OF
KILIMANJARO
by Ernest Hemingway
0-02-550940-3 $20.00

SPOON RIVER
ANTHOLOGY
by Edgar Lee Masters
0-02-581780-9 $20.00

TALES OF THE
SOUTH PACIFIC
by James A. Michener
0-02-584540-3 $25.00

THE THIN RED LINE
by James Jones
0-684-15555-9 $20.00

YOU KNOW ME AL
by Ring Lardner
0-02-568440-X $30.00

Literature/Biography

MY EARLY LIFE
by Sir Winston Churchill
0-684-15154-5 $27.50

MOZART
by Marcia Davenport
0-684-14504-9 $30.00

THE BEST SHORT
STORIES OF RING
LARDNER
by Ring Lardner
0-684-14743-2 $25.00

THE RING LARDNER
READER
by Ring Lardner
0-684-15365-3 $40.00

THE ART OF THE NOVEL
by Henry James
0-684-15531-1 $27.50

TALES FROM A
TROUBLED LAND
by Alan Paton
0-684-15135-9 $20.00

CRY, THE BELOVED
COUNTRY
by Alan Paton
0-684-15559-1 $22.50

History/Religion

DAWN OF CONSCIENCE
by James H. Breasted
0-684-14741-6 $35.00

A HISTORY OF EGYPT
by James H. Breasted
0-684-14510-3 $40.00

JESUS AND THE WORD
by Rudolf Bultmann
0-684-17596-7 $20.00

EVERYDAY LIFE IN OLD
TESTAMENT TIMES
by E. W. Heaton
0-684-14836-6 $22.50

MAN'S QUEST FOR GOD
by Abraham J. Heschel
0-684-16829-4 $22.50

FOLK AND FESTIVAL
COSTUME OF THE
WORLD
by R. Turner Wilcox
0-684-15379-3 $45.00

F. Scott Fitzgerald

AFTERNOON OF
AN AUTHOR
0-684-16469-8 $22.50

THE BEAUTIFUL AND
DAMNED
0-684-15153-7 $27.50

THE LAST TYCOON
0-684-15311-4 $20.00

TENDER IS THE NIGHT
0-684-15151-0 $25.00

Ernest Hemingway

GREEN HILLS OF
AFRICA
0-684-16481-7 $20.00

THE HEMINGWAY
READER
0-684-15164-2 $45.00

IN OUR TIME
0-684-16480-9 $20.00

ISLANDS IN THE
STREAM
0-684-16499-X $30.00

TO HAVE AND HAVE NOT
0-684-15328-9 $25.00

Edith Wharton

THE AGE OF INNOCENCE
0-684-14659-2 $25.00

ETHAN FROME
0-684-15326-2 $20.00

Write for brochure with complete listing of titles
available from Hudson River Editions

MACMILLAN PUBLISHING COMPANY
Special Interest Books,
866 Third Avenue, New York, NY 10022